INNOCENCE AND DECEIT

BRIGID COLLINS   STEFON MEARS

JAMIE FERGUSON   LEAH CUTTER

SHARON KAE REAMER   TODD FAHNESTOCK

GILES CARWYN   DEB LOGAN   ANNIE REED

DAYLE A. DERMATIS   DIANA BENEDICT

DEANNA KNIPPLING   KAREN L. ABRAHAMSON

PAM MCCUTCHEON   KRISTINE GRAYSON

Edited by
JAMIE FERGUSON

BLACKBIRD
PUBLISHING

COPYRIGHT

Innocence and Deceit

Published by Blackbird Publishing

Cover and interior design by Jamie Ferguson/Blackbird Publishing
Cover art copyright © prometeus/DepositPhotos

Enter the magical, unpredictable, wonderful world of fairy tales!

CONTENTS

INTRODUCTION

What if Cinderella was the wicked one, and manipulated her kind, loving stepmother and stepsisters?

Is being a handsome, charming prince really as effortless and trouble-free as it seems?

Would you be alarmed if you realized that the beautiful red shoes you're admiring change their appearance to appeal to whoever is looking at them?

And speaking of shoes, how did Cinderella manage to dance in glass slippers without them breaking and slicing her feet to shreds?

Enjoy the magic and wonder of the fairy tales retold, reimagined, and reinvented in *Innocence and Deceit*.

—Jamie Ferguson
Editor

CLAWS AT HAND

BRIGID COLLINS

All things considered, Tobi's life as a cat was simply not as idyllic today as it was before.

He paused in his contemplative bath, his paw still curled beside his face, his toes still splayed from his washing between them, and craned his neck so he could peer at the young woman across the room without moving from his lazy sprawl on the rug.

Robin Weatherwax, the young American girl who had come to study magic under Tobi's housemate, Baba Yaga, had certainly caused a fair amount of upheaval in their lives. Even the way she sat now, tucked in a plump upholstered chair by the fireplace with a heavy tome spread over her lap and satellite radio playing from her cell phone lying on the armrest, spoke to the changes. Baba Yaga had never been fond of having too much in the way of furniture, but Robin had bent the old wizard to her whims on that subject, and now overstuffed chairs, dainty tables, and tall sets of shelves crowded their little hut in the woods.

Tobi didn't mind that change so much. If he were truthful, he rather liked the new spaces to climb on. Sometimes he'd sit on top of the high bookshelf and watch the goings-on by the fireplace like the benevolent landlord he was.

Plus, Robin gave the best chin scratches, and she never squawked or grumbled the way Baba Yaga did when he climbed into her lap.

No, on the whole, Robin herself was a positive change in Tobi's life. Most of the time, she made him the happiest cat he'd ever been.

If only she hadn't rescued that damned prince.

Unlike most cats, Tobi hadn't had the benefit of being born a cat. For the longest time, he'd been mistaken for a human, and it had caused him no end of stress and depression until, finally, he'd risked a visit to the fairies. He'd been willing to pay any price to inhabit the proper body. They'd given it to him—well, almost: he'd wanted to be a gray tabby, and here he was, a tabby of the orange variety, but it hardly seemed worth fussing about—and in return, he agreed to serve as a messenger between the fairy court and the powerful wizard Baba Yaga.

But the fairy king had warned Tobi the spell could be broken.

"Beware, should you ever win the hand of a prince. If that event comes to pass, your true form you will assume, and we shall be unable to reverse it."

Tobi returned to washing his paw with a vigor that left his toes raw. Prince Ivan had the power to destroy everything Tobi loved about his life, and the idiot boy didn't even know it. He couldn't take a hint, either, given how often he still attempted to pet Tobi despite the ribbons Tobi would make of his hand.

Tobi didn't want those royal hands anywhere near him, thank you very much. He knew the fairies' penchant for taking things literally.

Of course, Prince Ivan's affection for Tobi was part Tobi's fault. He shouldn't have spent so much time sitting by the prince's bedside in the immediate aftermath of Robin's rescue. But the poor boy had looked so lost and scared, with his fresh-burnt face still healing and the haunted gleam in his eyes still lingering. The prince had spent a long, long time in a body that wasn't his own, following instincts that sickened him, and he'd only been able to get his curse broken by threatening and deceiving Robin.

Tobi could relate with a lot of that. And maybe he'd taken a little pride in the way Ivan's nighttime shivers would subside whenever Tobi curled up against his side. Baba Yaga and Robin knew what Ivan had gone through, but they didn't *understand*. Not the way Tobi did.

But it didn't matter. He and Ivan simply couldn't be friends without risking Tobi's very identity, and that was that. With a few more harsh licks, Tobi declared his bath finished, if not entirely satis-factory, and he heaved himself up from his spot on the rug. Maybe he'd saunter over to Robin's chair and vie for space on her lap.

The hut's door opened with a loud bang, and a swirl of cold, pine-scented wind swept through the room. Tobi yowled at the sudden chill. Robin squeaked in surprise, too, and the heavy book she'd been holding fell to the floor with a deep thud.

In from the cold staggered the source of Tobi's angst, Prince Ivan. His shoulders hunched in his coat, and he moaned in pain as he crossed the threshold. His face shone pale in the flickering light of the fire, even through the mess of scar tissue on the left half of his

4

face. He appeared only a few breaths away from fainting, vomiting, or both.

The spicy scents of pine and earth dulled under a heavy lacing of blood in the air.

Robin leapt from her chair and rushed to Ivan's side as the prince slumped to his knees. "What happened? Where are you hurt?"

Ivan only moaned again, but Robin fumbled to open his coat, and gasped. His clothes were a bloody mess, and a small puddle was already forming by his knees. Tobi couldn't see the wound from his angle, but the tang of blood increased.

"Went looking for monsters," Ivan finally forced through gritted teeth.

Tobi flicked his tail at this admission of stupidity.

Robin gaped. "Ivan! Baba Yaga told us not to confront anything in the thicket while she's gone. She can't fix our mistakes all the way from Italy."

"Some are not so hard to scare away," Ivan said. "And it's...nng... my fault they're here in the first place."

"That's not true, we've been over this. Here, lie down. I've got to stop the bleeding."

Robin's voice rang with authority, but her hands fluttered around the front of Ivan's coat. Her own face had grown paler since she'd gotten a look at whatever grievous wound the prince had taken, though Tobi knew she wouldn't faint. She was made of stern stuff.

"Tobi, would you—?"

But Tobi was already trotting into the back room where Baba Yaga and Robin worked their spells. With Baba Yaga out, it fell to Tobi to see to the needs of their housemates. He might keep his distance from Ivan's spell-breaking prince hands, but that didn't mean he would let the poor boy bleed out.

Poor Ivan. The boy couldn't take a hint, not from Tobi, and apparently not from a disgruntled monster.

The workspace was darkened in Baba Yaga's absence. This didn't bother Tobi any, of course. He knew the room by heart and whisker, not to mention he could see in the dark just fine. While he had no

5

interest in casting magic himself, Tobi took great pride in his role as wizard's assistant. He knew where every scroll, parchment, and scrap of paper with an incantation scrawled upon it lay.

It took the time of a tail twitch for him to jump onto the work-table, paw the book of healing incantations from its space on the shelf, and catch it in his mouth. Robin was lucky this book was light. Tobi didn't often deign to carry things. He wasn't a dog.

But an emergency called for all able paws.

The scent of blood had grown, as had the cold rushing in through the open door. Ivan lay on his side by the doorway, and Robin knelt beside him, holding his arm up to examine it. Tobi wrinkled his nose as he approached Robin, and, careful to avoid the spreading puddle, placed the book by her knees.

"Meow."

"Thanks, Tobi."

Robin reached for the book, and Tobi finally got a good look at the prince's wound.

His right wrist ended in a bloody stump.

Through the mess of crimson, Tobi read the odd signs of the wound. The skin around it had sustained none of the tearing which would have accompanied a bite or slash, nor any bruising from being crushed or twisted. By all appearances, Prince Ivan's right hand had simply been attached to his wrist at one moment, and then the next moment it had not.

"Don't let him pass out while I cast this spell, Tobi."

Tobi crouched beside Ivan's face. Ivan's scarred left cheek was smooshed against the floorboards, and his eyes had gone glassy, but he still managed a lopsided smile as Tobi settled beside him.

"Hello, cat," he slurred. "Seems I'm hurt enough to be your friend again."

Tobi set to washing Ivan's cheek with rough strokes. The silly idiot had a smear of blood under his eye.

Robin's arcane mumbles preceded a warm, green glow and the scent of fresh mint. The light lingered for a few heartbeats, and Ivan's cheek heated under Tobi's tongue.

"Doesn't hurt so bad now," he said. He tensed as if to rise.

"Don't get up yet," Robin said. "The new skin is still fragile. I *wish* you hadn't gone monster hunting without Baba Yaga here. What if this is poisoned or something?"

Ivan shook his head, the motion awkward against the floor. "It was a fairy. I thought it was a minor troll at first, and I've scared those off on my own before." He sighed and closed his eyes. "It was a sprig-gan. The moment the nasty thing saw me he snapped his fingers, and suddenly my wrist was gushing blood. He popped through a ring of fairy mushrooms with my hand in his knobby fist."

Tobi's heart sank. Now that Ivan had said so, the oddness of the wound obviously pointed towards fairy mischief. Only fey magic could rearrange a body so neatly. And if the thief was a fairy, then, by their own convoluted rules, the hand was reclaimable.

Someone would just have to go win it back.

Tobi remembered the lilt of laughter in the fairy king's voice as he'd administered his warning so long ago.

"Should you ever win the hand of a prince..."

Robin glanced at Ivan's wrist. "We can't wait until Baba Yaga comes back. If we're going to reattach your hand, we'll have to get it before this new skin gets too set."

"You can't go into the Fairy Realm alone," Ivan said.

Robin protested, and the two bickered while Robin helped him over to the plush sofa by the fireplace. With Ivan settled, Robin scurried about, jamming her phone in her back pocket, then gathering her coat and the backpack she had used when she first arrived in Russia. Once she had both slung over her shoulders, she pulled a silver thimble from her coat pocket and placed it on her right first finger.

Tobi lashed his tail back and forth. He, more than Robin, wished Ivan had committed his follies while Baba Yaga was home. Without the wizard's help, Robin wouldn't be able to open a way into the Fairy Realm at all.

But that wouldn't stop her from trying. She wasn't the sort to leave their poor, silly, idiot prince to suffer, and, seeing the awkward way the boy cradled his wrist as he lay on the sofa, Tobi didn't particularly want her to. But any attempt she made to get into the Realm was sure to end in mortal disaster for her.

Tobi's paws were tied. For the wellbeing of his housemates, he'd have to step up, even if doing so risked his very cathood.

Baba Yaga's house stood, at present, on the edge of a dark thicket in the heart of a forest in the Russian taiga. During the centuries of Prince Ivan's curse, the tangled brambles and gnarled trees had festered into a haven for dark, maligned creatures. Most were monsters who had come to bask under the shadow of the curse's power, but some of the more wicked fey creatures had also felt the lure. Once Robin broke the curse, some of the monsters had fled, but many remained within their hideaways deep in the thicket.

Though the monsters hid from Robin and Baba Yaga, and even from Prince Ivan most of the time, a walk through the thicket still featured a cacophony of horrendous growls, unnerving chitters, and distant roars. A pervasive odor of rot hung in the misty air deeper in, and the crown overhead grew so densely the branches and needles blocked out the sun.

So as Tobi and Robin crept towards a huge pine deep in the thicket at midday, Robin held her cell phone out as a flashlight with one hand and pinched her nose shut with the other.

Tobi padded over the icy ground with his nose held high. The scent of decay bothered him too, but the over-sweet smell of the fairy mushrooms had nearly covered it. The circle that led to the Fairy Realm grew in the shadow of the long, draping boughs of the big tree. In his role as messenger, Tobi had rounded this pine often enough to have worn a little trail through the underbrush.

But this was the only time the heavy beat of finality had dogged each step. This might be the last time he made this journey as a cat. It wasn't fair. He'd worked so hard to stave off the prince's affections, and to be caught by a technicality of wordplay now stung more than a claw to the eye.

Behind him, oblivious to his growing misery, Robin crunched through the thinning growth. The light from her cell phone glinted off icicles and frost as she searched. She probably didn't realize Tobi was leading her yet. But her light finally fell on the circle, setting the pale, blood-speckled mushroom caps glowing, and Tobi moved to the far side of the ring. He sat down directly opposite the great pine trunk and curled his tail around his feet.

"Oh, this is...you knew this was here, didn't you, Tobi?"

"Meow."

Robin ducked under the low-hanging branches and stepped towards the circle.

"Meow!" Tobi half stood, his back arching, and Robin backed away immediately. Good. Robin was a smart woman. A mortal human should never step into a fairy ring before it had been properly opened. Tobi didn't fancy negotiating with the fairy king to release his friend from a trap.

Once he was certain Robin wouldn't approach the ring again, Tobi resumed his sitting position. He curled his tail around his paws once more, then, with a few notes of cat song, he coaxed the magic of the mushrooms to brush at the bark, to peel back the veneer that hid the doorway into the Fairy Realm.

The bark creaked open, exposing the raw wood and flowing pine tar beneath, as well as the glowing, amber arch of the open doorway. A warm breeze gushed forth, sweet with the perfumes of flowers in bloom.

Robin's eyes widened and her knuckles grew white as she gripped her cell phone, but she did not step forward yet.

Tobi remained in his sitting position. Usually, when he visited the Realm in the colder months, he wasted no time bounding straight over the mushrooms so he could revel in the warmth of the fairy summer rippling through his fur. Now he contemplated letting Robin go in alone. She was resourceful, and knew how to keep her head in a tough situation. She'd really only needed his help to open the door. Now that it was open, he could trust her to work through the fairy riddles while he went back home to curl up by the fire.

Back home, where Ivan lay on the sofa, recuperating from the loss of his hand and probably worrying aloud about Robin's welfare as she faced malicious fairies for his benefit.

Tobi didn't think he could bear the guilt. Pesky human emotion, that. He'd never been able to shake it, even though he knew a cat had no need to answer to anybody.

Well, Robin *was* a smart woman. Most likely, Tobi's presence as chaperone would prove symbolic at most, and Robin would reclaim the stolen hand without the need for him to so much as twitch a whisker. Then she'd be the one who won a prince's hand, Ivan would be whole once more, and Tobi's status as cat would remain safe.

As reassured as he figured he'd ever be on the issue, Tobi walked around the circle and brushed against Robin's leg.

"Are you coming with me?" A tiny quaver in Robin's voice betrayed her nervousness, and Tobi knew he'd made the right decision. She might be a capable human, but that didn't mean she couldn't do with some moral support. Tobi remembered she'd had to go it completely alone when she broke the curse on Prince Ivan.

Crossing the threshold into the Fairy Realm felt like slipping into a pool of thin honey, but with a zing of magic that raced along the spine and tingled at the ends of toes. The Realm crackled with more energy than the mortal world, and yet something in the breeze urged one to slow down, don't rush, there's no hurry. Tobi knew it to be deadly, a treacherous way of luring the unwary into a stupor that would allow the fairies to drain them of their essence.

As Robin scanned the summer-green meadow they had emerged into, she slid her phone back into her pocket and unzipped her coat with languorous motions, but she also ran her right thumb over the thimble on her finger. Tobi knew the thimble granted her the power to see the location of any soul, represented by a little floating candle flame. She retained her alertness in the fey miasma, and she was keeping an eye out for any sign of an ambush.

"The trees are full of pixies," she said, her voice hushed, "and there's something bigger beyond those birches."

Maybe their spriggan thief.

Tobi pressed against Robin's leg once more, she nodded down at him, and the two of them took off together for the silvery trunks. Sunlight spilled warm and faintly emerald through the fluttering leaves overhead, a pleasant change from the close darkness of the thicket. No less dangerous, of course, with pixies laughing their high cackles behind every branch and the soporific perfumes of wildflowers dancing on the zephyrs, but still pleasant.

A dirt trail materialized beyond the trees, and they followed it until it carried them around a hillock blooming with clover and daisies, where they discovered a hut made of mud and dirty stones, and thatched with bundles of long, yellowed grass. A rank, fishy smell emanated from the open doorway along with a plume of gray smoke.

From the branches of a large bush by the door dangled a plethora of disembodied hands, twisting in the wind on ropes spun from bloody strands of sinew like a gristly set of chimes.

Robin clenched her fist over her thimble. "He's just inside the door."

No sooner had she spoken than the spriggan stepped out into the sunlight. The fishy odor billowed in its wake, and Tobi held back a sneeze.

The spriggan did look rather trollish at first glance, with its knobby gray skin and heavyset body. But a crown like tree branches mottled with splotches of fungus and its rootlike fingers betrayed its true heritage.

The spriggan seemed unsurprised to have visitors, judging by the toothy grin that spread across its face the moment it spotted them.

"Welcome, friends, welcome. I'm just about to start a spot of soup. Got a choice piece of flesh to serve as a base, I did, only an hour back. Won't you stay a bit, friends?"

Robin remained where she and Tobi had stopped, outside the bounds of the spriggan's "yard."

"I'm afraid we'll have to decline your offer. We've come to reclaim something that was stolen from a friend of ours, and it appears to have fallen into your keeping, somehow." Robin gestured to the dangling hands and contorted her face into a mask of good-natured confusion.

Tobi approved of her careful diplomacy. He added his own hint of nonchalance by sitting and washing the mud from his paw.

The spriggan glanced at the bush of hands, then stroked its chin with its twiggy fingers. "Hmm, this pale, dainty one, I take it? Well, the thing is, such a tender cut, obviously from a specimen of royal lineage, makes the most delicious broth. I couldn't possibly part with it. Not for nothing could you persuade me to give up tonight's dinner!"

"You'll part with it for something, then? Perhaps we can make some kind of trade."

Tobi purred against his paw. Robin was handling this fairy like she'd been doing it for decades. She didn't need his help in the slightest.

The spriggan stamped its foot, apparently uninterested in keeping up the game of words with so skilled an opponent. "Fine, yes, a trade will do. I've just remembered a substitute I can use in my recipe. If you can get it for me, I'll let you go with this prime piece of meat."

Robin nodded. "What is the ingredient?"

"The items I need are three: a bronze mouse from the earth, a silver fish from the river, and a gold bird from the sky. No hand but yours may collect these. Bring them to my yard by the time the sun touches the top of that hill, and you shall have your prize. Now be gone!"

The spriggan turned and stomped back into its miserable little hut, leaving Robin and Tobi alone on the road.

Robin looked at the hill, and her face fell. The sun had already sunk low enough to send the first pink streaks of sunset across the sky.

"But it was midday just a few moments ago!"

Tobi, who was used to the illogical flow of time in the Fairy Realm, nevertheless struggled to breathe as the weight of the task bore down on him. Anger flared in his throat, and he growled low. Had the fairies set him up? He'd worked hard to uphold his end of the bargain, but had they decided it wasn't enough anymore? Had this whole quest been designed specifically to break his spell? The spriggan's task seemed tailored to force Tobi to win Ivan's hand himself, and he couldn't see any way to wriggle out of it now. Not unless they were willing to abandon the quest, but Robin would never leave a story unfinished. Tobi couldn't stomach the idea of letting his poor, silly housemate go handless for the rest of his days, either. The idiot boy had only ever wanted to be one of Tobi's friends, after all. He didn't understand the circumstances that had driven Tobi to deny him.

Robin fretted as she paced back the way they'd come. "These animals must exist, if the fairy asked for them, but then how to catch them? I'm a folklore and botany major, not a hunter. And there's no time! Ugh, this is awful."

Tobi swallowed down the anger—it wasn't doing anything for him anyway—and trudged after her. "You don't have to do a thing. I'll catch them, and it won't take me more than a few minutes. The metallic ones are sluggish."

Robin spun around and gaped. "Tobi! You can talk?"

"Of course I can talk. We're in the Fairy Realm."

Robin closed her mouth, blinked, then nodded. "I guess that makes sense. But the spriggan said no hand but mine may collect the ingredients. How...?"

Tobi lifted one paw and splayed his claws. Of all his feline attributes, he was going to miss having claws the most once the spell was broken.

"I haven't got any hands, have I?"

Leaving Robin to shake her head, Tobi slunk into the trees. He had one last hunt to run, one final set of prey to stalk, and he was determined to enjoy it.

~

As Tobi loped down the hillside for the third time, Robin drummed her fingers along her forearm, and she kept her eyes glued to the sinking sun. The sky had turned a brilliant mix of pink and orange, with the first hints of purple appearing on the far horizon. The bronze mouse and silver fish lay dead at Robin's feet.

The golden bird fluttered weakly in Tobi's jaws, but he didn't bite harder. The thing was almost dead anyway, and if it wanted to cling to the few fragile heartbeats it had left, who was Tobi to deny it?

He tried not to resent Robin's look of relief when she saw him.

"Oh, you did it, you did it! Hurry, let's get these to the spriggan."

She scooped up the mouse and the fish without even a tiny flinch and strode along the dirt path. Tobi followed, happy to keep the bird in his mouth. It gave him a good excuse to avoid any conversation.

They reached the malodorous mud hut and entered the yard just in time. The spriggan waited outside, scowling at the sunset behind them, but he couldn't deny that the full disc of the sun still hung a hair's breadth above the hilltop.

Robin dumped the mouse and fish at the spriggan's feet, and then put her hands on her hips. Tobi approached more slowly. They'd already made it to the yard, as specified by the wording of the request. The spriggan couldn't complain if Tobi wanted to dawdle now.

And, turning his indolent cat attitude to its sticking point, Tobi did dawdle.

The yard stank enough to make his eyes water, but still he savored the strength of the smell. The mud under his paws was slick like slime, but he curled his toes in it just to feel his claws cut into the sloppy earth. The breeze that ruffled the fur on his back crackled with mischievous fey magic, but he simply relished his possession of the fur in the first place.

Would this reeking place even register to the nonexistent sense of smell in his human form? Could he keep his balance at all in this slop once he was back on his clumsy human feet? How cold and naked would he feel with no fur to protect him?

But the questions served no purpose now, except to torment him at the end of his spell. There was no question in Tobi's mind. For all Tobi had suffered in his human shape, Ivan had suffered more, and for far longer, in his monstrous one. If one of them deserved to be whole and at peace, it was Ivan.

He wished he'd let Ivan pet him all those times before. He wished he hadn't slashed and hissed, that he hadn't wasted every opportunity to snuggle against the prince's side or rub his own scent against the prince's ankles. Those were the things he liked best about being a cat, not the hunting of prey or the haughty attitude.

He wished he'd trusted himself enough to claim Ivan as a friend.

Tobi opened his mouth and let the golden bird, dead now, fall to the top of the pile of creatures he'd caught.

The spriggan moved to the bush of hands and cut down Ivan's, then brought it over to where Tobi and Robin waited. He thrust it into Robin's arms, and she took it without a grimace or wince at its cold, bloody touch.

"The trade is done," said the spriggan.

A writhing, roiling sensation sprang to life like snakes under Tobi's skin, running from the top of his head to the tip of his tail. Pain blossomed in his limbs so sharply he couldn't hold back his screams. Through the roaring in his ears and the dimming of his vision, he had a vague sense of Robin rushing to kneel over him, concern etched in the lines of her face and the hunch of her shoulders.

"Tobi! Tobi!"

But a great spasm of pain wracked his body, and he closed his eyes in a vain attempt to block it out.

When the pain subsided, he didn't know how long after, he lay in the mud, panting, but otherwise unmoving.

"Tobi!"

Slowly, afraid of what he would first see now that he had been thrust back into his misshapen, inelegant human body, he opened his eyes.

Robin hovered over him still, her face pale, but a wavering smile tugging at the corners of her lips.

Tobi cringed. "Don't look at me. I'm ugly."

"I think you're beautiful," she said. She reached towards him.

"Don't!"

But her fingers brushed his side, and at their touch, Tobi knew they'd met not bare skin, but fur.

Robin's smile spread. "You're all silver now. It's very pretty."

At once, the last of Tobi's pain receded, and he scrambled to his feet. Though he'd lain in the mud, not a speck of it clung to him. Sure enough, on his paws, tail, and everywhere he looked, the coat that had been orange from the moment the fairy king laid his spell upon him now practically glowed a silvery gray. Just the way he'd always longed to be, the way he'd always known he was meant to look.

His true form.

Tobi laughed, then pranced about Robin's ankles, and then laughed some more. There was nothing else to do, except, of course, to go home and curl up on someone's lap for a long, luxurious catnap.

Reattaching Ivan's hand took a lot of concentration on both Robin's and Tobi's parts, but the spell went without a hitch, and Ivan was soon flexing the stiffness from his fingers while Robin went to make a pot of tea.

Ivan turned his hand over, running his left along the site of the reattachment. With a little laugh, he smirked at Tobi, who sat on the sofa beside him.

"It's good work. Not even a tiny line left. But look, I still have the scar on my thumb from the last time I pushed my luck with you. Maybe it will help me keep from mussing your pretty new coat, eh, Tobi?"

Tobi hated the wistful look on the silly idiot's face. Without an ounce of his usual feline loftiness, he clambered onto Ivan's lap, and then butted his head against the prince's chin. While Ivan spluttered in happy surprise, Tobi turned about a time or two, until he found the perfect position and settled in for a nap.

Ivan used both hands to scratch at Tobi's cheeks, and soon had him purring hard.

All things considered, Tobi thought as he drifted off to sleep, his life as a cat had never been more idyllic.

ABOUT THE AUTHOR

Brigid Collins is a fantasy and science fiction writer living in Michigan. Her short stories have appeared in Fiction River, The 2015 and 2016 Young Explorer's Adventure Guide, and the *Chronicle Worlds: Feyland* anthology. Books 1 through 3 of her fantasy series, Songbird River Chronicles, are available in print and electronic versions on Amazon.

Find out more about Brigid at:
backwrites.wordpress.com

 twitter.com/purellian

 bookbub.com/authors/brigid-collins

THE FENNIGSAN'S CHALLENGE

STEFON MEARS

L loxup awoke to the feel of rain on his face. Hard, driving rain that worked quickly to freshen the mud of the roadway around him. The back of his skull keened pain through his jaw and down his spine. Hard to tell exactly where the bandits had struck him.

Bandits Lloxup had hired, thinking they were mercenaries who would guard his wagon. But then, Lloxup reflected as he lay there refusing to open his eyes, stealing those spices no doubt paid better than guarding them.

Lloxup forced himself to sit up, slanting his world left in a hard spin that left him on his hands, breathing fast and shallow, sweat mixing with the rain on his scalp. But he refused to vomit. Lloxup had no way of knowing when he would next eat, and he could not risk surrendering anything more than he had already lost.

Bad enough he had failed yet again, ruined another attempt at a career as much as he had ruined the clothes on his back in the rain and mud. He would not add regurgitation to the list of indignities.

He would not.

He could already hear his father, Duke Szedo of Lliost Reach, admonishing him not to compound his error any further. But that was life for the fourth son of the Duke. The eldest would inherit, the second went to war, the third dedicated to the gods and the fourth... was forgotten.

A groan to Lloxup's right, just loud enough to hear over the rain. Lloxup blinked his eyes wide, straining to see in the afternoon dimness: Torvius!

Gritting against his pounding head, Lloxup pushed against the softening mud to get his feet under him, but his knee screamed at the attempt to stand and down he went, face first.

But Lloxup had no time to worry about the mud caking his face and hands, the downpour freezing his back and plastering his thin shirt and pants to his shivering skin, the pain in his head and knee. His best friend, his oldest friend, was hurt.

On all fours, or at least three of them, Lloxup managed to reach the taller, stronger man and found him bleeding from his right shoulder but rubbing the back of his head. He had the dazed look of a drunkard trying to remember why he was on a tavern floor.

Lloxup tried to drag his friend off the road to a copse of bowl trees, so called for the gnarled branches that spread upward with spreading leaves filling the gaps to catch the rain so they could drink it over the course of weeks. But his chilled fingers managed only a weak grip, and his angry knee refused to cooperate.

"Help me, you great oaf, or you'll drown here in the road."

"Bad enough...you drag your name through the mud..." started Torvius, but he had a faint smile as he spoke and started kicking with his feet. Between the two of them, they finally managed to reach the protection of the bowl trees.

Lloxup started to tear his own shirt to bind Torvius' shoulder, but his friend said, "Your father would never forgive you."

"Just another entry in a long ledger," said Lloxup and tore the tail from his once fine, shadowthread shirt. He bound Torvius' shoulder, and began collecting water in bowl tree leaves, both to drink and wash the worst of the mud away. Both had taken blows to the head, but aside from the pain they did not seem as though they would cause lasting trouble. Torvius' right arm would accomplish little until the shoulder healed, but as he pointed out, he no longer had a sword to wield anyway.

Lloxup's knee had come out of it the worst, and after they rested and waited out the rain, Torvius had had to break a branch from a bowl tree for him to use as a cane.

"Now what?" said Torvius. "Our goods are gone, along with our money and food. It's a wonder they didn't kill us."

"Wouldn't dare," said Lloxup in an absentminded tone. He saw no easy answer to his friend's first question, so he addressed the implied question instead while he thought. He pointed to a large rock in the vague shape of a giant wing, off the east side of the road. "Not this close to the Fennigsan."

Torvius stared at Lloxup from where he stood, trying to warm himself in the late autumn sun. "You're not going to start in on that nonsense again."

"It's not nonsense." Lloxup sipped from another leaf, but saw the incredulous look stay steadfast on Torvius' face, so he said, "Llond said he saw her."

"Llond." Torvius made the name a curse. "He may inherit your father's title, but he's a pale imitation. Probably has highwaymen working for him."

Lloxup cleared his throat. Loudly.

Torvius started laughing, and soon Lloxup joined him. But the laughter was brief, banished all too soon by the realities of their situation.

"We're only a half day out from that last town," said Torvius. "We can probably get a temple to take us in and feed us while you send word to your father."

"No," said Lloxup. "I'm not going back to my father a three-time failure." He shifted his weight on his makeshift cane. "Besides, I'm not sure my knee will make it."

Lloxup pointed again at the wing rock. "All the stories say that the Fennigsan's house is near a rock that looks just like that. I say we go find out the truth."

"Be reasonable, 'Xup. We need food and shelter."

"Whether the Fennigsan is real or not, there has to be a house of some sort. Something people can point to and say, 'And that's where she lives.' So there will be shelter. As for the rest, I'm going to find out."

"You hope to claim the wonder." Torvius made the statement an accusation.

Lloxup met his friend's eye with as blank a look as he could manage, but knew he could not fool Torvius. Anyone else perhaps, but not Torvius. They had known each other too long and too well. And they both knew the stories: whoever could meet the challenge of the Fennigsan could claim a great wonder. The stories varied about the wonder, but they all implied one thing.

Magic.

Possibly magic enough for a fourth son to find his place in the world.

Lloxup steadied his cane and started limping across the road, then paused and looked back at his friend. "Coming?"

Torvius sighed and did as he had always done: followed Lloxup.

They traveled due east from Wing Rock, the way the stories all said to. From what Lloxup could see through breaks in the bowl trees, another batch of storm clouds would move in sometime that evening.

The sun might be peeking at them now, but more rain was coming.

The wind seemed to confirm this for him. It grew stronger, carrying hints of soft bark and moist earth. It rustled through the trees, agitating the birds and persuading some of them to move elsewhere.

But at least the ground beneath the bowl trees stayed stable enough that Lloxup could make good use of his cane.

Which was good. He could see Torvius watching his progress with a worried eye.

Torvius had just cleared his throat to say something when Lloxup saw the second sign of the Fennigsan's house.

"Look!" he cried, shifting his weight to his good leg to point with his cane.

Ahead of them lay the Tree That Hung Upside Down: a bowl tree that grew backwards. It spired in the center like a common nottle tree or wintwin tree, and its bowl leaves grew inverted all the way down to the ground, forming a giant green-brown dome in the forest.

Lloxup and Torvius stared at the wonder. The Duke's gardeners had all insisted such a tree could not be real. Everyone knew that bowl trees fed from the skies, but such a tree as this could not feed. It would die.

And yet there it was in front of them, every leaf as lush and green as those they had seen beside the road.

Lloxup gave his friend a significant look and corrected their course toward the north, doing his best to ignore the persistent throb of his knee and the grinding ache it added to every step. But he had to admit, unlike the pain in his head, his knee was growing worse.

Still, whatever Torvius had intended to say floated away behind them, forgotten.

An hour or two before dusk they found something every bit as welcome as shelter from the coming storm: an apple tree. The lowest branches had lost their apples to some of the local animals, but Torvius managed a one-armed climb onto the lower branches and used Lloxup's cane to knock down a half-dozen apples for them to share.

They lazed for a time under the tree, enjoying the pleasant sensation of food in their stomachs for the first time since before dawn.

But they knew they had limited time before dark would fall and the storm would rise. So they stood to continue, and Lloxup needed both his cane and the trunk of the apple tree to get to his feet.

"Truth now," said Torvius. "How is your knee?"

"Never mind my knee," said Lloxup, a faraway tone in his voice. "Do you see that?"

"What?"

"Give me a moment."

What Lloxup tried to see clearly was something he saw from the corner of his eye: the Lasting Mist, a column of soft gray mist that was said to never fade or strengthen. They said that the mist could be seen on the hottest day of summer and during the deepest snow of winter and during the torrents of rain that might fill any spring or autumn day.

Lloxup turned to see the mist directly, but when he did the mist vanished. At first he shook his head and turned back to the tree he had used to mark his direction, but the moment he turned his head away, there it was. A mist in the corner of his eye.

Two more tries and each time he could only see the mist when he directed his eyes elsewhere.

"That's it! The last marker," Lloxup sang out. He tried to point with his makeshift cane, but the moment he lifted it his knee buckled. Torvius grabbed his collar, but used the wrong hand and a moment later both friends sprawled in the dirt, clutching their respective wounds.

"I...should beat you...with that stick," said Torvius.

"With...one good arm?...Good luck." Lloxup used the stick in question to push himself to a sitting position. Torvius' shoulder had started bleeding again, and they needed a few minutes and more of Lloxup's shirt to re-bind the wound.

"Better," said Torvius at last, though Lloxup did not care for the ashen pallor of his friend's face. They would both need real rest soon, and Torvius would need a poultice for his shoulder.

Torvius continued, "Now, what were you going on about?"

"The last marker." Lloxup, safely on the ground, used his branch-cane to point at the Lasting Mist, and spent a couple of minutes first instructing and then persuading Torvius to see it in the fading light of the late afternoon.

Finally, Torvius had to concede that they had found the last marker.

Getting Lloxup to his feet again was not easy. His knee had decided it liked having Lloxup leaning against the apple tree, and had added stiffness to the swelling. He could try to ignore it, but he could not pretend it was not getting worse.

But with Torvius' help—and his poorly hidden concern about the state of that knee—together they made their way east by southeast from the Lasting Mist.

They drove themselves on through the dying afternoon, until, under the light of the setting sun, they pushed through the thick undergrowth of a copse of wintwin trees into a clearing.

When they did they found themselves in the presence of what could only have been the Bowl Tree House. The house where the Fennigsan was said to live.

The house looked to Lloxup exactly as he had always imagined it from the stories his nurse had told: a bowl tree wider than the duke's great hall with windows like hardened sap hinting at rooms scattered over at least three stories.

And front and center where one might expect to find a door, a single great leaf inset in the trunk, almost as tall as a man and easily twice as wide as a horse.

"Still doubt?" asked Lloxup, trying to keep smugness out of his tone, but despite his pain and exhaustion he could not keep his smile from showing what his tone might have hidden.

"All right," said Torvius, more hesitation than wonder in his voice, "we've seen the Bowl Tree House. Now let's get out of here before it's too late."

"Ridiculous! We've come all this way..."

Lloxup started forward, but Torvius grabbed his shoulder. "We need to leave. Now."

"But—"

"Lloxup, what happens to those who fail the Fennigsan's challenge?"

"They die, of course," said a creaky old voice behind them, like the sound of a tree just beginning to fall. The two friends turned and saw a skinny, slanted woman with skin the color of the scum that grows on a stagnant pond, a color that matched the odor she gave off.

"Even the Fennigsan must eat."

"We apologize for interrupting your day, Dark Lady of the Forest," said Torvius. "We are but humble travelers who have lost—"

"Dark Lady of the Forest," said the Fennigsan in an impressed voice. "You have the manners of one who has served in a castle. And you,"—she looked over Lloxup with an appraising eye—"have the bearing of noble upbringing, even if you look like a twice-robbed farmhand."

She cackled then, driving from Lloxup's tired mind the words he knew from his childhood stories, the words that would have taken up the Fennigsan's challenge. Her assessment struck home, and all he could say was, "Once robbed, by my own hired guards. I am Lloxup, fourth son of Duke Szedo of Lliost Reach. But I was trying to sell spices, not farm."

"Honesty? From a noble?"

She narrowed her eyes at him, leaning just close enough to give Lloxup a whiff of her foul breath, like pork belly left to spoil.

"Tell me, Lloxup of Lliost Reach, suppose I offered you the prize you seek without facing the challenge. And I said that all you had to do was offer me your manservant for my supper pot.

"What would you say to that?"

"Take the deal," said Torvius quickly. "We're both dead the other way—"

"Silence, manservant!" The Fennigsan's voice cracked like fire snapping a huge log. "I asked the noble."

"His name is Torvius, not manservant," said Lloxup, forcing himself to stand straight without the cane and gritting his teeth against the fiery pain in his knee. He held the cane like a weapon, but not yet menacing. "And I have come for your challenge, but I would sooner die myself than sacrifice him."

"Yes," the Fennigsan said softly with a series of slight nods. "I believe you would." She drew a deep, rickety breath and said, "All right, fourth son of a duke, you may face my challenge."

She turned to Torvius. "And you may leave."

"I will not abandon him," said Torvius.

"Have a care. If you fail I shall claim you both for my pot, but if you succeed only one can claim the prize."

Torvius stepped up behind Lloxup in a show of solidarity.

"Very well," said the Fennigsan, with another cackle. "More meat for my pot."

She twirled a wrist with popping sounds like wet wood on a fire, and the great leaf front door of the Bowl Tree House rolled wide open. "Come with me."

She led them inside, where the wood of the tree had been carved into dark, twisted furniture. Just inside the door sat the mockery of a fine sitting room, with hard, knotted couches set before a fireplace complete with a mantel carved to emulate stonework. Even a candle-less unlit wooden chandelier hung from a chain woven from twisted leaves. Around the edge of the room ran a spiral staircase that led up.

The sap windows let in dim, amber light, and the swamp smell of the room made both men gag and the Fennigsan chuckle.

"Wait," choked out Lloxup. "The sun has set. How..."

He could not finish the sentence, only point at the windows that clearly seemed to let in outside light. He turned back to look through the doorway, but that leaf had vanished. The trunk seemed to have covered it over.

The Fennigsan laid an affectionate hand on the stair's handrail. "This old house keeps its roots in many places, only one of which is near the place you call Lliost Reach."

She started up the stairs, looking back at them over her shoulder and not trying to hide her smile. "The challenge is this way. Don't worry about your knee, there won't be more than a few thousand stairs."

There were four thousand six hundred twenty nine stairs. Lloxup knew. He counted.

The ascent had taken hours. The Fennigsan had trudged along at a slow yet unyielding pace. For the first thousand steps, the two friends had managed to keep up, despite the pain in Lloxup's knee growing from difficult to severe. He found the rhythm of her stride and matched it with his cane.

But during the second thousand, they fell behind and the Fennigsan slowly pulled away. By now the pain in Lloxup's knee had grown intolerable and he began using the broken-branch cane in place of his foot. This slowed them down further, but he had no choice. When he let his bad leg carry any of his weight, each beat of his heart throbbed more pain through his body.

Meanwhile, Torvius' ashen pallor grew steadily more clammy.

Lloxup distracted himself from his own pain by worrying about that shoulder wound. Had it begun to fester? Had some befouled mud gotten into the wound?

Or was it some feature of this horrid staircase? It smelled bad enough to fester a wound, like a place in the swamp where the animals all went to die.

Lloxup wished he had thought of another comparison.

How stupid had Lloxup been to come chasing children's stories when they could have returned to town? Right now they could have been resting with their wounds treated and their bellies full, instead of climbing some interminable staircase. Only counting every painful step kept him focused, kept his mind where he needed it to be.

During the third thousand, the Fennigsan only made herself known through echoing complaints that any young men so slow as to fall so far behind an old woman would lack even enough muscle to produce well-marbled meat.

But her taunts meant nothing to Lloxup. He scarcely heard them above the pound of his own heart, his own squeaks of pain with every labored step. The agony from his knee seemed to spread to his hip, and somewhere shy of the two-thousand-six-hundred-seventy-fifth stair, Torvius had been forced to support his friend.

"You're compensating too much," said Torvius, putting his good shoulder under Lloxup's to brace him, even though he had to walk backward to do it. "You'll ruin your hip and back."

As they passed the three thousandth step, they had to stop. Just for a while. Just for a short break. They leaned against the outer wall of the tree and tried not to think of what appeared to be noonday sunshine past the sap window.

But then the Fennigsan stepped out of the inner bark of the tree and said, "No dawdling now. If you can't manage to even reach the challenge, you forfeit."

Lloxup and Torvius looked at each other, and Lloxup could see that his friend was considering the forfeit. Anything to end the torment of the staircase. At least death would be rest.

"No," said Lloxup. "We can make it."

Leaning heavily on his cane, he gritted his teeth and started up the next step, leaving his friend no choice but to follow.

By will alone the two friends managed to reach the top of the Bowl Tree House to stand among the great leaves of the bottom of the bowl itself. Each leaf looked as large and felt as solid as the one that served as the house's front door. The sky above them shone bright blue and clear as hope, though they could not see the sun.

Here they left behind the fouler smells of the house's interior for clean, fresh air and sunlight, a fact that alone helped hearten both Lloxup and Torvius.

Lloxup had finally had to tear the pants of his left leg to give his poor, abused knee more room to swell. He had seen cooked game birds smaller than his swollen knee, but he tried not to think about that.

And roasting his knee over a fire could scarcely have felt worse than it already did after all those stairs following the long day's march.

But more immediately concerning was that Torvius swayed on his feet, one hand always near his wounded shoulder, and his teeth clenched against his own pain.

"Oh dear," said the Fennigsan, seeming to step out of a large leaf. "I do believe it's beginning to fester." Then she smiled wide enough to shown large, yellowed teeth. "That always does interesting things to the flavor."

"You'll never...find out," said Lloxup. "Where's the challenge?"

"Don't you see it?" The Fennigsan pointed. "Look for the dew."

The two men stared, and after a moment, Lloxup thought he saw something in the way the light glinted off the dew.

"Is that a rainbow?"

"Very good, duke's son." The Fennigsan nodded with something like approval. "Not everyone who makes it this far manages the

33

simple task of looking. Now, follow me across it to the other side and you may claim your prize."

"And if we fail?" said Torvius.

"Then I come back in a week or so to collect your bodies. They'll be nice and ripe by then."

And with that the Fennigsan darted forward and the two men watched with amazed eyes as she twirled up the barely discernible rainbow and away.

Torvius looked around, and when Lloxup realized what was missing he joined in the search: the door they had come through was gone. Torvius made a half-hearted attempt to peel back a leaf, but could not budge it.

"I guess we die here," he said. "At least the scenery is pleasant."

"We're not dying here. There has to be a way."

"Of course there is, for a creature of magic like her," said Torvius, lying down on a leaf with a sigh that might have been pleasure. "For us, there is only starvation and death. At least our wounds should speed the process."

"There has to be a way," Lloxup said again, though he did not see how. He stared and stared at the rainbow he could barely see in the dew on the other side of the bowl.

"Maybe we'll get lucky and it will rain," said Torvius. "Then we can drown nice and quick."

"Enough!" Lloxup turned on his friend. "I am not giving up and neither are you. We will find a way through this. There has to be one. What did the stories say?"

"They told of heroes overcoming the impossible. Because even in stories you have to do the impossible before you get to have magic." Torvius shook his head. "But you and I aren't heroes, and we can't do the impossible."

"Maybe doing the impossible is what makes you a hero."

"Lloxup, I love you like a brother, better than your own brothers love you. But you have failed everything you have ever tried to do." Torvius sat up, leaning heavily on his one good arm. "What makes you think you can do this?"

"I haven't failed everything. I made it up those thrice-damned stairs. All I need to do now is one more impossible thing."

Torvius got a laugh out of that. But then he shrugged. And then he sighed. And finally he got up and joined his friend. "So how do we do this?"

"We look for an answer."

And so they looked. And they looked. They tried different angles and looking from different spots. They debated the path that they remembered the Fennigsan taking and they tried to follow her exact steps. But they could not agree on those exact steps, and Lloxup's knee hurt so badly he refused to take any steps he did not absolutely have to take.

Torvius, under pressure from Lloxup, made a few attempts to cross the tiny rainbow, but each jumping step only brought him back down among the bowl tree leaves.

The sky above them had grown darker blue with hints of the oncoming dusk when they next sat and rested. Though Lloxup did not so much sit as use his cane to lower himself to a supine position.

"I still haven't found any stairs," said Torvius, "nor any way to crest it like a ramp. How are we supposed to cross a rainbow if we can't set foot on it?"

"That's it!" said Lloxup, sitting up and wincing as his hip and leg protested. "There are no stairs. It's not a bridge." He scrambled to get his cane under him, but could not find purchase in the smooth leaves.

"Help me up!"

Torvius helped his friend to his feet. "I still don't see what you—"

"We've been looking for something to walk on." Lloxup hustled across the space between himself and the fading sight of the dew-made rainbow, Torvius following in his wake. "But we don't have to walk on it. We walk through it. Just cross it." He paused just before the rainbow.

"It's not a bridge. It's a curtain."

Lloxup reached into the rainbow and swept it aside.

Suddenly they were no longer in the bowl of leaves atop the tree.

Instead they were at the top of the staircase in an otherwise empty room on the third floor of Bowl Tree House. The sap windows in the room continued to let in their murky sunlight. The awful swamp odor returned full force, which would have made them gag if not for the pain each man endured.

In Lloxup's right hand was the curtain he had drawn aside: a single huge bowl tree leaf.

Heartened by his success, Lloxup barely felt the screaming pain in his knee as he led his staggering friend down a much shorter staircase. They passed the second floor where they saw a bedroom that made them shudder, and finally reached that entry room again, where the Fennigsan stood waiting.

"Very good, duke's son. You are the first to pierce my illusions, whatever the stories might tell you."

"You owe us...a wonder." Lloxup managed to keep himself upright despite his knee, despite every weary bone in his body.

"I do indeed, and have no fear. You have beaten my challenge, and magic has some rules that even I will not break. And one of them is hospitality. Since the challenge is done, I must behave as a proper hostess."

She held up her hands and two steaming mugs of soup appeared. Lloxup smelled beef, real beef, and carrots and onions and... She handed the men those mugs and they drained them quickly enough that broth slopped over onto their cheeks and trickled down to add more filth to their clothes.

As they finished their soup, each man sighed with relief and pleasure as he felt his wounds knit. Lloxup's knee shrank and eased, as did the almost forgotten knot on the back of his skull, and warm health seemed to flush through his system. Out of the corner of his eye he could see Torvius moving his right arm as though the shoulder had never been injured.

Neither man could help smiling at the other for the first time in what felt like weeks.

"And now for the wonder you have earned," said the Fennigsan.

She reached one hand into the air and plucked a ball of bright, blue-white light from nothingness.

"You, Lloxup, fourth son of Duke Szedo of Lliost Reach, have been unable to find your place in this world. And so I present to you your guiding star."

She held out the star, and Lloxup took it with a trembling hand. "How do I use it?"

"Only you can answer that," said the Fennigsan. And with that she waved her arms and the tree swirled around them, so bright and dark and fast that both men squinted closed their eyes.

When Lloxup opened his eyes again he was standing next to Torvius on the muddy road. Their clothes were still muddy, and their cart and belongings were missing, but in his right hand Lloxup still held his star.

"So that was real," said Torvius.

Lloxup only nodded.

"Is this where we started from? I don't see the wing-shaped rock."

"It's gone," said Lloxup. "Roots in many places..."

"So what do we do now?"

Lloxup looked at his guiding star, wondering briefly why Torvius seemed to squint against its light when to him it seemed gentle, welcoming.

"Does that give you any ideas?"

"I could throw this in the sky and it would always be there to follow." As Lloxup said the words, he knew in his gut they were true. "I could sleep with it under my pillow tonight, and I would dream of what I should do next."

"So what does it tell you now?"

Lloxup looked at his friend, then swallowed the star whole while Torvius cried out, "No! What have you done?"

"I have swallowed its power. And I will make my own way."

Lloxup started on down the road, and, after a moment, Torvius followed.

ABOUT THE AUTHOR

Stefon Mears grew up in California, Middle-Earth, and Amber. He went to U.C. Berkeley intending to major in Genetics, but the call of storytelling compelled him to graduate with a B.A. in Religious Studies (double emphasis in Mythology and Ritual). He later earned an MFA in Creative Writing from the Northwest Institute of Literary Arts, with a Fiction major, and has published many short stories, poems and essays.

Stefon has been an invited guest at a major Vodou ceremony in New Orleans, taught classes in the Brazilian martial art of Capoeira, spoken on a panel at one World Fantasy Conference and given a reading at another, and engraved his own set of Norse runes.

Stefon has worked as a professional audio engineer and played straight pool for money. He is an avid, lifelong fan of the San Francisco Giants. He lives in Portland, Oregon, with his wife and three cats, and when not writing he can often be found playing roleplaying games.

Find out more about Stefon at:
stefonmears.com

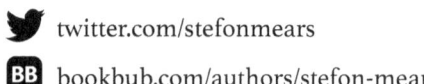

twitter.com/stefonmears

bookbub.com/authors/stefon-mears

INSIDE A FAIRY TALE

JAMIE FERGUSON

I leaned against the warm stone wall of the fourth floor restaurant's balcony and gazed out at the foothills on the west side of town. The sun had just gone down behind the mountains, and the jagged shapes of the Front Range were dark against the orange-red glow of the western sky.

Today was Midsummer, and had been an unusually hot day for June in Boulder, Colorado. I'd spent the morning escaping the heat by hiking in the mountains with my two dogs, the afternoon burning incense of sage, mint, basil and mistletoe to celebrate the solstice, and joined a few friends for happy hour in the evening.

Now it was almost nine o'clock, and while my friends had left the bar, I wasn't ready to go home. I knew I should. I had an important meeting at work far too early the next day, and I was nowhere close to being a morning person. But I didn't want to go back home yet. I wanted to stay out, to enjoy the last few hours of the longest day of the year with someone else instead of going home to my empty house. I loved my dogs, but there was a hole inside of me they'd never be able to fill.

And maybe nothing else would, either.

I pressed my lips together and stared at the foothills.

I'd grown up celebrating the solstice with the coven outside of Telluride, braiding circlets of clover and flowers, doing the ancient dances around a bonfire, and, when I was younger, sneaking off with my cousins to drink mead made from honey. But now I spent my days studying climate change—and working to pay my mortgage, which was no easy task on a research scientist's salary. When the head of my department finally read the report I'd slaved over for weeks, and liked it so much she asked to meet me in person to discuss it, I called my mom and told her I couldn't make it home for the coven's celebration.

Of course, my mom was supportive. She promised to light a candle for me and overnighted a protective amulet she'd made of rue, rowan, and basil—even though I told her I'd make my own for Midsummer. She also reminded me yet again that while my name, Valentina, meant 'strong and healthy,' I should keep in mind that as a woman in my mid-thirties, my strong and healthy child-bearing years were flitting by.

I'd long since given up on explaining to her that it had been barely a year since Matthew and I had gotten divorced, I had yet to meet anyone I was even remotely interested in dating, and I also didn't want to have children—just dogs. So instead I'd made polite, non-committal comments until she moved on to the ever-fascinating —to her—topic of my twin sister Daciana's three-year-old triplets. I loved my sister and my nieces, but was as interested in the intricacies of the dresses Daciana had made them for the solstice as my twin would have been if I'd told her the details of the Midsummer garlands I'd woven for my dogs out of harebell, bergamot, and leafy cinquefoil.

I sipped my glass of water as a woman in a bright blue dress with spaghetti straps walked up to the stone railing a few feet away from me. Her high-heeled sandals were made from a sparkly silver material, and she held a small purse made of a blue and green flowered print in one hand. I shot an envious glance at her silky, strawberry blonde hair, which hung in gentle waves to just above her shoulders. My own hair was a riotous mass of tangled curls that became more unruly the shorter I cut them, so I usually wore my hair pulled back in a ponytail—or, like tonight, in long, thick braids.

"Oh, wow. What a view!" she said. "Aren't the mountains spectacular? I just moved here in February, and I can't stop looking at them."

One of the straps of her dress fell off her shoulder, and she tugged it back into place, her breasts jiggling with the motion.

"Yeah," I said, pulling my eyes away from her cleavage. "They're pretty cool."

She turned to me and held out her right hand. Cheery little pink and white dots of acrylic paint decorated her fingernails.

"I'm Brianna," she said. She had a slight but noticeable gap in between her front teeth that somehow managed to make her more, not less, attractive.

"Valentina," I said, shaking her hand. Her skin was soft and smooth, and she smelled like vanilla. "Welcome to Boulder."

She beamed. Long, light brown eyelashes framed her eyes, which were a warm green flecked with bits of amber. A light pattern of freckles ran across the bridge of her nose. I found myself warming up to her in a way that was unusual for me. Not that I wasn't friendly, but being a witch in a world full of non-witches—where I had to be careful not to slip up and let people find out about my true self— made me a bit hesitant about developing new friendships.

"Thanks! I still can't believe I live here now. I keep having to pinch myself." She glanced over her shoulder, and then turned back to me and lowered her voice. "Do you ever feel like you're never going to meet your soul mate? Like you've dated like a million guys, and maybe he doesn't even exist?"

I blinked. "Um. Yeah. I've been married three times."

"Three? Really?" Brianna's mouth hung open, forming a perfect pink O. "What do you—"

She closed her mouth and glanced over her shoulder as a tall, dark-haired man walked up behind her. He wore expensive jeans, an untucked, buttoned-down, pinstriped shirt, and leather sandals. His dark brown hair was artfully tousled, and he had just the right amount of stubble. He was the kind of guy who'd look handsome and sexy and perfect while naked and lounging in bed, sitting in a meeting with a bunch of venture capitalists, or sniffing coke in a sleazy strip club. The back of my neck prickled.

"Here's your amaretto sour, babe," he said.

His eyes lingered just a little too long on Brianna's breasts as he handed her a cocktail. In his other hand he held an extra-dirty martini. He glanced at me as if evaluating my cute-but-practical cotton dress, low-heeled sandals, simple silver jewelry, and backpack purse, and then his gaze slid away from me and back to Brianna. I felt as though I'd been judged, failed some mysterious test, and dismissed.

"It was nice to meet you, Brianna," I said, enjoying the fact that a muscle in the man's cheek twitched in irritation. I was confident in my spot assessment of him, and pretty sure he'd been included in her 'a million guys' comment.

"You too, Valentina," Brianna said.

She gave me a smile as warm as the summer sunshine and then turned to her companion, her countenance becoming more serious—although I might have imagined that, since I'd taken an instant dislike to the man. As he appeared to have done with me.

"Thanks, Griffith," she said. She pulled the maraschino cherry out of her glass and popped it into her mouth.

I set my water glass down, rested my elbows on the smooth stone railing, and pretended to stare at the foothills while I listened to their conversation, which I couldn't help but hear since I only stood a few feet away. I felt a little rude at not saying hi to the guy, but I didn't like the way he'd looked at me. In contrast, he watched Brianna—who, to be fair, was a knockout—as if she were a scrumptious piece of candy he wanted to devour.

Thanks to my eavesdropping, I learned they'd met right after Brianna had moved to Boulder, and had only been dating for a few months. Her mom had gone to college with Griffith's aunt's brother-in-law, or her sister-in-law's cousin, or something like that—it was a bit hard to follow. Whatever the relationship, her situation sounded painfully similar to mine: well-meaning relatives had encouraged—more likely insisted—they date. I couldn't imagine Griffith resisting the idea once he laid eyes on Brianna, of course, but from what she'd said to me earlier, I wondered how much of her motivation was obligation and duty and being unsure what to do, instead of true interest.

They clearly had some chemistry but, as I'd learned with my own failed marriages, that wasn't enough. I could see their path together as clearly as if I was able to see the future like my Aunt Almha: they'd get married, Brianna would put her career 'on hold' while they had a couple of children, and then Griffith would fall for his hot, twenty-two-year-old yoga instructor. He seemed like the kind of guy to make a sweet, kind girl like Brianna sign a pre-nup, talking her into doing so 'for her own protection.' By the time they got divorced she'd have been out of the work force for long enough to have impacted her earning potential, and thanks to the pre-nup she'd get totally screwed in the deal.

At least all three of my ex-husbands were decent guys. I ran into them every once in a while, at a fundraising event for one of the local animal shelters, or at a STEM event, or something. I sometimes wondered if the problem had been all me. Each situation had been different, but how many people go through three divorces by the time they're in their mid-thirties?

You'd think Aunt Almha would have warned me, but no. Last summer, after I'd filed the papers for divorce number three, I finally called her and asked if she'd foreseen all of this—and if so, why she hadn't told me. She'd chuckled and said this was all part of my path through life.

I'd wanted to ask her how many more failed relationships I'd have, but decided she probably wouldn't tell me—and I wasn't sure I wanted to know the answer.

I certainly wouldn't marry anyone like Griffith. He kept talking about himself—how many startup companies he'd helped found and/or funded, how people came to him for advice on entrepreneurship, how many countries he'd vacationed in over the past year. I could tell that some of what he said was intended to impress Brianna, but he had that sleazy vibe that made it clear he was used to talking about himself on a regular basis. I had yet to meet anyone who did so because they were as awesome as they thought they were.

The sun was completely gone now, and the moon hung high in the eastern sky, bathing the town in that warm, silvery glow that only happens in Boulder in the summertime. The warm breeze ruffled the skirt of my cotton dress, and felt like a caress on my face and the back of my neck. I could feel the magic of Midsummer in the air, and wished I'd been able to go back home and dance around the bonfires with my friends and family.

I took a deep breath, and then exhaled. As much as I wanted to stay out and enjoy the night, I knew I should go home and get some sleep so I'd be awake for my morning meeting. I reached down to adjust the strap on my right sandal.

"Let's spend the night at my house," Griffith said. His voice was light and playful, but there was a hard element to it that made my ears perk up. "You've never been there, and it's about time. Come on —I'll take you there right now."

It wasn't any of my business where he was taking Brianna. Boulder was a small town, but not *that* small—I'd probably never see her again. Besides, she was a grown woman, and they'd been dating long enough that she was clearly comfortable with him. But there was something about his voice that sounded off.

"It's kind of late to drive up into the mountains," Brianna said, in a tone any woman would recognize as *I don't want to do this.*

"It's not even ten yet," Griffith said. "And it's not like you have to go to work tomorrow."

He clearly wasn't getting the message.

"The view of the Indian Peaks from the deck is spectacular," he said. "Come on, Babe. It'll be fun. I'll drive you back down in the morning."

I looked at Brianna out of the corner of my eye. She took a deep breath, and then gave a little laugh and shrugged.

"Sure, I guess so," she said.

They headed across the patio back toward the restaurant. Griffith placed one hand in the small of her back, a gesture that appeared gentlemanly, but which made my jaw tighten. When they reached the edge of the patio she glanced over her shoulder, and our eyes met. She smiled and gave me a little wave, and then turned the corner and was gone from my sight.

I could understand her not having been to Griffith's house before, especially if she lived in town and he lived up in the foothills. It wasn't like you started dating someone and immediately checked out each other's homes. But Griffith's insistence about seemed a bit odd.

I felt a strange sense of foreboding, like a tickle inside my head. Was I following in Aunt Almha's footsteps and developing the ability to see the future? Was I concerned about Griffith mistreating Brianna, even though they'd been dating for months and she seemed comfortable with him? As a three-time divorcée, was I concerned that Brianna—someone I didn't even know—would follow in my footsteps?

I bit my lip. I had no idea why I felt the way I did, but I couldn't ignore it. I grabbed my bag and walked across the patio after them, my pace quickening with each step.

By the time I made it through the restaurant and to the elevator, they were gone. I hurried down the stairs and out onto Walnut Street, and then stood on the sidewalk scanning the street for a glimpse of the couple. Finally I spotted Brianna's strawberry blonde hair as she passed under a streetlight about a block away.

I trotted down the street after them, forcing myself to keep my steps slow enough that I didn't look like I was following them. They stopped at a red Porsche convertible that parked on the street. I turned around and pretended to look at a shop window, so they wouldn't notice me if they looked in my direction. Griffith held the door open for Brianna, and she slipped inside. He headed around to the driver's side.

I took a deep breath and resumed walking toward Griffith's car, rummaging around in my bag. I pulled out my phone, lip balm, an energy bar, a cotton scarf, a *sleep-now* charm wrapped in flannel, a packet of tissues, and a tube of sunscreen.

Finally, I found the Midsummer amulet my mother had made for me. She'd placed the herbs in a cotton bag and tied it closed with a strand of yarn she'd spun out of alpaca wool. I held the amulet close to my face, breathing in the scents of basil, rue, and rowan, and cast a *find-me* spell on it, whispering the familiar words. I finished the spell just as Griffith pulled out of the parking spot. I tossed the amulet into the back seat of his convertible, and then I turned and ran toward 6th Street, where my little blue Subaru was parked.

I didn't know where Griffith was taking Brianna, but thanks to the amulet my mother had made for me, I could now follow them.

I reached my car and got in, saying the words to trigger the finding part of the spell I'd just cast as I turned my key in the ignition. A thin line of silvery light appeared in front of my car, invisible to anyone but me. I pulled out of my parking space and headed west, following the faint, sparkling thread that led to the amulet—and to Brianna and Griffith.

I felt like a stalker, but I was going to follow them nonetheless.
I just wasn't entirely sure why.

~

About thirty minutes later I switched off my headlights and pulled off the winding, two-lane road onto a gravel shoulder. I looked up the at the large, two-story house that stood at the top of a steep hillside; the thin trail left by the *follow-me* spell led straight up the long, winding driveway.

Light streamed from several of the windows on the second floor, but the first floor was dark. This spot was far enough back in the mountains that the glimmer of light from Boulder and the Denver metro area was a faint glow in the sky to the east; most of the light came from the moon and the starry sky. A few houses were scattered along the hills on the side of the road, but they were so spread out it looked like the lots were probably at least twenty acres each, so it seemed unlikely anyone would notice me even if it weren't so dark.

I got out and stretched my shoulders, breathing in the scents of pine and earth while the soft June breeze tickled the back of my neck. It felt at least ten degrees cooler than it had in town. I grabbed my backpack, slung it over my shoulders, and closed the car door as quietly as I could. One advantage of my car was that there were so many Subarus in Colorado that mine didn't stand out, even on this isolated mountain road. Just to be safe I cast a *look-away* spell on it. Now anyone passing by wouldn't run into my car, but also wouldn't consciously register that it was there at all.

I began to walk up the driveway, wondering if I should cast a *look-away* spell on myself as well. But even with the light from the moon and stars, the night was dark enough that it would be hard for anyone to spot me unless they knew exactly where to look.

A mountain lion, on the other hand, would spot me in a heartbeat.

I shivered and continued walking.

The house was huge, probably 6,000 square feet, and had a four-car garage. Like many mountain homes it had been built into the hillside, so the back part of the bottom floor was below ground, but the front door sat at the level of the driveway. A wide wooden deck jutted out from the second story and wrapped around two sides of the house. A flagstone pathway led from the door on the first floor out to a stone patio with a firepit. It all looked beautiful and expensive and fake, like Griffith.

I reached the corner of the house and stood there for a moment trying to figure out what to do next. Should I try to break in? Peek through the windows? What if there was an alarm system, or a security camera, or both?

Before I could formulate a plan, one of the garage doors opened. I ducked into the shade of a lilac bush and held my breath, peeking out through the branches. Griffith backed his convertible out of the garage and headed down the long, sloping driveway. The passenger seat was empty, so Brianna must be inside the house.

I dashed across the pavement and ducked under the descending garage door, managing to make it inside before it shut. I peered out the glass window and watched as Griffith's car reached the bottom of the driveway. He turned right past my Subaru, revving his engine, and then turned around the bend in the road and was gone from sight. The faint glow of the finding spell now led down the hill and along the mountain road to the amulet in the back of Griffith's car.

My heart thumped so loudly it felt like having a tiny drum beating inside my chest. I'd moved up from being a stalker, and had added breaking and entering—or at least entering—to my list of crimes. And why was I even doing this? Brianna was probably happily ensconced inside watching television, or sleeping, or something completely normal. Griffith had talked her into staying at his house without going home to get her things first, so maybe she'd asked him to go buy her a toothbrush or something. That seemed reasonable.

But I still felt the tickle in my head that I'd felt at the restaurant. I couldn't turn back until I knew for sure that she was okay.

I jumped as the garage lights flicked off, leaving me standing in the dark. Light from the moon streamed in through the narrow windows on the garage door, but didn't penetrate very far. I had my backpack, but had left my phone in the car, so I couldn't use it as a flashlight. And while there were certainly plenty of spells to call light, I didn't have any of the necessarily ingredients with me.

I grimaced and walked toward the far wall, holding my hands out in front of myself and careful to keep my steps short and slow lest I run into something. My sandals made tiny scuffing sounds on the concrete as I shuffled across the floor. I tried not to think about the fact that there might be spiders crawling around by my bare toes, or hanging from the ceiling on tiny strands of silk. I gasped when I bumped into what felt like a wooden workbench, and then I gripped the edge and followed it until I hit the wall. I trailed one hand along the wall until I felt the edge of a doorframe. I fumbled about for the handle and took a deep breath, hoping Griffith hadn't activated the house's security system when he left. I pushed the door open, sighing with relief as alarms failed to sound.

I stood in a wide, tiled hallway lit by light streaming in from an archway to my right. The rest of the hall was dark, but I could make out several closed doors. Through the one open door there were two dark, blocky shapes that looked like a clothes washer and dryer. I passed through the archway, squinting as my eyes adjusted to the light. It opened on a wide, carpeted area with two sofas, several chairs, and a giant television screen hanging on the far wall—but Brianna wasn't there. A wooden staircase with an elaborately carved banister led up to the second story. I headed up the stairs, which led to a great room that must have been at least thirty feet long, and almost as wide. The tall, wide windows let in so much moonlight that I could see clearly without having to turn on any lights.

I walked past the sofa and chairs in the great room and entered the spacious kitchen. The countertops were made of concrete, the gas range was twice as wide as the little stove in my own house, and the air smelled like rosemary and spearmint. A large dining room sat off the kitchen; a silver candelabra sat in the center of the heavy teak table. I padded down the carpeted hall and peeked in all the rooms.

The three guest bedrooms—each with an elegantly decorated private bathroom—looked as though they'd never been used. The den had a large, mahogany desk with a fancy fountain pen and a jar of what appeared to be ink next to it. Plaques on the wall proclaimed Griffith James Saunders had degrees in business and law. Floor to ceiling windows lined the southern wall of the master bedroom that had a walk-in closet as large as my own living room, and a private balcony that looked out at the Indian Peaks mountain range to the west. The master bath had shiny chrome fixtures, black-tiled walls, a marble floor, and the largest bathtub I'd ever seen. I headed back to the great room, opened the French doors, and walked out on the deck, breathing in the rich, pine-scented night air. I even looked in the hot tub.

Brianna was nowhere to be seen, but I knew she was here.

Sure, Griffith's fancy convertible was far faster than my plucky little Subaru. He could have stopped along the way and dropped her off. But where? We were well up into the mountains. There were no towns, or shops, or anything along the way. Besides, why would he let her out on the side of the road in the middle of the night? It didn't make any sense.

I went through all the rooms on the second story again, and then headed back down the polished wooden staircase to the ground level. I walked around the sofas in the living room, and down the tiled hallway that led to the garage. The open door I'd noticed earlier did indeed lead to a laundry room. Behind the other doors I found a bathroom, a large storage room filled with cardboard boxes and wooden crates, and a cool and very well-stocked wine cellar.

Where could Brianna have gone?

I took a deep breath, closed my eyes, and tried to sense her with my magic. I pictured her cheery smile, her hazel eyes, the way she'd leaned against the stone railing of the restaurant patio, how her eyes had lit up when she looked out at the mountains, the—

There. It felt as if I'd caught hold of a tiny bit of silken thread, and I had to concentrate on the gossamer material or it would slip out of reach.

I kept my eyes shut and concentrated on being calm so I didn't lose her. I pressed my lips together, remembering her vanilla scent, the waves in her reddish-blonde hair, how she'd given me that last glance before leaving with Griffith. The more I concentrated, the stronger and more solid the link became. I followed it, my eyes closed and my hands outstretched, walking as if in darkness even though I knew the lights in the hall were on. One part of me heard the sound of the wooden soles of my sandals on the tiled floor; another felt Brianna's essence, like a tickle on the tips of my fingers. My hands bumped into the hard, solid wood of a door. I rested my left hand on the cool metal handle and opened my eyes.

I stared at a blank wall.

I could feel the door's handle in my hand, but couldn't see it. It looked like my hand was curled up, with my knuckles resting against the wall.

Chills ran down my spine as I realized the door I'd found had been hidden by a *look-away* spell.

I blinked as the illusion disappeared; now that I was aware of the spell, I could see the door. It stood in the middle of the hallway—I must have walked past it a dozen times. Now that I thought about it, the second story had a significantly larger footprint than the first. It seemed obvious that there was missing space, it just hadn't occurred to me until now—which was undoubtedly due to the spell. Griffith must have cast it. Or had Brianna?

Why had I come here, anyway? Why was I inserting myself in the lives of people I'd just met, instead of getting sleep before my meeting tomorrow morning?

Why would anyone hide a room in their own house with a magic spell?

I gritted my teeth, turned the handle, and pushed open the door.

Behind it lay a large room, a little smaller than the great room upstairs. The floor boards were made of hickory, and the walls had been painted a pale purple. Magical paraphernalia filled the room: wands made of ash and hawthorn hanging from a rack on one wall; shelves of neatly labelled jars containing herbs, sand, and salt from beaches around the world; a large bowl of charcoal sat in the middle of a workbench; bunches of dried rosemary and sage and lavender hung from the ceiling; a crystal ball stood in an elegant filigree stand made of silver; a giant glass box shaped like a coffin rested up against the far wall on a low, wooden platform.

My heart thumped as I realized someone lay in the coffin.

I'd finally found Brianna.

I walked over to the coffin and looked through the clear glass. Brianna wore the same summery blue dress she was wearing when we met on the restaurant patio earlier in the evening. Her sandals and flower print handbag sat on the floor next to the wall. Her eyes were closed, and she looked as if she were asleep, but I knew better. This was Griffith's house, and this was his workshop. He wasn't just some rich, egotistical jerk.

Griffith was a warlock.

The coffin looked just like what I'd envisioned many years before, when my mom had read the fairy tale "The Glass Coffin" to me and my twin sister Daciana. This situation didn't fit the fairy tale, of course. Brianna's brother hadn't been transformed into a stag—or at least I had no evidence that he had been, assuming she even had a brother at all. And while Brianna was certainly a beautiful maiden, I wasn't a tailor's apprentice, like the man who'd saved the girl in the fairy tale by opening the lid of the chest she lay in.

I undid the latch on the chest, took a deep breath, and pushed the heavy lid open. Brianna's hands, with her polka-dotted fingernails, were clasped across her stomach, just below the curve of her breasts. The strip of freckles that ran across the bridge of her nose seemed darker, her skin more pale, and her lips rosier than I remembered, but her soft vanilla scent remained the same.

But even though I'd opened the coffin, her eyes remained shut.

The spring mechanism in the glass lid held it open, but just to be safe I propped it up with a thick, carved stick of ash that lay next to the coffin. I reached a hand out, grabbed Brianna's cool, bare shoulder, and shook her—gently at first, but with more force after she didn't wake up. Finally, I stopped and put my hands on my hips.

This was not working out like the fairy tale.

I ran my hands through the air, searching for traces of magic that might explain why she hadn't awakened. My fingers prickled as they caught the edge of a spell. I rolled my eyes as I realized Griffith was being true to yet another stereotypical fairy tale trope.

I took a breath, and then bent over and kissed Brianna on her lips.

It felt as though I'd been struck by lightning. The electricity coursed through my body, making me feel full of energy, and feel more alive than I ever had. I lifted my head up and stared at Brianna.

Her eyes flew open. She blinked at me, and then smiled.

"Valentina," she whispered.

She reached a hand up and touched my face. My breath quickened. I'd never even thought about kissing another woman until tonight, but now all I could think of was kissing her again. I swallowed as her fingers ran down the side of my cheek, and then my neck.

"What are you doing?"

I jumped up, banging my head on the lid of the open coffin, as Griffith's angry voice boomed throughout the room. I whirled around to see him standing at the door behind me, a pizza box in one hand. Out of the corner of my eye I saw Brianna push herself up to a sitting position.

"You're messing everything up," he said. He scowled at me and set the pizza box down on the workbench nearest the door. "It takes *hours* to create the spell that keeps her asleep until she's kissed. Now I'm going to have to make it all over again. How did you get in here, anyway?"

"Sorry," I said. I grabbed Brianna's arm and helped her out of the coffin. "I don't think she wants to sleep for a hundred years."

He slammed the door shut and crossed his arms. My eyes scanned the room, but what I saw confirmed what I'd already figured out—this room was in the part of the house that had been built into the side of the hill. There were no windows, and no more doors. Griffith blocked the only way out.

And not only was he a warlock, he was clearly very angry.

"I told him I wouldn't marry him," Brianna whispered. Her warm breath tickled my ear, and made my insides tingle in a way that seemed highly inappropriate given the severity of the situation. "And that I'd actually been thinking about breaking up. Then he made me fall asleep."

"You don't happen to be a witch, do you?" I asked, keeping my voice low.

"No," Brianna said. "Are you?"

"Yes," I whispered back, trying to sound strong and confident in spite of the fact that my insides felt full of butterflies. I'd never been in a magic battle and was pretty sure that the witchy duels my sister and I had fought when we were kids, where we did things like change the color of each other's hair, was not going to be much help here.

"I don't want her to sleep for a hundred years," Griffith said. "I want her to agree to marry me. And until she does, she stays in that casket."

"I already told you no," Brianna said, her voice strong and firm. "I'm not marrying you."

"I love you, Brianna," he said. "I'm keeping you here until you realize you love me too."

"But I don't," she said. She crossed her arms. "And I won't. Ever."

Did he really love her, or did he just need a trophy wife for some reason? I shot a glance at Brianna, and then pulled my gaze away as I realized my thoughts had begun to go in a direction that was new and surprising for me—and also rather distracting, since the only thing I should have been thinking about was how to get us out of here.

"How do you expect her to breathe inside that thing?" I asked. "If I hadn't opened it, she might have suffocated."

Griffith glared at me. Would he kill me over this? That would make Brianna even less likely to agree to be his bride.

Of course, he could always cast a spell to make her fall asleep, jam her back into the coffin, and the next time he woke her up to propose pretend that I'd gone somewhere. "Somewhere" could be the bottom of an old mine shaft somewhere in the mountains. I swallowed.

"I realize you couldn't possibly understand," he said. "The glass chest is enchanted. Anyone inside of it will stay alive—and asleep —indefinitely."

He stepped over to the workbench, keeping his eyes on us, and opened a drawer pulling out something small and metallic. I had no idea what it was, but was sure it was something magical.

"But you made me fall asleep before putting me in there," Brianna said.

"Of course I did. It was a lot easier to do that than wrestle you over to the chest and put you in it while you were awake." He raised an eyebrow. "Although I have quite enjoyed the other times we've...wrestled..."

"I can't believe I went out with you in the first place," Brianna said. She wrinkled her nose at him. "Let us go. I'm never going to marry you."

My eyes scanned the workshop, looking for something I could use to help us escape. The only way the crystal ball could be useful was as a distraction if I knocked it over. The jars of herbs and sand and things were ingredients for spells, but weren't magic themselves. Magic wands were tuned to individual people, so I wouldn't be able to use any of them—and worse, if Griffith grabbed the wand from me, then *he* could use it against *us*. The room was chock full of spell material, but I didn't see anything that could help. I clenched my hands into fists.

"Of course you'll marry me," he said. "I'm smart. Rich. Powerful. And I'm a warlock. You'll come to your senses."

He grinned and began walking toward us, his leather sandals making tiny scuffing sounds on the hickory floorboards. Brianna and I both stepped backward, but of course the coffin was right behind us, and the wall behind it, so there wasn't anywhere to go. My backpack purse pressed up against the side of the coffin, pulling the straps tighter across my shoulders. Minutes from now Brianna would be asleep again, trapped within the coffin for who knew how many years, and I would be—well, probably dead, or on my way there. He certainly wasn't going to put *me* to sleep, at least not temporarily.

I caught my breath as I realized one thing I could try.

I shrugged my backpack off, knelt down, and dumped the contents out on the wooden floor. I ran my hands through the little pile, pushing aside my cotton scarf, a tin of mints, a tiny notepad. Out of the corner of my eye I could see Griffith's leather sandaled feet approaching.

My fingers touched the soft flannel that held the *sleep-now* charm. I grabbed it and leapt to my feet. I pulled the tiny silver charm free and flung it at Griffith. It hit him square in the middle of his forehead and stuck there.

"You can't possibly think that throwing your jewelry at me will help," he said. He chuckled, and then his eyelids began to droop. He took an unsteady step forward, and then another. I pulled Brianna out of the way. "Hey...what did you do?"

"You're not the only one who knows magic," I said.

"I'm...so...sleepy..." he said. He began to sway, and grabbed the edge of the glass coffin to steady himself.

"Help me get him in," I said to Brianna.

We pushed Griffith's upper half into the chest, and then lifted his legs in. He blinked once, twice, and then his eyes closed.

Brianna grabbed the edge of the lid and held it while I removed the ash stick that had propped it up. We lowered the lid, and then stepped back to stand side by side and stared at Griffith through the glass.

"I had no idea he was a warlock," she said. "I didn't think magic was real. But I guess I was wrong."

"I've never seen anything like this," I said, waving a hand at the glass coffin. "But magic is definitely real."

"It sure is," she said. She scratched the side of her head. "What should we do with him? Should we call the police?"

"I'll call my mom," I said. I crouched down and reassembled my backpack. "She and her coven will know what to do about him. He said the coffin is enchanted to keep whoever's in it alive and asleep, so he'll be fine overnight."

"Thank you for saving me, Valentina," she said. She put her

sandals on and picked up her flowered purse. "But how did you know to rescue me?"

"I'm not sure," I said. I stood up and slid the straps of my backpack over my shoulders. "I had a weird feeling when you left the restaurant. I don't really know why. It's Midsummer, and there's a lot of power in this day. So maybe I tapped into some ancient bit of magic without realizing it?"

"Now I understand why it never seemed like I could meet the right man," Brianna said. She rubbed the side of my arm. My skin tingled where she touched it.

I stared at her and blinked.

"I mean, I—you—when you kissed me..." Her voice trailed off. She bit her lip. "I must have misunderstood. I thought... I've just never felt like that before. It was like being filled with sunshine. But I... I'm really sorry."

She tucked a lock of hair behind one ear and looked down at her feet.

"I felt the same way," I said, my voice low and scratchy. I reached out and took her hands in mine. She looked up and smiled at me. It felt like a ray of sunshine coming out from behind the clouds.

A sudden buzzing sound made us both jump. We turned toward the glass coffin, and then began to giggle.

The evil warlock was snoring.

"If you aren't too tired, I'd love to hear more about you being a witch," Brianna said. She grinned. "Well, really, I'd love to hear anything about you."

"Do you like dogs?" I asked.

"I *love* dogs," she said.

We grinned at each other. I might not get as much sleep as I'd planned before my morning meeting at work, but I knew it would go well nonetheless.

Brianna and I turned our backs on the coffin and the evil warlock and walked toward the door, hand in hand.

I'd been caught up in a fairy tale, but it was *our* fairy tale. And Brianna and I were going to figure out what happened next together.

ABOUT THE AUTHOR

Jamie focuses on getting into the minds and hearts of her characters, whether she's writing about a saloon girl in the American West, a man who discovers the barista he's in love with is a naiad, or a ghost who haunts the house she was killed in—even though that house no longer exists. Jamie lives in Colorado, and spends her free time in a futile quest to wear out her two border collies since she hasn't given in and gotten them their own herd of sheep.

Find out more about Jamie at:
jamieferguson.com

facebook.com/jamie.ferguson.author

twitter.com/jamie_ferguson

instagram.com/jamie.ferguson.author

goodreads.com/jamieferguson

pinterest.com/jamieauthor

bookbub.com/authors/jamie-ferguson

THE LIZARD HORSES

LEAH CUTTER

Change had crept through my little village of Bakonybél over the years, particularly once the Soviet Union collapsed and Hungary tore down the barbed wire along her borders.

We now learned English and German at *gimnázium*, not Russian. Foreign goods—mostly imported from nearby Austria, though some American- and Chinese-made things as well—were regularly for sale at the local green grocers.

Tourists, too, now sat at the *kávé* shop, particularly when the weather was nice, spreading out their maps and their books, taking up extra tables and chairs, more space than any Hungarian would, as well as always drawing attention to themselves, their voices filling the air with foreign words.

Even outside the village, beyond the picturesque white houses with red clay roofs and the thin, winding lanes, things had changed. The forests were protected—though some would claim "again," as they'd been hunting grounds for the Habsburg royalty ages ago, and peasants caught poaching in them meant death, then, merely fines, now. Electricity flowed into even the smallest huts, and TV brought its western culture, too. We no longer had to wait, like in the bad-old-days, for a phone line—cell phones gave us instant contact.

Yet, some things remained the same. Our little house at the base of Köves Mountain had foot-and-a-half thick walls, built over a century ago, to keep out both the winter cold and the summer heat. Mice rustled in the thatched roof at night, and birds stole pieces of hay from it for their nests. In the winter, I lay dreaming in the loft above the living room, kept warm by the hearth fire there, the little lame boy out of everyone's way and easily forgotten.

I did help Mother with the garden in the backyard during the summer. It produced tomatoes, cucumbers, strawberries, cabbage, and towering stalks of dill. Just beyond the stone wall, under the trees and the start of the forest, blackberry brambles rolled, tempting me to reach past the barrier of thorns to pick their sweet fruit.

Mother also kept yellow-legged, black brood hens, one of the many reasons why I wasn't permitted a dog. The hens roamed freely through the yard, terrorizing me as a child, moving faster than I could on my crutch, with sharp beaks and large wings. I always celebrated in the fall when we turned them from brooders into stewers.

When one of them stopped laying eggs in the nest box, Mother gave me the job to go find the hen's new nest.

Summer had just settled in, with deep blue skies and long hot days. School had let out a month before and I filled as much time as I could tucked away in my loft, reading about faraway lands, like Earthsea and America, colonies on Venus as well as in India. The rest of the time I did the chores set out for me, sometimes better, sometimes worse than what was expected.

The grass in the yard, closest to the house, had started to brown. It wasn't long enough to catch at my single wooden crutch —not yet, anyway. As I was finally big enough to use the push mower myself—despite only one good foot to balance with—the chore of mowing the grass had been passed from my older brothers to me.

That was something else that had changed. In the bad-old days, my birth defect would have been called an *ördög láb*—a devil's foot. The old women at the market, in their kerchiefs and black skirts, wouldn't have sold me anything, and made signs with their hands to ward away the bad luck I carried.

Now, I was merely teased, called *Nagybácsi Sánta*—Uncle Lame— despite being only a teenager.

I snagged a sun-warm tomato as I limped past the rows of vegetables, biting into the sweet flesh with relish, the seeds dribbling down my chin. Nothing ever tasted as fresh at the market.

I passed out of the bright sunlight and into the shade of the trees that grew just beyond the stone wall that marked the border of our property. In the corner of the yard leaned a ramshackle hut, once a garden shed for storing tools and the occasional barrel of wine. One of the walls had collapsed over the winter, changing the square doorway into a stunted triangle.

Balancing on my good, right foot, I banged on the door jams with my crutch, making sure they wouldn't collapse suddenly. Then I knelt down and stuck my head into the hut. The smell of molding hay and the sulfur of rotten eggs rolled out to me. I held my breath, blinked, and peered into the darkness.

Sure enough, there was the missing hen, clucking and cackling. As my eyes adjusted, I saw movement in her new nest. She hadn't just laid eggs there, no, she'd hatched them. Though I didn't hear any peeping, the nest rustled as if half a dozen chicks lay hidden.

I knew I should go back to the house to get a basket to collect up the chicks. Even if I'd had two free hands and hadn't needed one to handle the crutch, I couldn't have caught and carried them all.

Still, I decided to catch at least a few now. I slid my crutch across the threshold and poked at the nest, startling the brood hen. She stood up and hissed at me, spreading her wings wide.

Five lizards sped out from loose collection of hay and grass under her.

I pushed myself back, startled, landing on my ass in the dirt.

Stupid *tyúk*. Lizards ate eggs. Bird probably had been keeping *them* warm for a week, not her chicks.

I grabbed my crutch and struck at the lizards coming out of the hut. Missed the first one as it raced away, and the second one as well. I ended up smacking the ground hard, jarring my arms as I pounded the dirt.

But the next three came out in a straight line. *Whack.* With a single stroke, I stunned them all. Then I took my crutch in both hands and smacked them again and again, until they were all dead.

They were some of the ugliest lizards I'd ever seen. Gray-stone colored, with nobby heads and matching points running down their spines. Their jaws were funny as well, over developed, like they could unhinge them to swallow something bigger than their heads.

The brood hen came strutting out of the hut like she owned the yard. I pushed myself forward and grabbed her, tucking her under one arm firmly. Then I slid my crutch across the grass, cleaning away the lizard guts, and struggled to get my feet under me.

Mother wasn't going to be happy about losing the eggs. At least I had the hen, and she hadn't been hurt.

I glanced over my shoulder at the three dead lizards. Where had they come from? Someone's pet, maybe, that had gotten loose in the forest? Escaped across the border from Austria? Who knew?

I got myself back across the yard, then deposited the hen behind the gate of the coup. She could just stay there for a week or so until she started laying eggs in the right place again.

As I walked toward the front of the house, I heard a long, low whistle, coming from the lane out front.

I pushed my way past the roses, peonies, delphinium, and the rest of the wild blossoms that Mother grew in the front yard, stumbling all the way to the wall.

There, just beyond the iron bars of the gate, stood a boy I'd never seen before, though I'd guess he was my age. He wore all black, like the old women at the market, though his clothes were more modern, with a long sleeved shirt and jeans. Over his shoulder hung a black leather messenger bag that bulged with books. His hair was as black as everything he wore, but his eyes reflected the blue of the sky.

"Jó napot kivánok," he said, giving the old fashioned, formal greeting.

"Jó napot," I replied, still wary. Too many salesmen had come to our gate, believing the lies their city cousins had told them, looking to sell shoddy wares to unsuspecting peasants.

"Have you seen my lizards?" the boy asked.

"Your lizards?" I said. "Yes, I have. They killed our chicks!" I complained to him, suddenly angry.

"No, not my lizards," the boy assured me. "They might breed with a hen, but they wouldn't hurt her brood."

Breed with a hen? How stupid did this boy think I was? That was just an old wives' tale.

"Yes, I saw them," I told him coldly. "I killed them, too."

"You what?" the boy asked, turning his huge eyes toward me.

I couldn't believe it. He actually had tears in his eyes! I *knew* they'd been someone's pet and had escaped.

"How could you kill them?" he lamented. "They were my babies! My chicks to watch over, until they'd grown."

"I didn't kill all of them," I grudgingly admitted. "Two of them got away."

"Where?" the boy asked eagerly, wiping his eyes with the back of his hand.

I shrugged. "Out of the yard, probably over the wall and into the woods," I told him. I gestured toward it with my crutch. "They didn't escape too long ago."

"No, no," the boy said, shaking his head. "It's too late, now that they've reached the trees. I'll have to catch them later. When they've grown into my horses."

Horses? Obviously the boy was touched. It made me feel closer to him, actually. An old man at the market once told me that I'd been touched by the devil, that he'd grabbed me by the ankle to keep my soul from escaping into this world. That was why my foot was so twisted and bent.

The boy paused and gave a great sigh, like one of the old timers thinking about the great deeds of his ancestors and how today's youth could never measure up. "I will be back in seven years," the boy said after another moment.

"Really?" I asked. I'd never heard of such a thing. It just confirmed that he was *bolond*, as crazy as Old Hajmás who lived up in the hills and was still armed against the Russians returning.

Though given the way the people had been voting recently, maybe Old Hajmás wasn't that crazy.

"Before I go, could I have some milk?" the boy asked.

"Sure," I said, though I thought it was an odd request. I passed into the cool house, got out one of my cups with a lid on it, filled it with milk and brought it back out into the heat of the afternoon.

The boy now sat on the dusty road outside the gate, one of his books open in his lap. He clutched at a necklace drawn outside his shirt collar, his hand wrapped tightly around whatever was strung from it. His eyes were closed and his lips moved, as if in prayer.

I sat down awkwardly on the other side of the gate and waited. The warm smell of freshly cut hay came on the wind. Cicadas sang in the nearby trees. I put the cup of milk outside the gate, then drew my arm quickly back to safety and waited.

What kind of boy would ride lizards as horses? Would he direct them to battle, their huge jaws crushing tanks and castles alike? Would they move slowly, ponderous as dinosaurs? Or quicker than a wink?

When I looked up, I saw the boy smiling at me from his side of the gate. "I'm Csörsz," he said, pronouncing it the old fashioned way with two syllables—*Chur-urs.*

"Jelek," I told him. We shook hands through the gate. His palm was rough, like tree bark, and strong.

"What's wrong with your foot?" Csörsz asked, his eyes as wide and innocent as a boy half his age.

"Birth defect," I said, surprised, giving him the short answer. It was good enough. Maybe some year we'd have enough money and I could go to Budapest to have it operated on.

Maybe someday Old Hajmás' pigs would fly, too.

"The old folk say the devil touched you, don't they," Csörsz stated. He held up his necklace—an odd shaped hammer, with one hand, while holding open the collar of his shirt with the other. "Me too!" he said.

A long jagged scar ran down the center of his chest, like a lightning bolt. The skin was softly pink, as if it was newly healed. But there wasn't any puckering around it—it wasn't really a wound, but a birthmark.

"This mark was why my *nagynéni* sent me to study, far away with my brothers," Csörsz confided. "Where I learned...everything."

"Like what?" I demanded.

Csörsz shook his head at me, then reached for his cup and finished his milk. "Thank you," he said. "Though you killed my lizards, you were still kind to me. For that, I will warn you. Be sure to keep all your hens in tonight. The storm will be bad."

"What storm?" I asked. The sky was clear and hot, and the barometer probably wouldn't change for the next month.

"You've been warned," Csörsz said with a smile as he stuffed his book back in his bag.

I tried to see the title, but Csörsz moved too quickly.

All I caught a glimpse of was one of those ugly lizards, done in gold on the cover.

And maybe a single word. *Sárkány.* Dragon.

Seven years passed easily. I didn't spend much time thinking about Csörsz, or how he'd played at being a *garabonciás*, a Hungarian wizard with magic books who drank only milk.

More changes came to Bakonybél: more tourists visiting the beautiful forests, the mountains, and the old abbey; the picturesque streets growing wider to handle the summer traffic; broadband internet arriving and even a club-footed boy finding he could make a living on the web.

My brothers moved out but I stayed, my old wooden crutch replaced with stronger metal ones. I still worked with Mother in the garden through the long summer days, chasing chicks and hens and wondering about lizards growing to horse-size in the nearby trees.

Mother had just hung up the laundry and gone to take her afternoon nap when I heard a long, low whistle coming from near the lane.

I didn't remember Csörsz, not until I saw him again. Then I recognized the call, the same as he'd given before. He was all still in black, with the same messenger bag slung over his shoulder.

"Jelek," Csörsz said, smiling. "I told you I would come back."

"Has it been seven years?" I asked, though I knew it had been. "Have you come back for your horses?"

"I have," Csörsz said. "But first, may I have another glass of your excellent milk?"

"Of course," I told him. I still used a cup with a lid—habit from the old crutch, when I was a teen and less steady on my one foot.

Csörsz sat on the ground outside the gate again, eyes closed and lips moving in prayer.

I boldly opened the gate this time, set his milk down, then leaned against the jam, the warmth from the stone sinking deep into my sore back muscles, encouraging me to close my eyes as well.

When I opened them, Csörsz was staring at me. "You've grown into a fine young man," he said, as patronizing as any uncle from the market.

"Thanks," I said, unwilling to tell him the same. "Where are you going to look for your horses?" I asked.

"Up Köves Mountain. I know a spot, where they might be hiding," Csörsz said. He finished his milk, then caught my eye. "You should get your mother to take her laundry down. There will be another storm this afternoon. Worse, much worse, than the last one."

I remembered, now, the storm that had blown up out of nowhere the afternoon Csörsz had first come looking for his lizards. Ancient trees had fallen and blocked the road leading out of the village. It had taken three days before they'd been cleared. All our hens and their chicks had survived, thanks to Csörsz's warning.

"I'll make sure it gets put away," I told him. I took the cup, then stood as he did, pushing myself up against the warm wall.

"I've thought about you," Csörsz suddenly told me. "How you were marked, like I was. How you could have been a brother of mine."

"But your mark is hidden," I complained. "Mine—everyone can see."

Csörsz nodded slowly. "Yes. That's probably why you weren't chosen. Why you can't be." He held out his hand. "But I'd still be honored to call you brother."

I took hold of his hand and shook it. It still felt like rough bark, though even stronger, now.

Before I could escape, Csörsz pulled me closer and whispered in my ear, "You can still fly," he promised. "You already do." Then he let me go and walked away, up the road toward the trees, whistling a jaunty folk tune.

I went back into the yard and closed the gate, locking myself inside. *Bolond*. Crazy. I was safer here, inside my walls, with my mother and our thin connection to the rest of the world.

The sun beat down with familiar heat. I looked around the proliferation of flowers, everything known, nothing new.

Nothing really changed.

Suddenly, the yard seemed too small and I had a hard time breathing.

I knew I had to follow Csörsz, to see his horses. Even if he was just crazy and not a real wizard. I'd spent too much time dreaming as a boy.

Maybe it was time for me to fly.

I raced along the clothesline, pulling everything down, damp and dry alike, before throwing it all into a basket and dumping it inside the door. I grabbed my second crutch, then I ran out the gate and up the road.

Of course, I wasn't really running. I couldn't even jog. The way my foot twisted, riding a bike was impossible too.

But with the second crutch, on smooth ground, I could make good time, swinging myself like a pendulum, leaping forward with an easy gait.

The road curved up the mountain easily. It was paved, now, making it easier for tourists and their cars and bikes. The smell of pines filled the air. Songbirds happily cheered me on, along with a chorus of crickets. I passed from bright sunlight into shade and back into the sun again as the trees dictated. White snowdrop flowers with their double cups bobbed their heads in the cool mountain breeze.

I only caught sight of Csörsz just as he stepped off the road, onto a trail. Had he been waiting for me? Did it matter?

I followed eagerly, plunging into the shade under the trees. I had to go much more slowly now. The trail wasn't wide enough, or smooth enough, for me to swing along easily. I debated stashing one of my crutches along the side of the path, but in the end kept both.

The trail wound up and up. I was surprised I didn't meet any tourists hiking. The afternoon grew still under the trees. Not too far off the path I spotted the red caps of *csípős gomba*, Mother's favorite mushrooms. I'd have to remember to come back, or to tell her about them.

Though I was used to the long walk into the village from our house, my arms and shoulders still ached after a while. I had to pause and breathe, sweat flowing from me in the humid air trapped under the trees.

I didn't spot Csörsz again until after the trail broke, up on a grassy plain, far above the village. While Csörsz walked over to the very edge, gazing down, I stayed apart, under the trees. What was the crazy *garabonciás* going to do now?

Next to the cliff stood two boulders, gray colored and nobby. Csörsz sat down between them and took out one of his books.

I was too far away to see, but I would have bet that it was the same book I'd seen before, the one with the picture of the lizard on the cover, done in gold.

Csörsz closed his eyes and prayed, rocking back and forth. A cold wind sprang up, chilling the sweat still gathered across my back. Beyond the clearing, clouds rolled in, covering the sky.

I shivered, knowing I was about to get soaked. I wasn't looking forward to making my way down a muddy trail on my crutches in the rain.

I stubbornly stayed where I was.

This would be my only chance, I knew.

Csörsz continued to rock and pray, keeping his eyes closed as if oblivious to the coming storm. Groping blindly, from inside his bag, Csörsz pulled out a short leather cord. He shook his hand once, twice, three times.

Suddenly, the short cord grew, curling out of his hand. It stretched out long and thin, turning into a set of reins.

The rain started then, cold and biting. Wind pushed at me. If I'd been standing, it would have knocked me over. I pressed my back firmly against a tree, and kept wiping the water from my eyes.

I had to see.

Suddenly, one of the nobby rocks next to Csörsz shifted. It grew, forming an ugly snout first, with huge, over-sized jaws and cold lizard eyes. Csörsz moved faster than lightning, tossing the bit of the reins into the mouth of the lizard and jumping behind it, staying out of its way while it unwound, forming legs and spiny back and...wings?

The creature tossed its head from side to side, but it couldn't dislodge Csörsz's bit. With a great leap, Csörsz landed on its back, yanking the creature's head up. It shook itself all over like a wet dog, but it couldn't throw Csörsz from its back. Finally, it settled down, its muscles bunched and tense, as if about to take off.

Csörsz shouted his prayers to the sky now. Most of the words were lost to the wind but I caught a few, entreating saints I'd never heard of before, as well as words of power that I didn't understand but recognized all the same.

Maybe I could have been his brother, in another life, in other circumstances.

Another set of reins formed in Csörsz's hands, silver and lean, made out of chain. I was ready for the other rock when it transformed. Csörsz caught it with more difficulty, first tossing an end of the chain around its neck and forcing it to the ground before finally driving the bit into its mouth.

I pushed myself up, ready to race across the clearing and leap on the second dragon's back. This was my chance to fly.

Then I realized my crutches were gone.

Csörsz had used them for the second set of reins.

With one leg now on both steeds, Csörsz tugged on the reins of his lizards—his horses, his dragons. They leaped off the cliff, into the storm, carried away on the winds. His wild yell echoed across the valley. Thunder responded and they disappeared into the clouds.

I found a downed branch to use as a make-shift crutch to get myself off the mountain. The worst of the winds passed below me, though I was soaked through, shaking and sick by the time I got home.

Things changed a little more after that. Within the month, my web business took off and I was finally able to afford the operation to rebuild my club foot. I'd always limp, but instead of a crutch, a cane sufficed.

A year later, a package arrived, containing a beautiful cherry-wood cane that had a silver dragon's head handle. No return address, of course, but I knew it had come from my brother.

As for flying, I continued to soar the same as I always had, traveling to faraway places in my books and stories and myths, dreaming in my loft of dragons and magicians and stone-colored horses and lizards that could fly.

ABOUT THE AUTHOR

Leah Cutter writes page-turning fiction in exotic locations, such as a magical New Orleans, the ancient Orient, Hungary, the Oregon coast, rural Kentucky, Seattle, Minneapolis, and many others.

She writes literary, fantasy, mystery, science fiction, and horror fiction. Her short fiction has been published in magazines like *Alfred Hitchcock's Mystery Magazine* and *Talebones*, anthologies like *Fiction River*, and on the web. Her long fiction has been published both by New York publishers as well as small presses.

Find out more about Leah at:
leahcutter.com

BB bookbub.com/authors/leah-cutter

THE RED STILETTOS

SHARON KAE REAMER

Heinrich and Hagen stood together in the clearing in the Schattenreich. Early morning here. Heinrich took in the pastoral-quality scene around them, breathing deeply. The grass was already bright green, spring well landed. Tiny pink and white daisies dotted the meadow. Many of the trees in the forest in back of them had begun to leaf out—willow and oak, maple, and beech. The air was redolent of sweet violet and strong with the scent of pollen. Nearby, the River of Life sang merrily as it coursed over stones lining the bank.

Heinrich knew the illusory appearance was of nature in its most harmless aspect. Illusion it was, even if a good one.

Back in the waking world, in northern Europe in early March, the earth was still slumbering, just beginning to think of stretching and throwing off her winter blanket. Burg Lahn, their ancestral home located just a few tens of meters from the Rhine river, possessed a favorable microclimate, and narcissus bulbs were already in bud. But spring still hadn't poked her head in fully.

Just a few minutes earlier, Heinrich had entered Hagen and Caitie's bedroom at Burg Lahn. Hagen had been slumbering with Caitie.

Heinrich stood there quietly so as not to wake Caitie, and, after watching their contented sleep for a few envious moments, tapped his brother on the shoulder. Hagen had opened his eyes immediately and nodded when he saw Heinrich standing over him.

Just a few minutes later, he and Hagen sat together in Heinrich's training room and crossed the veil to reach the Schattenreich.

Hagen must have understood it was urgent. Heinrich would never have disturbed them in their bedroom otherwise.

Heinrich handed one of the pair of red shoes to his brother.

Hagen raised an eyebrow at Heinrich. His almost-shoulder-length hair was still mussed from sleep, marring the arrogance of the gesture. He turned the shoe over, sniffed it.

"Well?" Heinrich asked.

"*Guten Morgen*, to you, too, Heiner."

"Is it already *Morgen*?"

81

"It's always *Morgen* somewhere." Hagen traced a finger across a shoe. "Shiny. They're well made."

"Great. I'll pop off a note to the manufacturer and let them know," Heinrich said with a growl.

"Are they Louboutins?" Hagen asked.

"My best guess is *Medieval*," Heinrich said. "The medieval version of Christian Louboutin must have put some time into shadowcrafting them."

"Funny." Hagen did laugh a few seconds later. "How do you know they've been crafted with shadow?"

"Describe them to me," Heinrich said.

Hagen paused and then launched into the details of the shoe. The sides were transparent plastic, the upper rim sprinkled with strass. He ran a finger over what he described as the smooth burgundy-colored patent leather surface of the heel and toe. The deepness of the red, the perfection of the clear plastic, the form of the stiletto itself that would show off a woman's ankle to perfection. "They would look lovely on Caitie. She has such lovely ankles."

Heinrich laughed. There were such a lot of lovely things about his brother's wife. "Yes, she does. Now, Hajo, I'll tell you what they look like to me."

Heinrich, holding up the shoe he was still holding, described the sinuously smooth red silk straps and the tightly stretched satin of the pointe shoe itself, the drawstring in a fine thin lace of matching color, a deep burgundy, much the same color Hagen had described in his version of the shoes.

"Wait...you see a red ballet shoe?" Hagen asked.

Heinrich nodded. "And you see a red stiletto."

"Hmm. Where did you get them?"

"Helena acquired them as a gift from another singer, an acquaintance of hers. She doesn't actually call her *friend*, but they've known each other a long time."

"And?" Hagen made a spirally gesture with his forefinger.

"Helena says they are cursed."

"So? Good cursed, bad cursed, just plain-old cursed—whatever *cursed* even means—I don't understand the importance?" Hagen rubbed a hand over his brow, the sign that his brother knew trouble was on the way.

Heinrich knew better. Trouble was already here. "Jacqueline confided in me—made me swear to secrecy—that she tried them on. Just for a few seconds. She said they were Mary Janes with a low blocky heel. Deep red velvet, wonderful, a perfect fit. And she would like to have a pair *exactly* like them, pretty please, for her tenth birthday."

"*Verdammt,*" said Hagen. "Heiner—"

"Yes. And no. No time for a lengthy explanation. I have to go on stage this evening. And that's why I need your help. Or more precisely. Someone who can imbue a pair of shoes with the power of runes. *Before* tonight."

Tonight. Before he and Helena were to perform. To forestall said trouble. Or it might be too late. And he would do everything in his power—considerable as his own shadowcraft was, Heinrich knew it would not be enough—to make sure that trouble did not include Hagen and Caitie's daughter Jacqueline. Or Caitie.

"Ah, you mean Ankou," Hagen said. "Seems this will be a long night, then."

I sighed at all the glitz and finery and held back a sneeze from the excess of hairspray. Here I was, backstage at the *German Music Night* competition. Caitlin von der Lahn, mother of four and wife to a German baron. I kept telling myself, yes, that counts. You are someone.

The door to the Green Room slid open and shut for the ten-thousandth time in three minutes, allowing entrances and exits of performers, their hangers-on, and television people carrying techy bits. It was one of those fancy-schmantsy doors. Semi-transparent white glass with concentric glazed white circles of glass all throughout and framed by luscious sheer white curtains. It could have been the one-way entrance to the Pearly Gates or a private cosmetic clinic (they all seemed to have extravagant doors and prices). My nine-year-old daughter, Jacqueline, giggled and made whooshing noises to mimic the door.

Heinrich, my teacher of the arcane, soulmate, and brother-in-law, sat next to me on one side of our designated, supposed-to-look-comfortable-but-wasn't, semicircular couch. In white plush. A round glass coffee table was in front of us. It contained a bottle of champagne in a bucket of ice surrounded by four glasses.

"Heiner..."

Heinrich von der Lahn, who we all called by his nickname, pulled himself back from wherever he'd been. Heiner, mysterious poet, gifted musician, maker of my kids' lunches, glanced at me.

I pointed to the champagne bucket. "Very funny. As if I am going to let my nine-year old daughter drink champagne."

He pointed to the bottle of mineral water next to it.

"Oh. Okay." Was the champagne for later? I sure hoped not. I wanted a glass. Right now.

Jacqueline—Jax—sat on my other side, her beautiful blonde hair let down for the evening. She sat ramrod straight on the couch, trying to look grown-up in her sleeveless peach dress of lace and satin and matching satin bolero. Jax sat like a lady, already well on the way to developing her performer persona, her blue eyes alert and her gaze darting everywhere. The dress had been expensive and, in addition to her being backstage at *German Music Night*, was the reward she had chosen for skipping a grade ahead in school last year.

I would have loved to have a white couch at the castle. Maybe a tad gentler shade, like cream. White was a Very Bad Color for a couch in a household full of kids, and although I loved plush, it wasn't at all practical. But what did I know? With four children all under the age of ten, almost nothing in Burg Lahn, our cozy castle near the Rhine, and I'd amend that to absolutely nothing, had been done up in white since our children were old enough to crawl and spill and throw up on everything. Durable (and washable) neutral-colored fabrics, bulletproof floors, and a growing collection of plastic eating utensils formed a large part of our contemporary, not-so-noble decor.

Heiner popped the cork on the bottle. "Caitie?" he asked.

I mouthed, "yes, please," and held out one of the glasses. He poured. He opened the mineral water, no bubbles, and poured a glass for Jax and himself.

Heiner's orange and sandalwood perfume, custom-made of course, was subtle but pleasing. His skin, drenched with early March sun, looked fabulous against the couch. He wasn't winter-pale like the rest of the German population this time of year. He looked great, as usual. No cowlicks or stray hairs. His tight but not too tight faded black jeans (hot!) and stretchy close-fitting black silk shirt, the sleeves already rolled up, accented his athletic build well.

I tsked at him. "Good thing we packed a second shirt. That one will be wrinkled before you even go on," I said.

Heiner took a slow sip of water and shrugged, awarding me with a crooked smile. "Sorry. Where is Helena?"

"Femme fatale singers need longer to dress, especially for their first *German Music Night* appearance."

I fingered my champagne glass and took a sip. Very dry and very nice. I'd have to be careful not to swizzle too much too quick or I'd be smashed before we even got through the first half of the six performances. Why not a dozen or more? Got me. What did I know? I just did numbers for a living, and six was not a number I'd pick. Seven was better. It was a prime, for one thing and it had a mystical, lucky, quality to it. Enough said.

I hoped Heiner hadn't twigged to Helena's nervousness when we arrived this afternoon. Jacqueline and I had a relaxing morning at the Regent Hotel in downtown Berlin. We'd opted not to stay in the same hotel with the other performers. Even though he wasn't joining us, Hagen had splurged (and that's putting it mildly) on the suite.

Helena didn't want to miss out on the networking among the singers, and so chose not to stay with us, even though there were three bedrooms. That was *perfectly* fine with me. Jacqueline had her own room. And I had had two blessed nights without all the kids underfoot plus a chance to play dress-up with my daughter. I went for a massage and mani-pedi this morning and, until just a few minutes ago, had been feeling relaxed, pampered and (nearly) a decade younger. So *not* early-forty-ish.

Unreasonable panic was the right word for Helena's not-so-subtle body language when we'd arrived together at the studio where the competition was being held. She kept looking over her shoulder and pulling on the carry-strap of her designer bag. I had pulled her aside on the way to the dressing room she'd generously allowed Jax and me to share. Her short platinum blonde hair that went so well with her elfin facial features was mussed and not in an 'I'm really a famous model' way, and her cheeks were flushed. She wasn't very tall, but she looked even more shrunken in her scruffy ballerinas and harem pants.

I'd never seen her so frazzled before a performance. Helena Musac was addicted to being on stage and had never shown a jot of nervousness before.

"What's wrong, Helena?"

She glanced to make sure Heiner had disappeared into his own dressing room.

"I can't do this," she said.

I took a deep breath. "You can't do what?"

"I can't go on tonight," she said, her voice lowered to a raspy sigh. "I've lost them..." She shook her head.

"You lost your voice? Did you strain it practicing?" That was the worst thing I could imagine, and panic shivered through me.

She shook her head again, hard, her lips in a straight line. "My voice is in great shape."

I pulled her into the dressing room, Jacqueline crowding in with us, closed the door, and gave Helena a dressing down. She finally agreed that she would go on. I wasn't convinced. She wasn't either.

Helena wouldn't tell me *what* she had lost. Her prized collection of Jimmy Choo heels? Her earrings? Her contacts with that music company she'd been trying to land? The last scenario was the only one that seemed realistic to me. Getting a recording deal was what had driven her relentlessly the last half-dozen years.

I had to give her credit. She'd taken her singing career from a few decent paying performances for friends and family, weddings, parties, etc. to managing her schedule, writing her own songs, and keeping herself true to a certain style.

Helena's songs were somewhere between Gloria Gaynor and Celine Dion, and not a bad place to be for this kind of contest with its emphasis on pop music. The Germans called it *Schlager* music. The winner would be the German representative for the annual *European Music Contest* to be held later in spring, this year in some Scandinavian country.

To be honest, I found Helena's disco lite style more suited to weddings and parties than the big time. But when she sang folk rock with Heiner, she shone. It was a shame she didn't recognize that his kind of music was the key to her success. Both in her professional career and her relationship with Heiner. Yes, I was jealous. No, I had no right to be jealous. None whatsoever.

I dressed and made room for Helena when her make-up and hair styling crew came in. They glanced at me questioningly, but I had done my make-up earlier at the hotel with the help of a very small glass of pink champagne. I waved in my daughter's direction and told them just a bit of make-up for Jacqueline. Then I made my way out to the couch to wait. And drink. And hope that things were going to go down all right. For Heinrich's sake.

Jax followed shortly after me, all done up and pretty in peach.

"You look fabulous, Jax," Heiner said.

Her face glowed at the compliment.

Then Heiner growled. "First and last. Why did I agree to this?"

His short dark brown hair had just a touch of gray at the temples. Triplets will do that to you, even if you were just an uncle, and I had triplets plus one, a son almost a year older, and that made everything all that much more challenging. To two of my children, my sons, Heiner was more than 'just an uncle', but no one else in the waking world knew that except Heiner and my husband Hagen (and my father). I so did not want to think about complicated paternity issues right now. I wanted to enjoy my touch-of-glamour night with Jacqueline.

Heiner had compelling dark blue eyes, an unusually pure color, and an exact match to Hagen's, even though they were fraternal twins. He closed those eyes now and appeared to be meditating. I knew better. He was *mediating*. A small but important difference: he was enhancing his song with *Schattenwerk*. Shadowcraft.

It was probably an unfair advantage, but I wasn't about to inform anyone, especially the judges, about Heinrich von der Lahn's talent as a modern-day druidic Bard (yes, with a capital B) the likes of which the world hadn't seen since the Iron Age. He had no problem wowing crowds with his music and his voice. But I didn't think he was particularly worried about that part.

Scarlet Heart, the song Helena was going to sing tonight with Heiner backing her on acoustic guitar, was an excellent example of Celtic fusion. He'd worked on it for weeks, not even intending to compete in this contest. Heiner worked hard on all of his music, although it always looked to me like he wrote songs effortlessly. They just came out of his endless well of creativity. It was what he *did*. Singing and songwriting, were a large part of his magic. He produced his own music in addition to babysitting duties, breeding horses, and helping me organize life at the Burg.

But he'd made the mistake of airing his song at a performance where the producer for the annual *German Music Night* was in attendance, and Heiner had been encouraged to enter the competition. A music contest wasn't his thing. At all. But since a good portion of his royalty monies went to the charity foundation he'd set up with Hagen, he had a moment of weakness and agreed to enter his song, thinking he could boost music sales and thereby promote his charity through the publicity.

I patted his arm. "Because you, songwriter of the very first caliber, could not resist. Am I right?"

He snorted.

"Stop that. There are probably cameras everywhere. Snorting on camera is something only I can do."

Heiner didn't have the easy elegance of Hagen von der Lahn, his fraternal twin, but he made up for it with charm, irresistible animal magnetism, and genuine niceness. Not that my husband wasn't nice... we had lots of nice moments. Especially after the kids were in bed. But it was easier to be around Heiner; there wasn't as much sexual tension between us, at least not all the time.

My not-so-platonic relationship with Heiner was not something anyone—anyone—needed to be judgmental about. It was my decision. One I'd made long ago, before the children were born. And I'd (almost) never regretted it.

"Swish," Jax said, imitating the door sliding open. Another musical hopeful with their entourage had just (re)entered the Green Room.

Hagen texted me that he was already ensconced on the couch in our large living room. The Burg's single big-screen television set had been installed there for the evening and surrounded by the rest of our darling progeny. They'd been given leave to stay up for Heiner and Helena's performance. I'd already texted Hagen a dozen times about what everyone was wearing, the average cup size (37.72—mostly C width—with high standard deviation) and more than the usual number of twenty-something back-up singers with prominent cheekbones (hair color, variable—not all of them were blonde).

I'd donned a sleeveless black evening gown. It had wide over-the-shoulder straps and a high-waisted flow, slit up to the knees, and a crossed-strap open back. I'd made sure it looked good with me sitting down—since that's what I'd be doing for the evening—and was comfortable. I wanted to look nice but didn't want to compete with Helena. It was her and Heiner's big night. Most importantly, I wanted to look good in case Hagen caught a shot of me during the very few moments the camera would be on us after the performance when it swept through the Green Room.

"Swish. Klunk," Jax sang. And again, with rhythm.

The third time she did it irritated me enough that I glanced at the door. It was stuck, as if something was blocking it from closing. Heiner still had his eyes closed.

The bad feeling that tingled my spine had nothing to do with tonight's performance. Experience had taught me to trust those kinds of feelings. I rose, wobbling a little on my high heels (not the champagne, nope), eased my way past Heiner and Jax, and took a few steps towards the door. Just on the other side of the door, which was blocked by something I couldn't yet see, a warbly scream came forth. Was that how singers screamed?

A few steps more, and I saw the reason for the door blockage and the scream.

Someone—a woman—was lying down, halfway into the Green Room and halfway not.

My stomach gurgled with acid. *Please don't let her be dead. Please.*

Her head was face down on this side of the door, her long black hair splayed. She had on an elegant black gown with what looked like a gauze cloud puffed up around her waist.

Her feet stuck out past the other side of the entrance.

Her shoulders were what was blocking the door. Which was the first good thing about what was in front of me. If it had been her head, I would be feeling even more nauseous than I already was.

The woman was very still. I didn't see or smell any blood. Two good things, then.

"Mama, what is it?" Jax came up to stand next to me.

Helena stood across from me on the other side of the door, just behind the woman's feet. She was the source of the scream. She wore her dress for the evening, a red—four layers of fine, delicate tulle—thigh-length skirt with see-through lace bodice encrusted with black and red beadwork over a red bustier. Shiny. Bright enough to make me wish for sunglasses. She put a hand to her mouth to stifle another scream and quickly bent to the unknown woman's feet.

I turned and tried to push my daughter back towards the couch. "Jax. Go sit with Heiner. Now."

She looked up at me, pleading. I understood the feeling and could completely sympathize. Her eyes had teared up. Jax shook her head. I gave up and pulled her close, trying to hide her face against my waist. Was the woman dead? Automatically drawing the worst conclusion, I hoped—I wanted to be wrong. Maybe she had fainted. Performance stress? Or she'd fallen and knocked herself out.

Helena bent to kneel at the woman's feet, and that's when I saw *them*. The unfortunate woman was wearing red stilettos. *The* red stilettos. The ones I'd seen two days ago right before Heiner and Helena's dress rehearsal at Burg Lahn.

It had to be the same ones. I'd never seen shoes like that before. They were a deep click-your-heels-three-times ruby red color with three-inch heels and covered in black lace in a triskele pattern so delicate, it seemed impossible. And that didn't even begin to describe how gorgeous they looked.

My fingers itched to have them. To wear them. I'd only had them on for a few seconds that evening, but the desire for *those* shoes was enough to take over my entire body—and soul. That made it official. There was something supernaturally bad about the red stilettos. And there was Helena kneeling there, staring at the shoes intently.

"Mama, why does that Frau have on Helena's shoes?"

Jax held onto me tightly, her head turned to the scene in front of us. Her eyes had gone wide and bright. She had tried on the shoes too, had them on for a few seconds, just as I did. I squeezed her closer, not just to calm her. I was not letting her go.

Helena removed one of the red stilettos from the woman's foot.

I opened my mouth to speak. But not a thing came out.

Then she took the other one off. She quickly stepped out of her own black pumps and laid them by the woman's feet. And then put on the red stilettos.

"What are you doing, Helena?" My voice finally came out in a hard-edgy whine.

People were coming up behind us now. Gasps. Moans. An exclamation of, "Oh, no, it's E!" And, "Where's security?"

An elegant slender man in a tuxedo with equally elegant thick silver hair bent to the woman, laying a hand on her neck. "She has a pulse," he said.

Jax began to shake. My hands trembled.

Heiner was there. Behind us. He put his hands, one on mine and one and Jacqueline's shoulder and gently tried to turn us away. I resisted at first. But forced myself to relax; turned my back on Helena. We pushed through the crowd and went back to the couch, neither of us letting go of Jax. I settled my daughter between me and Heiner. The three of us formed a small, tight packet that no one could invade. But it couldn't be far enough away from her. From Helena.

I couldn't stop the replay of that scene—Helena taking E!'s shoes, the shoes Helena claimed were hers. And that they had been cursed.

The reason a person would choose a stage name with a (silent) exclamation point has baffled me ever since I heard of her. E! burst onto the pop (*Schlager!*) scene just a few years ago. She had some African heritage (or African-American—I admit to *not* having read up on her in one of those glossy mags at my last dentist appointment) that gave her an exotic look. She can also sing.

Lustful, rather than lusty—she doesn't do pirate music—ballads, songs with a little rock'n'roll, and pseudo-rap numbers assured her quick rise to prominence. She started to amass adoring audiences early on and had not even approached the apex of her orbit of fame. Not much of a pop aficionado, I had heard of her from listening to Heiner and Helena discussing her style.

And, as I understood it, she not only sang pop music, she danced while doing it. And she was so good, some have remarked that she must have studied dance formally at one point.

Swish. Klunk. Swish.

Blessed silence.

Then she was there in front of the couch. Helena's face was a pasty white. Against her spiky blonde hair, she would have looked like a ghost. A svelte, very petite ghost. If not for the red dress. And those red stilettos.

Helena lowered herself carefully, not so easy to do in multiple layers of tulle, with a nervous glance and a full-blown frown. Heiner looked straight ahead, trying not to notice.

I leaned forward. "What was—"

"Something very bad," Heiner said. "And I suspect—"

He clamped up.

I glanced to Heiner and back to her, hoping for explanations. Or even clues. Jax still trembled next to me.

Helena sat on the edge of the couch, her eyes in full panic attack mode, way beyond rabbit-in-headlights. Her hands shook. She reached for the glass in front of her and tried to lift the champagne bottle from its bucket on the table, but lost her grip and it crackled back into the ice.

I was quite sure Helena had wanted to make a different entrance, smiling, looking straight ahead as if she expected everyone else to be looking at her. Well, her entrance did raise a few eyebrows from those who had stayed put on their identical white plush sofas scattered throughout the room in a semi-regular pattern. The performers, I assumed, not wanting to be troubled with what was going on over *there*. By the door.

The other couches were occupied with what Heinrich called 'performers who behave poorly': Singers. The room smelled of expensive perfume with an afternote of ardent egotism. Added to that was now a fog of perspiration-nervousness and dread. It rolled in and didn't look likely to clear.

My stomach had soured so quickly, I didn't want to drink any more champagne, but pervasive fear and my reaction to the shoes Helena was now wearing *made* me want to. Badly.

Security arrived. They dispersed the crowd in front of the door. Some people tried to leave but weren't allowed to. The man in the tuxedo argued with the security team, all speaking aggressively in low voices, a hard trick to pull off. *Security* was a man and a woman dressed in the types of utilitarian black suits that showed they weren't here to sing in front of a crowd. They shook their heads as if synchronized and gestured towards the couches.

Swish.

The med techs had arrived and moved the injured woman away from the fancy sliding door.

I looked at Helena's feet, encased in the shoes she'd taken from the poor woman. They matched her red dress perfectly, and Helena looked as if she was born to wear them. I felt my lips go into a line and shook my head to clear it. I looked again, couldn't stop staring. Helena jutted out her chin and this time managed to pour herself a glass of champagne. But her hand shook. She took an unladylike gulp and set the glass down hard on the glass tabletop.

I winced.

"They are *mine*," she said. "I wanted them back."

Heiner cleared his throat. "Helena, where did you get those shoes?"

She let out a sigh and eyed the champagne bottle. And then pushed herself back onto the couch, her shoulders stiff.

"E! gave them to me," she said.

Heiner pinched the bridge of his nose. "A little while ago you told me you were not going to wear them."

Helena shrugged. "Changed my mind."

"But you..." I said and paused. Heiner hadn't seen her steal the shoes. If he didn't know, then he couldn't reveal it to potential security questioning and then maybe they wouldn't know Helena had stolen the shoes. I certainly wasn't going to say anything because I had to believe, wanted to believe with a crazy-assed passion that Helena didn't have anything to do with what happened to E!. At the same time, I wondered why E!, why *anyone* would voluntarily give those shoes up. She didn't at the end, give them up voluntarily.

Helena shook her head in a way that reminded me of my horse when it refused to jump the box hedge at the tail end of the Burg Lahn property. I half expected Helena to push out a breath loudly through her nose.

Helena leaned forward, looking right and left. "When she gave them to me, E! said the shoes were making her ill." She poured herself a small glass of champagne. "I thought she meant they had injured her feet. She couldn't have worn them much."

I had to agree. They looked brand-sparkly-new and probably still smelled like they just came out of the box.

I glanced at the shoes again. Jax did too. And then my daughter

sat back, tossing her hair over her shoulder to show she wasn't interested. It was a very adult gesture, and I almost laughed. Where had
she learned that? Of course, Jax was still interested. So was I.
Intensely.

The pull of the shoes was an ache, like the beginning of a
stomach flu or something worse, and did not seem to lessen. Even
though Helena was wearing them. Maybe it was the proximity. And
the fact that the both of us had tried them on. If that was what caused
the yearning, then I couldn't imagine what it would be like to wear
them for any length of time and then lose them.

"What kind of 'ill'? Were they hurting her feet?" Heiner asked.

"No. I told you they were cursed. But you didn't believe me."

"Of course, I didn't believe you," Heiner said. "But you also didn't
explain it." He did not look at me. But I felt something from him, an
undercurrent of emotion.

"E!—she told me the shoes were cursed—and the only way she
could get rid of the curse was to give them to someone else."

I put a hand on my forehead. It felt warm. I felt Jax's. She was also
running warm, but not feverish.

"You accepted shoes from someone who claimed they were *cursed.*
Okay. I understand. But not really. You didn't believe her, right?" I
said.

"Wrong," Helena said. "I did believe her. But I wanted them
anyway."

My cell phone chimed. It was the sound of Hagen sending me a
text message that read: *What is going on? They've started running*
German Music Night *highlights from past years.*

I looked around then called him. "Hey," I said when he picked up.

"Is everything all right?"

"Um, no, not exactly. There's been an incident," I said.

"Incident. Tell me you're not involved."

I shook my head. Of course, he couldn't see that. "Not directly."

"I'm so *reassured* by your answer, *Liebling.*"

"Good. I'll let you know when we know something."

"Jax? It's not Jax, is it?"

"No, she's fine. She's sitting here between Heiner and me."

"Okay. That reassures me a little."

"Love you."

"You, too."

Heiner and Helena were glaring at each other. They stopped when I disconnected.

"Did I miss something?"

"Witches," Heiner said. "Helena believes in witches."

I tried to raise an eyebrow like Hagen, but wasn't very good at it. Most of the time it (apparently) looked like I had something in my eye or that something was wrong with my mascara.

"Something wrong with your mascara?" Helena asked.

"No. Witches?"

"Look. I was born in the Czech Republic. We only moved to Germany when I was ten. The small village I am from, they were very superstitious. Everyone believes in witches. There are good witches."

She looked pointedly at Heiner. But avoided eye contact with me. Did that mean we were a good witch, bad witch pair? What did that make Hagen? Über witch? Of course, Helena suspected there was something not quite ordinary about the von der Lahns. She'd have to be a total ninny not to. We weren't witches, though. Just different in a supernatural kind of way.

"Implying there are also bad witches," I mumbled.

"Your point being?" Heiner asked.

We had spoken at the same time.

"Bad witches curse people. Good witches help people."

He breathed out. "Okay. Let's just leave it at that."

A plain-clothes detective swung into the room. I'd had enough to do with them over the past decade plus to recognize the type right away. His suit didn't fit quite as good as hired security. And he just had that attitude. Mid-forties, touch of salt-and-pepper. No paunch but stocky in a former-athlete way, an unusual build for the detectives I had so far met. World weary expression and blue eyes. Detective Man talked with Security Man and Security Woman and then scanned the couches, his gaze lidded. Uh oh.

"They're not letting us out of here," I said.

Helena gasped as she realized what I'd said. "What?"

"It's a closed-door crime." I rattled that off as if I knew what I was talking about. True, I'd been reading a lot of *Krimis* lately. Good research material, seeing that I'd been (somewhat unwittingly) involved in solving my share of crimes including dead bodies, kidnappings, and similar kinds of whatnot over the past few years.

"You mean 'closed-room'," Heiner said with a smirk.

I wrinkled my nose at him.

Helena glanced at her shoes, putting her feet together, toe-to-toe, and curled her hands together on her lap. Jax was busy with her cell phone. No doubt keeping her siblings (and her father) informed about every little detail. She looked up, appraised Detective Man in a swift once-over and resumed typing on her phone.

The Security Pair nodded in our direction and Detective Man gave us Detective Eye. He headed our way without hesitation. Heinrich pasted on his performer face and its associated plastic smile. I tried to look like a seriously concerned parent (without *any* knowledge that Helena had taken shoes from the unconscious, injured E!). Helena would not betray her crime, if crime it was. Jacqueline was the weak link in our defense strategy.

We hadn't yet taught her enough about cultivating *hidden*, mainly because we hadn't thought we needed to. There was a certain element of hiddenness that all the children had learned from very early on: never to speak of the Otherworld, Ande-dubnos. All of our immediate family (and possibly distant cousins who constituted family but we had no knowledge of) had access to the Schattenreich.

That arcanely walled-in ancestral domain was our (mostly) private Otherworld sandbox, our very own supernatural outpost in a wildly unsafe world of entities—they were not really alive but existed —who fed on mortal blood, when they could get hold of it, and human dreams. Crossing the veil to reach the Schattenreich was a learned skill. I had first learned it in my mid-thirties. Our children had learned it at age four.

Detective Man stood in front of us and introduced himself as Hauptkommissar Grünberg while sizing us up individually.

"I've been told that you were the first to discover the singer E! in the doorway," he said by way of preamble.

A pause ensued. Not good.

"I saw her on my way from the dressing room," Helena said. "She was lying half in, half out of the door."

Grünberg looked at me, something like recognition infusing his expression. But I'd never met him before.

"I was sitting here, and noticed the door wasn't closing properly," I said and pointed, unnecessarily, to the sliding door, "and got up to see what was causing the problem."

"I went to see what my mother was doing," Jacqueline said and displayed her innocent, angelic-looking face to Hauptkommissar Grünberg.

I knew that face well. It usually meant that Jax had done something she didn't want anyone to know about, either the responsible adults or her siblings. I hoped that Grünberg did not have a daughter anything like mine. But I was silently gratified that my kids had acquired some street sense on their own that I had so far been unable to impart to them. I wasn't very good at lying. If we had been druid characters in a computer game, Heinrich and Hagen would be at least ten game levels above me when it came to stealth and camouflage tactics.

Heinrich shrugged. "I was concentrating on my upcoming performance and wasn't paying attention until I noticed the crowd around the door."

Grünberg grunted some kind of acknowledgement of our stories. Whether that meant he believed us or not, it wasn't clear.

Jacqueline asked, "Is she...E! okay??"

"She seems to be recovering remarkably quickly. But the doctors don't have a clue as to what happened to her."

"And you suspect foul play?" I asked, trying to project the same innocence my daughter did.

"Didn't you, when you saw her lying there?" Grünberg replied.

"I did."

"But you didn't summon help," he said.

"I...listen here, Hauptkommissar Grünberg. I was trying to comfort my daughter and was also panicked because I thought E! was dead and a bunch of people came up and then she had a pulse and then security came and then—"

He held up a hand. "Enough. I'll be here a while. If you can think of anything that you might have seen, let me know."

I nodded and smiled weakly. What I said was mostly true. Just missing some information. Like the part about seeing Helena stealing E!'s shoes? But I didn't look in her direction.

She owed me.

The party mood that had diffused through the Green Room earlier tonight had fizzled with the discovery of E!'s condition. And now it was quashed completely. It didn't look likely that the competition was going to go forward. The promoters must have been having ballistic kittens.

It reminded me of the time growing up in Fredericksburg, Texas, when my junior high class was performing a school play. It was a story with vampires in it, but the play itself was harmless. No actual human blood drinking. This was deep in the heart of Texas, after all. The fictional vampires preferred tomato juice. It was the stupidest play I'd ever been in. But the girls who wrote it were teacher's pets and so thought it was the best thing ever.

We all had stage fever the night of the play. Little Tammy Bailor, who was playing a vampire, fainted in the middle of her opening monologue, and had to be taken off the stage and put in a quiet room to recover. It was high drama for seventh graders—and their parents —and way more interesting than the play itself. I was just so happy we didn't have to go on with it.

But then other one of the girls with a lead role, Suzie Cray, who I hated with a passion because...reasons...made an impassioned speech that the play had to go on, that Tammy would have wanted us to. And, to my great disappointment, the play did go on.

I was wondering why something like that wasn't happening here.

Why the producers and promoters weren't pressing for *the show to go on*, insisting that E! would have wanted it that way.

My best guess was that E! definitely did not want it that way because she would have been out of the running. I turned to Heiner, wanting to share my analysis—

Swish.

"Look," Jacqueline cried and pointed.

E! swept into the room, her black dress looking like it hadn't suffered much. The black gauze train that had been bunched up around her waist, she now had draped across her arm as she walked in.

Wearing Helena's black pumps.

Everyone burst into applause, including Jax and me, the acclaim punctuated by whistles in addition to excited squeals and lots of chatter. E! made a dramatic bow and flung air kisses in all directions.

An entrance like that was hard to top.

E! started towards her designated white plush couch. She paused and turned towards us.

Then she winked at Heiner.

He didn't wink back.

Had I imagined it? Maybe she was winking at someone else. But there weren't any couches next to us. The next one was catty-corner and facing in the other direction. Was I the only one who saw that? Did she have something wrong with her mascara?

Hauptkommissar Grünberg swiveled on his booted heels. He hid the shock that had animated his face for a few seconds. Then he moved, heading off E! They exchanged a few terse words. Then Grünberg marched away, his exit (swish) followed by Security Duo.

Things were definitely looking up. At least that's how it appeared.

I reached for the champagne bottle, while typing a text message one-handed. Jax was typing with both thumbs and watching E! at the same time. Talk about multi-tasking.

The producer arrived. With him was the moderator, a hip-looking German woman with oodles of strawberry blonde hair who wore a tight evening dress (which overflowed with her figure in an attractive way). I probably should have known who she was, but since the high-end flat screen set, just the one, that we owned, was only ever turned on for *Formula One* races (Heiner's passion) and the occasional gardening show (Hagen's passion), I had no idea who any of the hip people were in the German Television World. Or any television world, for that matter.

The *German Music Night* producer, a stocky man who did not look as hip as the woman (possibly a surfeit of Neanderthal genes), but who had a dazzling white-toothed smile and oodles of shaggy blond hair, began speechifying. Sounded like locker room pep talk to me.

The show was definitely going on. I sipped champagne.

Helena and Heiner were up first. That was a good thing because Helena was about to implode from nervous energy. Couldn't have been the cursed shoes, could it?

We barely had time for good luck hugs before the two of them were ushered out of the Green Room.

Heiner had entrusted his guitar to the stage crew, and the big flat screen on the wall in front of us showed him backstage (I assumed the camera was not showing this to the television-watching crowd. Right?) taking his custom guitar (his prized possession) out of its custom-padded case. He tuned it while Make-Up did a touch-up to Helena and then tried to ignore them while they worked on him, and then they waited for the hip lady moderator to whip up the crowd into an acceptable frenzy. The audience, probably beyond restless while all the backstage drama was being sorted, had also possibly become just a bit angry. Unless they had enough champagne to go around.

Going first, the pole position, was in this case not the best way to win.

Maybe Helena and Heiner were being punished for my discovering E!

Maybe they would have gone first anyway.

Someone had to go first.

Jax and I held hands tightly. Perspiration threatened. At least I had on black.

While waiting for them to go on, I glanced next to me. Hauptkommissar Grünberg sat on our couch, appearing as if out of nowhere. He mopped perspiration from his forehead. He stopped and smiled at me.

"Herr Grünberg," I said, trying to find the right words. "Is something wrong?"

Jax grasped my hand tighter and then let go. She pulled her phone out of her fully accessorized peach clutch while I was left to deal with The Detective.

"I should have asked first," he said, "If it's all right to sit here. Do you mind?"

Maybe I hesitated a few seconds too long. What should I answer? Was he still investigating E!'s accident? If it was an accident. That one wink had produced serious doubts.

"I can go backstage, but thought it might be easier to see what's going on from here."

Careful, careful. The less words, the better. "See...what?"

"I remember where I've seen you before, Frau von der Lahn. That murder in Trier. The one you solved."

"You remember that?"

He grinned. Then he didn't. Even the smile disappeared. "You don't really believe that accident with E! was accidental?"

I sighed and shook my head. "No, not likely."

"Officially, I'm off duty."

"Well, then." I positioned a champagne glass in front of him and poured it full without asking. I refilled mine. We chimed glasses together before taking sips.

"Mama," Jax said.

"It's only my third," I said. "And they weren't even—"

My daughter elbowed me. I turned to the screen. Heiner sat on a low stool and had begun the opening chords to his song. Helena stood in front of him, facing the crowd, her feet already moving to the beat of *Scarlet Heart*.

But something didn't look quite right. Her legs did steps that preceded the accompanying body moves, like a computer simulation of a person where the programmer hadn't gotten the synchronization quite right. She smiled as if nothing was wrong, as if her body was obeying her, and belted out the lyrics just like she had during the dress rehearsal two days ago.

Heiner had a recording studio that he'd installed a couple of years ago in one of the Burg Lahn basement rooms. He knocked out a few walls to make it big enough. On the evening of the rehearsal, they'd made a quick recording of the song to test its fidelity and listen for ways to improve it.

But that wasn't the rehearsal. That was the run-through before the rehearsal. Heiner had planned for them to perform their song on the stage in another, older part of the Burg that we used for small, informal family gatherings. It was a floor-to-ceiling library that stretched the length of the room. Windowless, being in the very heart of the Gothic construction. Besides all the books, it was furnished with a baby grand piano, two antique settees and an heirloom rug. There was an open gallery above that had to be traversed before descending into the room. Due to that and the domed ceiling and thick paneled walls (and the rug), the room had great acoustics.

Perfect for a rehearsal or performance of any sort. And that's what we'd always used it for. Whenever Heiner wanted to test a new song, or for special occasions when we all gathered to sing, or when my Aunt Bertha told one of her incredibly intricate Celtic tales, this was the room we'd use.

Whoever constructed that room way back when, they knew what they were doing.

Jacqueline and I had been in attendance that evening. My other three children were with Hagen at a school science presentation. Jax, who worshipped Heiner and already burned to pursue the musical path, did not want to miss this rehearsal for a 'stupid science fair'.

We sat together on one striped-silk settee while waiting for Helena and Heiner to arrive in the *Salon* (our informal, so very French, name for the room).

A wooden box had been laid on the other settee. Jax opened the lid and peeked inside. I was as curious as she was and leaned over to look.

The red stilettos were inside.

We both gasped. I pulled them out.

I immediately kicked off my sneakers and slipped the gorgeous red shoes on. My head filled with music, with the longing to dance, dance forever, and never stop. I pictured Hagen and me dancing together, whirling, smiling, touching. I closed my eyes and felt the tingly craving all through me, my restless legs aching with the urge to dance.

"Mama? Can I try them, too?"

Jacqueline brought me out of the trance. With great willpower, I slid the shoes off. I attributed my dance dream to the fact that it had been so very long since Hagen and I had had the time to indulge in one of our most enjoyable shared pastimes.

My fingers didn't want to let go of them, but I handed them to Jacqueline, expecting her feet to swim inside, a child in grown-up shoes. I smiled at the thought even though my neck muscles tightened with the irritation of letting the shoes out of my hands.

To my surprise, the shoes fit Jax. But how could that be?

That was the first inkling I had, the suspicion that all was not right with those red stilettos. Heiner's voice rang out above us, from the gallery as he spoke with Helena.

"Jax! Take them off." My mother-command-tone whisper made Jacqueline jump.

Her fingers closed around the heel of the shoe on her left foot. "They feel so comfortable. I could wear them forever."

It was as if she, too, had to force herself to remove them. "Jax, quick. They're coming. The shoes probably belong to Helena."

She shook her head and shrugged; set her lips in a line. A very grown-up response. But that was my Jacqueline, ahead of her years, understanding and reacting, already leaving childhood behind. She tore the shoes off but then placed them gently in the hand-crafted wooden box. She began to lower the lid of the box, caressed the shoes one more time and then firmly closed them within the box.

I let out a huge breath. Heiner and Helena had already started down the stairs.

And now, *German Music Night* was here, and Helena was out there on the stage, performing the same moves as she had that night. The shoes looked the same. Helena didn't.

During the rehearsal, after she had put on the red shoes, Helena had glided, swung, stepped, and twirled, and the song flowed effortlessly along with her choreography. It looked perfect. There was no way she could lose the upcoming contest. Jax had murmured soft praise with words like, *cool, crazy wow, fantastic*. And lastly, *those shoes*.

But now. Even though Heiner's song sounded the same, and Helena's delivery, her dance, lost its beauty and power. The magic had gone astray. The tiny voice inside me whispered what I knew as truth. With every cell, every telomere of every chromosome, every surge of red platelets through my veins and arteries, I knew it shouldn't, couldn't be possible to dance badly with those shoes on.

Another quiet but compelling inner voice—it sounded strangely like Heiner—said, *there's been a swap. A swindle. A sting*. Those are *not* the shoes.

I filled my glass full and topped off Grünberg's, shaking out the last drops. The bottle was empty. And so was I.

Grünberg slugged back his champagne, nodded his good-byes, and left. Jax quickly occupied his place, curling against the arm of the plush couch, trying not to look tired.

Heiner returned to sit with me, make-up washed off, his face without even a sheen of perspiration. He still smelled good, manly with a lingering trace of his perfume. His performer smile was firmly in place and would likely remain so until the contest was over.

But I knew it; the contest was already over. Heiner's song would not be the winner.

We watched all the other performances. E! was up last, perhaps a concession to her accident. Before she went on, the hip lady moderator, whose name Jax informed me when I asked was Zöe Bienenfreund (Zöe, *friend to the bees*), announced a change to E!'s song. It was unusual, and possibly not allowed under the terms of the contest. But

E! had appealed to the judges and they had approved the change in song.

She was E!, after all.

None of the other singers had her status, many of them being amateurs, on the brink of professionalism. But here was the catch: the song's composer was to be listed as *Anonymous*. That, apparently, wasn't against the rules of the contest, but why would anyone want their song to be anonymous?

I thought I had a clue, and clenched my hand into a fist.

My suspicions were confirmed when E! emerged onto the stage, gave a bow, and then began to sing *Danger, Dancer*. Her back-up band and singers couldn't disguise the fact that it was one of Heiner's songs. One he'd been working on as recently as a week ago before he and Helena had begun devoting all their free time to rehearsals for tonight's contest. I didn't recognize the lyrics, which sang of shoes that compelled the wearer to dance until she died, unable to stop.

Lyrics written for E! Lyrics that described the red stilettos and their curse?

But when had he done that? And why would he jeopardize his own chances of winning with his officially entered song?

It was a lively, if a bit more commercial version of the song I'd heard him composing in his living room. Definitely could be construed as *Schlager* in its current pop-hip-hoppy version. Had it broken his heart to do that? But Heiner jumped musical genres with apparent ease. He played folk metal from time-to-time, and some of his performances (with a very diverse crew of musicians) could also be considered World Music.

I shivered and bit my lip, and felt tears forming. Helena had not returned from the stage after her performance.

"Where is Helena?" I finally managed to ask Heiner after E! finished to a T-Rex-sized roar of applause from the audience.

"She's not coming back," he said, turning his head to meet my gaze, the apology in his eyes. But still he kept his performer face on. Heiner had compromised his own chances of winning the contest. Why had he done that?

"Did you listen to the lyrics?" he asked me softly.

I nodded. "Are you going to tell me the rest?"

He took my hand and squeezed it while glancing at Jax, who was once again busy checking messages. She seemed oblivious to our conversation.

"After this is over. Back at the hotel."

I squeezed back.

Heinrich and Caitie stood together in the clearing in the Schattenreich. Hagen had agreed to meet them here. Heinrich was more nervous now than he had been on stage, and that had been bad enough. Caitie's ire was a force to be feared, way more powerful than a ticked-off audience-turned-nasty. They had also brought Jacqueline over with them and laid her in a soft bower of grass with a blanket and a pillow. She curled up as if that was the way she slept every night. Caitie kissed her forehead and adjusted the blanket.

Caitie stood and crossed her arms as she faced Heinrich.

"Well?" she said. "How did you do it?" She still wore her evening dress but had shadowcrafted it to be shorter, knee length, flaring out at the bottom edge. She was barefoot and adorable, her anger making her earlobes red at the tips.

"Do what?" Heinrich said.

Hagen appeared nearby and walked towards them.

Caitie flicked her wrist and a generic red shoe appeared for a brief moment before it disappeared. "The switch. The sting. And... the reason."

"The lyrics. I didn't make them up." Heinrich flicked his wrist and held out a book of fairy tales to Caitie. "*The Red Shoes* by Hans Christian Anderson. The real ones must have originated before Anderson wrote his tale. Possibly in the Middle Ages, is my best guess. They were apparently, and always have been, real."

"Or these shoes were a very good remake," Hagen said. "And

although that irks me to no end, we'll probably never know. Or how E! got them. Did she say, Heiner?"

"A gift from another performer," Heiner said. "One of those never-ending tales."

Hagen smiled and bent to kiss his wife. She smiled at him. Then she frowned. "You were in on this, too?"

"I was. It seemed prudent. I didn't want you to have to cut off your lovely feet to stop your dancing," Hagen said and pointedly stared at his sleeping daughter. "Or Jacqueline."

Caitie put a hand to her mouth. "So, Helena was right. They *were* cursed. But—"

Heinrich held up a finger. "The fake red shoes were shadow-crafted. By Ankou. He inscribed them with runes to do the job of camouflage. It was the only way to protect Helena as well. She'd already danced in them once. And she would eventually have reached the point where she wouldn't have been able to take them off."

"And E!—she wore them. They belonged to her," Caitie said.

"Yes," Heinrich said, drawing it out. "She began to realize their danger and was close to the point of no return—of never being able to take them off again. It seems just having them on once is not enough. But the effect is cumulative. The longer they are worn, the harder it is to take them off."

"Aha. That's why E!'s dancing got so good."

"She told me her career really took off once she started wearing the shoes."

"And…let me guess. In exchange, you gave her your song?"

Heinrich nodded. "In exchange for our subterfuge, which she pulled off beautifully."

"How—"

"I don't know what she took to pass out, but probably something fast-acting such as chloral hydrate. Followed by another drug to counteract its effects. I think she mentioned Ritalin combined with something else…that part was dangerous. But she was willing to risk it. She regretted giving the shoes to Helena. Didn't want to see her suffer."

"Or she didn't want supernatural competition from Helena," Hagen said.

"But, the song, the charity. I'm so sorry," Caitie said.

"Don't be. I've retained the publishing rights. And E! agreed to donate all the proceeds from the song to our foundation."

"Well, then." She paused and shook her head. "Fooled just about everyone. Except me. Oh, and Hauptkommissar Grünberg," Caitie said.

"I think Helena twigged to it after the performance. She was really angry with me," Heinrich said and shrugged.

"She'll get over it," Hagen said. "And her greed for fame overcame her reluctance to wear *cursed* shoes. So, she is not entirely blameless."

"Perhaps not entirely. But I still feel sorry for what happened to her tonight," Caitie said and put hands on hips. "And what happened to the real shoes?"

Ankou, Lord of the Dead, without doubt the most powerful deity still extant in Ande-dubnos, stood behind Caitie. He called her name softly. She whirled around.

"I thought you might want to wear them once more," Ankou said and bowed to Caitie. He held out his hands, which held the *original* enchanted footwear. "Before I take them away for safe-keeping."

Caitie gasped when she saw them.

Heinrich wondered what they looked like to her. He still saw the beautiful ballet shoes.

"Ankou!" she said.

"My name does not have an exclamation point in it," Ankou said with an Otherworldly smirk.

She laughed and then stopped. She didn't trust Ankou. She had many good reasons not to. She held out her hands for them and he pulled them just beyond her reach.

"One condition," Ankou said.

Caitie's hands returned to her hips. "What?"

"The first dance," he said.

She lifted her chin, looked towards Hagen.

"I concede to the request," Hagen said to Caitie. "If it's acceptable to you."

Caitie bit her lip. But then she nodded.

"May I?" Ankou asked.

She held out a slender foot. Ankou slid one shoe onto her foot. And then the other. The red from the shoes sparkled in the muted glow of early evening. Banked coals in the cool night air.

Ankou stood and held out his hand. "Milady."

She curtsied with a smile. "Milord."

Heinrich picked up his acoustic guitar, which he'd hidden behind the nearest tree, the grandfather oak that defined the entrance to the woods bordering the clearing. "What shall I play?"

"*Sacred Heart*," she said.

"Do you want me to sing?"

Caitie shook her head. "Without. I really like the instrumental version."

Heinrich strummed the first notes of the song.

And they began. Hagen stood next to Heinrich, his arms crossed. He probably hated the fact that Caitie was dancing with Ankou. But they needed to show some gratitude. And Caitie didn't look like she was minding it one bit.

Ankou danced exceeding well, an immortal who had no doubts about his place in this world, the Otherworld. Or any world. He moved with inhuman grace. And passion. That should be said.

But Caitie.

In the enchanted red shoes, she was not...no, not poetry in motion. That would be a cliché. And there wasn't a single clichéd thing about her, the woman who stirred his heart like no other. A von der Lahn by birthright and by marriage. His muse, his friend. His sometime lover.

She was Skaldic verse sung in that forgotten language with the voice of a thousand Germanic warriors bent on glory. Her movements rang a tribute to cadence and, imbuing Heinrich's music with her rhythm, an unfailing current of strong emotion and will.

She smiled with the joy of her dance, her long reddish-brown hair flying out, her dress swinging as she twirled to follow Ankou's precise lead. Caitie laughed, drawing an answering laugh from Ankou. Heinrich had never seen the Lord of the Dead so focused, so engaged. So enthralled.

Heinrich ended the song. Grateful to have been able to witness, to provide the impetus to bring Caitie to the brink of abandonment. Like making love, only, somehow, more intimate.

"Hajo?" he asked his brother. "Would you like to dance—"

"I would. You know which song."

Heinrich did.

Hagen strode off to take his wife back from the immortal deity who worshipped her. She came eagerly into her husband's arms.

Heinrich planned to let *this* song play out longer, for he did not begrudge them their pleasure.

But he would not be sad when Ankou took those red shoes away. He hoped that they stayed gone, for at least another human lifetime. Heinrich glanced at his niece Jacqueline, sleeping the sleep of the innocent beneath the grandfather oak's boughs that stretched over her head.

Make that two human lifetimes.

ABOUT THE AUTHOR

Now a full-time writer living near Cologne, Sharon Kae Reamer's speculative fiction is inspired by her participation in various archeoseismology projects during her twenty-something years as a senior scientist at the University of Cologne. Locations that include the Praetorium and medieval Jewish settlement in Cologne, ancient Tiryns in Greece, and Greek ruins in Selinunte, Sicily, provide perfect backdrops for creating fantasy stories rich with history and mythology, such as her *Immortal Guardian* and *Schattenreich Mystery* novelette series and her five-book *Schattenreich* novel series.

Her love for mixing and mashing science fiction and fantasy continues unabated. *Night Shepherd*, in the *Schattenreich* universe is a spinoff (one of many) of her soon-to-be-published first novel in *The Sundered Veil* series, a further conception of science fantasy.

Sharon plans to continue her pursuit of archeoseismology because the personal and professional connections she's made cannot—and should not—be deterred. She also cooks daily (German-English), gardens (chaotically, at best), knits (badly), does needlepoint (rather well) and reads (everything) all the damn time.

And, of course, she has cats.

Find out more about Sharon at:
sharonreamer.com

BB bookbub.com/authors/sharon-kae-reamer

TRUE LOVE

(OR THE MANY BRIDES OF PRINCE CHARMING)

TODD FAHNESTOCK AND GILES CARWYN

Some people blame poor Prince Charming for throwing Cinderella into the dungeon. They call him heartless for having little Snow White beheaded. Few know the real reasons Sleeping Beauty had to be burned at the stake. But that is because they have only heard one side of the story.

It is time the truth came to light.

The tale of Prince Charming begins, as all romances should, in the Enchanted Forest. Magic sparkles in the air. Zephyr breezes sway through the trees. Birds sing their sweet songs into the amorous ears of all who will listen...

Prince Charming—or Evil King Chuck, as he came to be known—was hardly the merciless and maniacal madman as many would like to believe. He was a big-hearted man, a man of strength and compassion, a man who did his duty. The prince married—all too frequently, in fact—for love, and fought for justice. In the end, he was forced to battle to save his wounded heart.

Have you ever noticed that fairy tales never continue past the last dance at the royal ball, the sumptuous palace wedding banquet, or love's first true kiss? There's a reason for that.

That first kiss eventually twists itself into a wedding, and marriage can bring out the worst in a person. Magical enchantments tarnish into nothing but lust. Those zephyr breezes can turn shrill and howl through the castle halls. And those birds—those damn birds!—can chatter loudly enough to drive a man insane!

Certainly, Prince Charming blames the birds for much of his own matrimonial disasters. Charming's lot was a sad one. His choices were difficult, but he made them with a stiff upper lip. And his thanks for all his sacrifices? A cold throne. The hatred of his subjects. Tales of his legendary cruelty spread throughout the land. A mockery made of his name. So how did it all come about?

Let me tell you the tale of the sadly misunderstood Evil King Chuck.

◦∿◦

Back in the Enchanted Forest, down there among the breezes and singing birds, a handsome young prince named Charming stood to inherit a fabulous kingdom. He considered himself the luckiest among men, and why should he not? Talking with the young prince Charming was like a dance with the summer wind. Conversation never lagged before Charming filled it with a witty jest or a fanciful tale. People flocked to spend time in his presence.

Charming was also a natural athlete. A strapping lad, he excelled at all the manly activities. By age eighteen, he'd out-jousted his father's strongest knights, outfought the most experienced men-at-arms. His physical endurance was without equal. He could run through the woods for days without tiring. On the hunt, Charming always killed twice as many beasts as any other man.

In politics, Charming was a fast study. From the time he was a boy he spoke freely and wisely during his father's royal councils. Charming had an uncanny ability to understand men's hearts and what forces moved them. Ambassadors and ministers sought his advice. The court all whispered that he was everything they could hope for in man, a friend, or a king. Every golden path lay before him.

Charming could have done anything, but there was only one direction his heart ever led him in. Charming was a true romantic.

He loved jousting with the knights. He loved matching swords with the men-at-arms. He loved out-thinking the generals. He loved making people smile and laugh, but he craved one thing above all: he wished to find his True Love.

Surely there must be some woman out there to share his life with, a lovely, sensible woman with wise eyes and gentle hands. Someone to rule by his side through the years, faithful and loyal to him and to his future kingdom.

Charming had seen into the hearts of the women at court. He heard their petty gossip. He saw them sing a friend's praises to her face and then speak poison of her behind her back. He wanted none of that. In their eyes he was nothing but a husband to be won.

Charming wanted to be loved for himself, not for the attached position and real estate. He wanted the kind of love that no one in the kingdom had seen in ages. He wanted True Love.

Charming searched far and wide. Sometimes he would leave the palace using the pretext of a long hunting trip, sometimes with the excuse of visiting relatives in other kingdoms, but always he searched for the perfect woman he just knew was out there, waiting, ready to love him and only him.

All his looking was to no avail. No matter how hard he searched, he could not find his True Love. Charming began to despair, to feel that perhaps he was setting his sights too high. Perhaps True Love was just a myth.

With the death of his dream, he began to sink into an unaccountable melancholy.

The king worried over his son and asked what was wrong. Charming did not want to alarm his father, but he could not hide the sadness in his heart.

"Surely you have not met with every woman in the kingdom?" the king asked his son.

"Father, I have traveled far and wide. Everywhere I go, it is the same. I speak with women. I laugh with them. We tell each other stories. They do that strange thing with their eyelashes. I wait for the spark that will warm the deepest corner of my heart, but there is nothing…"

"Surely you have not knocked upon every door in the kingdom and asked to meet the daughters of the house?" the king asked his son.

"No, Father," Charming admitted. "I have adventured high and low, but not door to door."

"Well, then," the king said, "So we shall."

The next day the king issued a proclamation. There would be a royal ball. All the eligible ladies in the kingdom were invited to spend a night dancing at the palace. The king sent his messengers door to door, presenting the invitation.

Charming could hardly wait for the night. The ball seemed to be the answer to his dreams. Surely he would find the woman he searched for.

The night of the ball arrived and the palace was filled to capacity with women of every sort. Prince Charming danced with tall women, with short women. He danced with golden-haired women, with red-haired women, with dark haired women. He danced chest to chest with heaving breasts, gut to gut with bursting girdles. He danced with women who could glide silently across the floor, with women who trod painfully upon his feet. He danced with silent women. With boisterous women. With demure women. Fiery women. Beautiful women. Ugly women.

He danced until the soles of his shoes wore through.

Charming's outlook was grim indeed. Was there not a single woman in the entire kingdom that he could love? As he pulled his tortured feet out of the scraps of leather that were his shoes, he knew that true love could not be found in such a manner.

Then *she* walked through the ballroom doors.

Charming's jaw dropped. She had hair of shining gold, ruby red lips and milky white breasts. His eyes traveled the length of that pearl-studded blue-on-blue gown which hugged and emphasized her wonderful curves. He lost his heart in an instant. Cinderella turned toward him and met his gaze with a lovely blush that tinted her cheeks the color of rose petals.

As the prince stood there watching her, he realized he was not alone.

For a short time, it was wonderful. In fact, it was the memories of that first night that kept Charming from insanity or even suicide in later years.

But that was the future. On that night, Prince Charming forgot there were any other woman in the palace. Arm in arm with Cinderella, he swept about the dance floor for hours. The blisters on his feet were forgotten. The bruises on his shins were a memory. Everything was perfect, or so it seemed, until, at the stroke of midnight, Cinderella suddenly screamed and ran for the doors.

Charming stood in shock as True Love fled from his arms. Too late he tried to give chase, sprinting across the dance floor and onto the grand staircase. Nothing was left of the woman of his dreams, save for a glass slipper on the steps and an enormous pumpkin rolling away into the night.

The glass slipper should have tipped him off. Cinderella's odd carriage should have nailed the coffin shut on her chances of marriage. There were hints all along of trouble to come, but Charming was smitten. He could see nothing beyond her beauty, her soft skin, her fine figure. Her dulcimer voice haunted his memories.

But what kind of a woman owns glass shoes? Shoes in which the slightest misstep meant severe lacerations? What kind of a woman shuttled herself around in a squash? From the moment she stepped out of the coach, Charming should have realized she was out of her gourd.

With that damn slipper, Charming managed to find Cinderella. He and his entourage went door to door, searching for the owner of the glass slipper. When he found it fit upon the delicate foot of a servant girl he could not have been happier. Two days later he was married.

No one truly knows what occurred on the honeymoon. As honeymoons should be, it was an affair between the young lovers alone, but Charming returned with a smile on his lips and light in his eyes.

Things went downhill after that.

Perhaps he had begun to learn of his new bride's eccentricities. Perhaps the fire of his idealism had dimmed. It is possible that Charming, with his keen insight, had seen where his relationship with his wife must certainly lead. If so, he blocked it out and continued on in the most noble manner.

He did not question his dear wife when she brought all of her pets into the palace. When the nobles fled the city due to the singing rodents in the west wing, Charming was concerned. Still, he had nothing in particular against mice and calmly pacified his father. When the seamstress complained that the little rodents were stealing her best fabric and thread to make hideous dresses, Charming hushed it up, bought new materials, and set the seamstress up on the other side of the palace.

Then the royal stables became infested with rodents and lizards, lounging in the mangers of the matched teams, draped across the ornate handles of the state coaches. The pests could not be chased off. As speedy as quicksilver, they would zip out of sight when the royal cats went after them, then resume their positions the moment no one was looking. The entire stable staff resigned after the first month.

By all rights, Charming should have immediately dealt with his wife's hobbies. When Charming discovered his mother's twelve prized Persian cats dead beneath the west tower window—a window filled with singing mice—he should have staged a mass rodent execution.

But Charming was a romantic. He was a man of honor, and he loved his wife above all else. He cleaned up these messes and covered for her. Charming held onto his illusions to the bitter end.

Then Cinderella invited that woman into the palace. Charming checked his sigh when she introduced the old hag as her Fairy Godmother. But the prince loved his wife and put on his most charming smile. The old woman was given her own rooms and whatever she might require to make Cinderella happy.

The old woman was plump and jovial. She sang silly songs, but that did little to hide the truth that she was the most criminally expensive dressmaker of all time. After long years of making do with the dregs from her stepsisters, Cinderella had some serious shopping to get out of her system. That sweet-smiling, rosy-cheeked fairy godmother inflated Cinderella's wardrobe to epic proportions. Charming's new bride ordered the finest fabrics from the ends of the earth. Diamonds from the far southlands, pearls from the west coast, even rubies from the east. Even Cinderella's undergarments glittered, shone, and could cut glass.

Then came the interior decorating. No chair satisfied Cinderella until it was worked by a master carver and upholstered in silk. No bed was fit to sleep in unless the headboard was inlaid with precious metals and mother-of-pearl. Even the royal castle was not up to the standards of this ex-scullery maid.

"The fixtures are too dull," she would say, "Replace them in gold."

Perhaps the old king should have done something before it got out of hand. He should have told Charming he was letting his wife run all over him, but just as Charming could deny his wife nothing, so the king denied nothing to his only son. They both waited in painful anticipation for Cinderella's next request.

The expensive balls began shortly thereafter, as Cinderella decided it was time to show off her new clothes. Money flew out of the treasury. Taxes were raised, slowly at first, then faster and faster, until the peasants began grumbling. Discontent among the people grew as quickly as Cinderella's wardrobe.

Within a year, the kingdom reached the edge of revolt. The peasants were taking up arms. Curses, and worse, were flung at the king when he rode through town. The peasants were starving, and Princess Cinderella had 5,000 pairs of shoes. Charming knew he had to do something. Balance had to be restored before an angry peasant mob attacked the palace gates.

Every man has his breaking point, and Prince Charming's came late one night when he went to his father for counsel on these brewing matters. When he walked he into the king's room and found the mice taking down the drapes to make yet another dress for Cinderella, Charming snapped.

He ordered every hungry cat in the kingdom to be set upon the mice. He trapped them, poisoned them, burned them out of their holes. The lizards became belts. The thieving fairy godmother was sent back to her Enchanted Forest, wearing a new gown of tar and feathers. Cinderella was finally thrown into the dungeons after psychiatric counseling and a series of expensive 12-step programs failed to curb her spending.

Prince Charming then began to restore the kingdom he'd nearly brought to its knees by his foolishness. He had Cinderella's dresses and shoes sold off, the rich furnishings and rugs returned or auctioned to the highest bidder. The palace's golden door handles were melted down, replaced by more serviceable brass ones. Soon, both the bellies of the peasants and the chests of the royal treasury were full again.

Life in the dungeon was not too bad for Cinderella. She made friends with the rats down there. She sang them songs and they wove her petticoats out of garbage and the remains of corpses...

Poor Prince Charming, however, was devastated by what had happened. Once the kingdom had been righted and riots no longer ravaged the streets, he went off to live alone in the woods. He hoped a little solitude would salve his badly wounded, too-trusting heart.

He lived a month alone in a small cottage, hunting for his supper, and chopping his own wood for the fire. In the evenings, with his belly full of venison, Charming would watch the sun set and marvel at the beauty of nature. Slowly, he put the insanity of Cinderella and her entourage behind him. He began to take long walks into woods. He would choose a different direction, a walk a different route every time.

And so it was he stumbled across the crystal casket lying alone in the woods. When Charming peered inside he was amazed. The prince had never seen a more devastatingly beautiful young woman. She was so radiant as she lay there sleeping. She had raven dark hair, ruby red lips, not to mention those milky white breasts barely concealed by a velvet gown.

Charming shook his head. He nodded gruffly and looked at her in what he hoped was a clinical fashion. She was beautiful, but the prince just had his fill of beauty. Still, his curiosity was piqued by her predicament. Why was this woman asleep in a crystal box out in the middle of nowhere? He considered tapping on the glass to ask her, but wasn't certain what would be polite in a situation like this.

As the prince stood there watching her, he realized he was not alone.

Charming's acute ears heard them scuffling. His hunter's eyes spotted the tiny men hidden in the trees.

Charming unsheathed his sword. "You may as well show yourselves!" he called, "If it's gold you're after, you'll find your work difficult enough this night! I've given up enough gold lately and, frankly, I'm in the mood for a fight!"

The little men came out of hiding, hands out and open in a pacifying gesture. There were seven of them, and each was stumpier and uglier than the one before. They swore they were not thieves and had no wish to fight the strapping young prince. Instead, they told him of a horrible curse that had been put upon their friend in the casket, the beautiful Snow White. Only the kiss of a real prince could break the spell.

Charming almost turned on his heel and marched out of the glade. He knew that would be a very unprincely thing to do, however. With power came responsibility, and he knew that princes didn't come by this neck of the woods every day. If he didn't help the girl, who would? Besides, the little men seemed so sad. They obviously thought of the girl as a daughter and cared very deeply for her.

Smiling a little, Charming announced that he was a prince. The dwarves cheered. Flipping open the casket's lid, he leaned over and kissed the girl. Her lips became instantly warm. Her soft arms wrapped snugly about Charming's neck, and he found himself in the midst of a deep kiss.

No, it was a legendary kiss.

Fire spread throughout his body as he kissed those ruby red lips and she pressed those heaving, milky white breasts to his chest. Finally, the kiss subsided like the tide receding from a beach.

Charming's breath came in short gasps as he looked down into the young woman's sultry, dark eyes. They beckoned him for more. He tried to think of sunsets alone by his cottage, of roasting venison over a fire. All of these memories blurred like watercolors in the rain and vanished.

Two days later, Prince Charming was married again.

No one truly knows what occurred on the honeymoon. As honeymoons should be, it was an affair between the young lovers alone, but Charming returned with a smile on his lips and light in his eyes.

Things went downhill after that.

Charming felt like he was revisiting a bad nightmare when Snow White moved her pets into the palace. He could not turn his head without seeing a bluebird twittering. He could not walk down the stairs without being passed by a pack of rushing squirrels.

But Charming was a patient man, and he had seen far worse. He let these things go by.

Then the dwarves moved in. They were loud and annoying. Charming tolerated it at the behest of his new wife, whom he could deny nothing. After all, the gnarled old men had taken care of her in her youth.

After the first day, Charming began to wonder if he had made a grievous error. He tried to take an interest in his wife's friends, but it was impossible to tell the little buggers apart. Some of them were chronically grumpy, others were manic. One of them went around sneezing on everyone. A few days after the dwarves moved in, half the staff came down with the flu.

The dwarves were horrible houseguests. On top of being ugly as sin, they had no table manners whatsoever. Burping, snorting, farting at the table! After the conclusion of the Cinderella debacle, the local nobles had slowly begun to sift back into the palace. They were still skittish and it didn't take long for them to start sifting politely back out. One dinner with a dwarf was enough for anyone to lose their appetite.

The dwarves dug up the basement. They dug up the yard. They would have dug up the ballroom floor if Charming had not physically disarmed them.

"It's just in their nature," Snow White would say sweetly and give him one of those deep kisses. Thoroughly pacified, Charming would nod and smile his charming smile. And so it went...

Perhaps things would have smoothed out after a while if those pacifying kisses had continued. Who can say how long a man can stay lost in the eyes of a lovely and willing woman?

But the kisses became less frequent, then stopped altogether. In the beginning, it would have been an understatement to say that Snow White enjoyed her wifely duties. As the months went on, however, she became less and less interested in poor Prince Charming. If she did not suffer from a headache, then she was simply too exhausted to muster more than a passing greeting to her husband before she slipped into slumber.

Every man has his breaking point, although Charming was a more patient, compassionate man than most. He wanted nothing more than his beloved wife's happiness, but when he found the long, gray hairs in his bed one morning, his blood began to boil. But Charming had no proof, so he held his tongue. Every day after that he suffered when he saw the smug little smiles on their wizened little faces, that rosy tinge to their wrinkled little cheeks.

Charming was a hunter, and began to hunt his wife. He found little muddy footprints in the Snow White's private bath. He noticed extra lumps in the feather mattress on her bed. It was only a matter of time before he caught her.

Charming could actually hear his heart split in two that night he walked into the apple orchard and found all eight of them together.

Though it made him sick at heart, Charming had no choice. The law is the law. He called the axeman and had the lot of them put to death.

Charming fell into a deep depression. The squirrel hunt he arranged in the palace made him feel better for a few hours, but it didn't last. All he could think about was Snow White's betrayal. What did those little bastards have that he did not?

Soon after, the executioner brought him the answer. Not every part of those dwarves was little.

Enraged, driven by the need to release his anger, Charming went on a quest, seeking out good deeds that needed doing. He hoped some adventuring would take his mind off of his troubles. He scuttled a pirate ship and rousted a pack of bandits, but they were only passing fancies. Then Charming heard tales of an evil witch who was keeping an entire kingdom encased in a spell of eternal slumber. It was rumored that the witch could metamorphose into a dragon with black fangs and burning yellow eyes. Charming's budding misogynist streak flared. He took it upon himself to rid the world of this evil bitch.

Prince Charming and the sorceress-dragon met upon a battlefield of thorns. The fight was long and bloody, but Charming emerged victorious. He stabbed the dead dragon body numerous times once she had fallen. He stomped on her head, chopped off her claws, made a necklace of them as he laughed into the wind.

Finally he tired and stood there empty and alone, staring at the dead witch.

As the prince stood there watching her, he realized he was not alone.

Struggling through the remains of the thorns was a skinny officious man. Charming had not had so much fun in almost a year, and he nearly lopped the offending man's head for interrupting. The prince stayed his hand long enough to listen to the man. He was a messenger from the kingdom that the evil sorceress had enchanted, and had been sent to report that the spell had not been broken with the sorceress's death. In order to truly free the kingdom, a prince must kiss Sleeping Beauty in the high tower.

"Oh, God," Charming spat, "I'm not going through that again. I'm just here to kill things. Find yourself another prince!"

Why the stupid girl had to go and get herself cursed in the first place, Charming didn't even want to know. The messenger cajoled and bribed. In the end, Charming had to admit that an entire kingdom shouldn't have to suffer just because he didn't want to kiss some sleeping tart stuck in a tower. Finally, after great deliberation, Charming swore to go into the high tower and break the spell.

Charming climbed the tower, threw the cover off of Sleeping Beauty and kissed her. He made certain to jump back before she could get her tentacles around him. She awoke slowly. Charming turned his head, not wanting to even look at her. He wanted to run, afraid of what would happen next. His damned curiosity caused him to pause.

Instead of igniting the fires of his passion, however, she began to sing. The melody of her voice filled the room and wrapped Charming up in its power. She sang of a daring prince who faced the horrible dragon of her nightmares. She sang of how he risked his very life to come to her aid, of how sweet and kind his lips were against hers. She sang of how she owed him everything.

Charming, poised to flee, slowly turned and looked into her eyes, which were brimming with tears. He smiled hesitantly and her song turned joyous. He looked down at her honey colored hair, her ruby red lips, her milky white breasts...

Two days later, Prince Charming was married yet again.

No one truly knows what occurred on the honeymoon. As honeymoons should be, it was an affair between the young lovers alone, but Charming returned with a smile on his lips and light in his eyes.

Things went downhill after that.

More pets. Getting dressed in the morning was tantamount to a full-fledged hunt. If it wasn't the damned owl stealing his shirts, it was the bunnies running off with his boots! Soon, even his own horse started laughing at him! But Charming bore it in smoldering silence because he was determined to be such a fucking good husband.

Charming soon noticed an even more frightening trend in his new wife. Beauty had spent her entire life being told that if she pricked her finger she'd die. She'd never even been allowed close to anything sharp until the moment she entered Charming's castle.

Perhaps it was the curse, or perhaps she had been warped long before because of being raised by fairies, but Beauty began to develop an obsession with sharp objects.

"Charming, be sure to bring the needles to bed with you."

"Charming, what a lovely new dagger you have."

"Charming, if you love me, you'll use that sword on me like a man, not a boy."

"Charming, meet me at the ballista again at midnight, you chicken-shit bastard!"

Hushed rumors began spreading throughout the servants quarters. Blood on the bed sheets. Strange rituals in the prince's rooms at midnight. Perhaps they were sacrificing chickens... goats... newborn babies!

This time, Charming wasn't going to wait until things became intolerable. He wasn't going to wait until he woke up, impaled with a fence stake by his wife's latest gesture of affection. Charming didn't want to do it, but he had no choice. He had to get rid of her and he couldn't be merciful about it. The headsman's axe would have excited the girl far too much. It would have been indecent. Instead, he had her burned at the stake.

Charming never left the palace again. He wouldn't risk it. He spent the rest of his days locked away from all women. When his father died, the once charming prince became the Evil King Chuck, the king who outlawed marriage. He had any passing love poets put to a painful death. Minstrels who strayed from a strict battle hymn into softer songs of the heart soon found themselves swinging from the gallows.

Much as Chuck wanted to ignore it, the inky smoke from Beauty's pyre lingered in the air. Snow White's little gasp at the falling axe echoed in King Chuck's ears. Sometimes, late at night, he could still hear Cinderella talking with the mice. Slowly but surely, the memories of his past weighed him down. As the dark years passed, Chuck developed a crick in his walk. His hair and beard grew wild and unkempt. His once broad shoulders curled over into a hunchback's lump. The few servants and nobles who had survived the first three brides of Prince Charming quietly fled the palace, and it became a dark, dank place. The peasants abandoned their fields and went in search of richer kingdoms.

It was said that Evil King Chuck was cursed.

~

Soon the king was all alone in his dismal castle. His fingernails grew into claws. He took to talking with the clocks and candlesticks to keep himself sane. But Chuck was not completely unhappy. Never did his yellow eyes look upon a woman. Never did his hairy ears hear the words: True Love.

But one day a stranger snuck into his castle. Chuck was up in the farthest reach of the west tower when he caught the scent of her perfume. He flew into an immediate rage. Grabbing two knives, he raced down the stairs, charged through the long hall and threw himself over the banister that led into the grand foyer. With a maniacal snarl, he fell upon the foul creature.

"Please, please!" she cried out, "Don't hurt me! My name is Belle. I mean you no harm!"

The young beauty looked up into the Chuck's bestial eyes. Fear marked her face, but courage held her fast. Chuck watched as compassion for him slowly entered her features.

No! He would not be swayed! Evil King Chuck grabbed his knives tighter and prepared to make supper of the girl.

And yet...

Chocolate colored hair... Ruby red lips... Milky white breasts...

"You don't have any pets?" he asked. His grip on the knives relaxed.

"Ah, just a horse," she said, keeping her composure despite the flashing knives.

Chuck paused.

"He doesn't sing goes he?" he growled.

"Uh, not so far."

He paused.

"I think this could be True Love." he said.

ABOUT THE AUTHOR

Giles Carwyn is a novelist, screenwriter, husband, father. He co-authored the Heartstone Trilogy with Todd Fahnestock published by Harper Collins in 2006-2008. While living in Los Angeles he worked as script analyst for Phoenix Pictures. He has presented workshops on various aspects of the writer's craft through Pike's Peak Writers and Delve Writers. His also a licensed Shadow Work® Facilitator and Coach who specializes in men's sexuality. He is a co-creator of the Eros Work Program and the Men's Sexual Shadow Transformation Weekend with Shadow Work® founder Cliff Barry. He currently lives in Asheville, NC and is working on a historical screenplay about the mentoring relationship between Merlin and the teenage King Arthur.

Find out more about Giles at:
gilescarwyn.com

ABOUT THE AUTHOR

Todd Fahnestock is a writer of fantasy for all ages. His bestselling The Wishing World series for middle grade readers began as bedtime stories for his children. His epic fantasy series include: *Threadweavers*, *The Heartstone Trilogy* and *The Whisper Prince Trilogy*. *Charlie Fiction*, a time travel urban fantasy, is his latest novel. Stories are his passion, but Todd's greatest accomplishment is his quirky, fun-loving family. When he's not writing, he goes on morning runs with his daughter, wrestles with his son, and practices Tae Kwon Do. With the rest of his free time, he drives the love of his life crazy with the emotional rollercoaster that is being a full time author.

Find out more about Todd at:
toddfahnestock.com

facebook.com/todd.fahnestock

twitter.com/@Todd_Fahnestock

goodreads.com/ToddFahnestock

bookbub.com/authors/todd-fahnestock

BEAUTY OR BUTTERFACE?

DEB LOGAN

CHAPTER 1

Fathers! What can you do with them? Nothing. That's what. You just go along with their mad whims and hope to all the gods the universe holds that they don't screw up your entire life. At least, that's what happens when your father is king and you're his only son and heir.

It's not like the old days, when magic ruled and every royal family had a fairy godmother to help them out. I know the legends; I've heard Dad's stories. To hear him tell it, my mother's fairy godmother was instrumental in their lives, but that's probably just another of Dad's tall tales. I've certainly never seen a fairy, but if I had, you can bet I'd've wrangled a wish for some way to make Dad ease off on the life-altering expectations.

Don't get me wrong. I'm no pushover. I pull off the occasional small rebellion. Sometimes even manage to logic my way around a few of his crazier ideas. But when it comes right down to it, I obey or the castle guard will see to it that I'm grounded for life. And in my case, grounded means a private cell in a dank, dark dungeon that smells of mold and rat droppings. Possibly with chains—just to make sure I get the point.

Yeah. I know who's boss...and someday, if I don't screw things up, it'll be me!

Dad's latest obsession is securing a line of succession, and since I'm his only son, that means I have to marry a princess and produce an heir. Pronto!

Great. The most important decision of my life and Dad wants me to make it in the next five seconds.

No pressure, son. Just make a choice. You'll only have to spend the rest of your life with her. Not to mention have sex with her on a regular basis so I can have a grandchild. Nope. No pressure at all. Just get on with it!

Thanks, Dad. Can't wait.

CHAPTER 2

"Philip, my boy! How are you this morning?" Dad beamed at me from his seat at the breakfast table. Sunlight streamed through spotless windows and sparkled off gleaming cutlery and polished serving dishes. A sideboard groaned under the weight of every possible delicacy a king could desire first thing in the morning. Platters of eggs (scrambled, fried, deviled, and poached), rashers of crisp bacon, salvers of thinly sliced beef and savory fish, stacks of buttered toast, waffles, pancakes, bowls of colorful berries, and, of course, my least favorite food, steaming, gluey porridge.

You'd think we were expecting an army to join us for our morning meal.

Dad looked unusually chipper this morning, which put me on edge. "What's up, Dad?" I asked, eyeing his perfectly tailored suit complete with purple sash of state slashed across his rotund torso. Dad can manage a dignified appearance if he has to, but most of the time he looks like a short, round, balding Santa relaxing in the off-season. Thank all that's holy, I take after my maternal grandfather, tall, slim, with a full head of wavy chestnut hair. "You're awfully well-dressed for so early in the morning."

I waved the butler, Jennings, away and stepped to the sideboard.

Dad was old-school. He preferred to sit in state while Jennings offered him dishes and then served the items Dad chose. Always seemed like a waste of time to me. Why sit there and wait when I was perfectly capable of scooping up my own scrambled eggs?

When my plate was enticingly loaded with fried eggs, bacon, toast and marmalade, and several slices of honeydew melon, I joined Dad at the table.

"Great news, Philip," Dad said, wiping a bit of yolk from his chin. "I'm finalizing a treaty with Lindesland this morning. A very advantageous one. I'm sending you to Stefan's kingdom. You're to marry his daughter, and when the two of us are gone, our kingdoms will be merged. You and, eh, uhm, what's her name will rule a new and vastly larger realm. Isn't that exciting?"

The blood drained from my face. My appetite fled, and a knot of molten lead formed in my belly. "You've chosen my wife? Without even asking me?"

Confused disappointment dimmed Dad's smile. He looked like I'd just refused the best gift in the world. Bewilderment glazed his eyes. He frowned momentarily before his gaze cleared and his smiled brightened.

"Not at all," he cried, slapping his palm on the table. "I've forgotten the best part. Stefan has *two* daughters. Identical twins! You'll have your choice of brides."

I groaned and buried my face in my hands. Why did I have to be born a prince?

CHAPTER 3

King Stefan's castle was much like our own: ancient in design but refurbished to include all the modern conveniences. My suite of rooms was suitable to my station. Luxurious bedroom complete with a king-sized (of course!) four-poster bed hung with velvet curtains in royal purple, a comfortable sitting room paneled in dark wood and overlooking a rose garden, and a private bath with Jacuzzi and sauna.

My royal guards and I arrived late in the afternoon. Dad referred to the guards as my retinue. I thought of them as jailers, there to make sure I didn't make a run for it. I mean, why in the world would I need four burly men to protect me from Stefan and his daughters? My best protection would be the destruction of that treaty, but that wasn't going to happen. I just had to resign myself to choosing between two identical girls.

I could hardly wait.

After being shown to our rooms, I was informed that dinner would be at seven, and that I would meet the family in the drawing room promptly at six-thirty. One of my men would accompany me, of course, but being a well-trained guard, he would fade into the background.

I had just finished adjusting my cuff links when a knock sounded on the door. David, my jailor for the evening, opened the door to a young man in Stefan's livery.

"Highness," he said with a precise bow, "I'm here to escort you to the drawing room."

I glanced out the window at the sunlight fading across the rose garden. Just like my freedom...rapidly disappearing.

"Highness?" said the footman.

"Yes," I said, turning to face my inevitable doom. "Of course."

We strode through carpeted hallways, down a sweeping staircase with a lavishly carved bannister, across a stone-flagged entry and paused at a richly polished mahogany door. The footman opened the door, stepped inside, and announced me.

"His royal highness, Prince Philip of Glencowrie."

Straightening my shoulders and inhaling deeply, I walked into the room. The tableau that met my eyes surprised me. King Stefan stood before the window, gazing out over the perfectly manicured lawns. His wife, Queen Isabelle, sat in a high-backed chair on the far side of the room. I'd expected two young women, but the king and queen were alone.

King Stefan turned when I entered and marched to meet me, hand outstretched. "Philip," he said. "I don't believe I've seen you since you were a small boy." He grasped my hand and shook it. "You've grown into a fine man."

"Thank you, sire," I said, gripping his hand, but not too firmly. No need to turn a hand shake into a duel. "I'm pleased to be here."

Stefan smiled and led me across the room to his queen. "Allow me to present my wife, Queen Isabelle."

I clicked my heels and bowed over the hand she graciously extended. "An honor, your majesty."

"You are welcome in our home, Prince Philip," she said. "I hope you will enjoy your stay."

Her words were courteous, but I thought I detected sadness in her eyes, a slight tightness at the edges of her mouth. Was something amiss? Had my arrival interrupted a disagreement? My own mother having died when I was still in diapers, I was unaccustomed to the nuances of a married couple, but something felt...odd.

I pushed the thought away and smiled. I was probably projecting my own unease onto Stefan's queen.

"I'm sure you're anxious to meet our daughters," Stefan said.

I nodded politely while trying to breathe past the sudden tightness in my chest.

Stefan gazed meaningfully at a door beside a large stone fireplace. A footman moved to open the it and called, "Their royal highnesses, Princess Dawn and Princess Aurora."

A rather plain young woman stepped into the room. Short dark hair curled around a face dominated by a bulbous, overlarge nose. Her lips were thin and uninteresting, but her eyes...her eyes were large and dark and surveyed me with wary intelligence. She wore a deep blue evening gown that failed to glamorize her angular, too-skinny frame.

I clicked my heels and bowed to her, my heart sinking. Identical twins. The next girl wouldn't be any more attractive.

When I straightened, I realized just how wrong a guy could be.

The second sister had entered the room and her radiance filled every shadowy crevice. The breath left my body and my lungs forgot how to function, until her gaze met mine and she smiled.

My heart pounded, the thrum of my own pulse drowning out every other sound in the room. I inhaled sharply, wondering what I'd done to deserve such a prize?

She was perfection personified. Hair so golden it looked like she'd captured the sun and pulled it into ringlets. Lips so full and red they made the roses in the garden look drab. Sapphire blue eyes twinkled mischievously in a face whose complexion was a glorious mix of peaches and cream.

Like her sister, she wore a gown of deep blue, but that was the only similarity. This gown clung to a lush bosom, flowed past a trim waist, and spilled over ripe, round hips. I burned to take her in my arms, run my hands over those curves, kiss those rose-red lips...

"Prince Philip?"

King Stefan's voice jolted me from thoughts rapidly descending into the lewd. I jerked my gaze from his luscious daughter and fought to focus on him.

"Forgive me, sire," I said, lowering my eyes and closing them for a brief moment. When I looked up again, my emotions, and my lust, were under control. Barely. "You were saying?"

Stefan smiled, a trace wanly. "If you will escort Princess Dawn," he said, glancing at the mousey sister, "we'll go in to dinner now."

I chanced a glance at Beauty, for that was how I thought of her, and saw her place a perfect hand on the stunned footman's arm to be escorted in to dinner. The young man looked like he'd been hit between the eyes with one of Cupid's arrows.

My own eyes narrowed with jealousy. I looked away quickly, caught my breath, and turned my attention to my assigned partner. A butterface, if ever I'd seen one. Crossing to her side, I held out my arm. "May I see you to the dining room, Bu...Princess?"

Good Lord! I'd almost said *Butterface* aloud! I was more addled than I'd realized.

Brown eyes sparkling good-naturedly, she rested a hand lightly on my forearm. "Of course, Prince Philip," she said. Her voice was soft and musical, a balm to my jangled nerves. "I look forward to getting to know you."

And suddenly, surprisingly, I found myself pleased to be her dinner partner.

Since there were only five of us, the grand dining table had been replaced with a small one. It sat rather forlornly at one end of the large room, looking as out of place in the grandeur of the dining hall as Butterface did beside Beauty. King Stefan took his place at the head of the table, Queen Isabelle on his right and Butterface, uhm, Princess Dawn on his left. Princess Aurora sat beside her mother, and I took my place beside Princess Dawn. Which placed me directly across the table from Beauty.

I couldn't have asked for better placement for that meal. I could gaze with besotted wonder at the stunning face and form of Beauty, while conversing quietly with her lovely-voiced and quick-witted sister.

For Dawn proved to be a delightful conversationalist, well-informed and not shy about sharing her opinions. Our topics ranged from racing—both cars and horses, to school experiences—we'd both attended prestigious boarding schools and were pleased to be finished with them, to the perils of royal birth.

I genuinely enjoyed listening to her speak, both for the musicality of her voice and the logical flow of her thoughts. As long as I didn't concentrate on her appearance, I found her lovely and engaging.

"So, tell me truthfully, Philip," she said as the butler served a lovely crème brûlée for dessert, "What do you think of this treaty our fathers have designed?"

"Well," I said, stalling as thoughts whirled through my head. Truthfully? How could I answer truthfully without giving offense?

"Come now," she whispered leaning toward me so that I breathed in a hint of lavender and roses. "You can't have been entirely pleased with this arrangement."

"No," I admitted. "Father's been after me for the last few months about choosing a wife and providing him an heir, but..." I hesitated, met her gaze and, recognizing a spark of irritation that matched my own, plunged ahead, "I never expected him to take the choice out of my hands."

She nodded. "I understand completely." A mischievous grin lit her face. "I suppose he tried to appease you by saying you still had a choice. Twins, after all."

I grinned. "Yes, he did pull that one out. Can't say that it made me feel a lot better." I stopped, held her gaze, my mood suddenly serious. "Of course, it's no help at all to you and Aurora. There's only one of me."

She sat perfectly still, an air of thoughtfulness wrapping around her like a cloak. Then she cocked her head and smiled at me, the playful expression making her features almost pretty. "You know, I think one might be all we need."

Her mother chose that moment to rise, ending the meal. So on that enigmatic statement my first encounter with Butterface came to a close.

CHAPTER 4

T he next day Queen Isabelle suggested that Aurora show me the castle grounds. The princess smiled at me and said she'd be delighted.

I forgot how to breathe again.

Fortunately, before I could die of asphyxiation, she moved to my side, placed a hand on my arm, and guided me toward the French doors. Between her touch and my own faltering gait, the paralysis of my lungs subsided and I drew breath once more.

We strolled through the rose garden trailed by a maid and James, today's guard. I'd never really needed a chaperone to walk around a garden with a pretty girl before, but then that girl had never been Beauty...

I was hyper-aware of her hand on my shirtsleeve. The heat of her small fingers burned through the fabric, nearly scorching my skin. I glanced at my arm, convinced that the cotton must be smoldering, but all I saw was a small, neat hand tucked into the crook of my arm. Perfectly normal. Except that it wasn't. Normal, that is.

Her hair was loose on her shoulders today, spun gold glistening in the morning light. Her dove grey silk blouse and light blue cardigan clung to her curves. My mouth alternated between too dry to speak and practically drooling. And those trousers! Dark grey, neatly pleated, and so perfectly molded to her gorgeous...uhm...assets.

I closed my eyes, concentrated on not stumbling over my own feet, and let her guide me through the garden.

And that's when I discovered it. With my eyes closed, when I couldn't see the golden perfection of her, my world fell back into place. I heard the breeze sighing through the trees, caught the blend of delicate fragrances of the garden's flowers: roses, lilacs, lavender and violets. Without the sight of her to distract me, I felt the good solid earth beneath my feet, the crunch of gravel on the path. My mind cleared. I realized that we hadn't spoken a meaningful word in all the time we'd been walking.

My thoughts and attention had been completely mesmerized by her beauty, by my desire to touch her, hold her, do other, more intimate things to and with her. But when I closed my eyes, I was hardly even aware of her hand on my arm. I certainly had no awareness of her as a person.

Something was definitely wrong with this whole situation.

CHAPTER 5

S everal days later, I still hadn't managed to figure out what was going on, but I had a wealth of experience with both Beauty and Butterface.

Beauty continued to dazzle my senses, but I had discovered ways to deal with the enchantment of her perfection. I'd learned to glance away, close my eyes, concentrate on a single thought. In short, my defense against Beauty's glamour was meditation.

Now there was a laugh. What red-blooded, healthy young male wants to meditate in the presence of a stunningly beautiful, perfectly proportioned female? Me...because I also wanted to keep my sanity and be able to speak in complete sentences.

Butterface was a totally different story. She was charming and sweet, but with a deliciously wicked sense of humor. I loved spending time with her and thoroughly enjoyed our conversations. But I couldn't get past her unattractive exterior. Logical debate or game of trivia? I wanted her on my team. But hold her in my arms and kiss her? No thanks. Let's play chess instead.

On the last night of my scheduled visit, King Stefan sent word that I should join him in his study. Expecting a manly conversation complete with drinks and cigars, I was surprised to find all three of the ladies present. Stefan rose from behind his desk when I entered and motioned me to the sitting area to join his family.

I hesitated. The furniture was arranged in a cozy conversation square: two sofas faced each other across a low rectangular table. At each of the other ends stood an overstuffed leather chair. Queen Isabelle occupied one chair and King Stefan stood beside the second.

That left the sofas, each of which held a princess.

Which would it be? Would I choose to sit beside Beauty or Butterface?

I declined to choose. Instead I strode across the room and leaned against the edge of Stefan's desk. This placed me behind Beauty, but I had the feeling I was going to need my wits about me, so that wasn't necessarily a bad thing.

Stefan covered his mouth with his hand, but not before I saw the grin he was trying to hide.

We subsided into tense silence. Queen Isabelle stared at the table, her fingers nervously pleating and unpleating the edge of her sweater. Butterface sat straight as a board on the leather sofa, her unblinking gaze glued to the floor. King Stefan fidgeted, clasping and unclasping his hands or twisting his royal signet on his finger. Only Beauty appeared at ease. I couldn't see her face, but her shoulders were relaxed and she sat quietly.

Finally, Queen Isabelle cleared her throat and gave her husband a very pointed look.

"Right. Yes," he said. "Down to business. Philip, we've asked you here to this private room to finalize the treaty between Lindesland and Glencowrie. As you know, the agreement calls for you to marry my daughter. The time has come for you to make your choice."

My face felt like I'd stuck it in a fire, but I managed to nod. What to do? What to say? How was I supposed to meet my father's expectations without screwing up the rest of my life? If I'd been one of those lucky royals of old and had a fairy godmother, I knew what I'd wish for in that moment: I wanted nothing more (or less) than to merge Beauty and Butterface into one person! Too bad that wasn't an option.

My heart pounded so loudly I was sure everyone in the room

could keep time with its rhythm. My palms were slick with sweat and my mouth was parched.

Rubbing my hands on my twill trousers, I straightened away from the desk and stepped to Queen Isabelle's side.

"Your majesty," I said, inclining my head to her. "Thank you for the honor of allowing me to get to know each of your daughters. Both of them are treasures." I focused my attention on the mother, knowing that a glance at one daughter would render me speechless, while catching sight of the other would weaken my resolve.

"Thank you, young prince," the queen said, her voice tight with strain, "but like my husband and daughters, I am anxious to hear your decision."

I nodded, closed my eyes and tried to think. *Don't look*, my heart whispered. *Just listen.*

Without looking, I leapt.

"I choose Butterface," I said. My eyes popped open in horror as I realized what I'd said. "I mean D-Dawn," I stammered. "I choose Dawn!"

To my utter bewilderment, everyone in the room burst out laughing.

The queen grasped my hand and cried, "Bless you, my boy!" while King Stefan staggered to his feet and raced to thump me on the back and pull me into a bear hug.

But most amazing of all? Beauty disappeared in a shimmer of sparkles and a glimmering woman appeared behind the sofa where she'd been seated. An ageless woman with wings and a wand.

"Wh-what's going on?" I cried, glancing to the one person in the room whose opinion I valued most, Butterface...who was a butterface no longer.

Dawn grinned at me with tears in her eyes. Her hair was still short, dark and curly, and her eyes were still deep brown and beautiful, but the rest of her facial proportions had changed. Her nose was no longer large and bulbous, but straight and just the right size for her face. Her lips were full, but not overblown, and her complexion was tanned and lovely with just the right blush of healthy pink. And the rest of her...well, let's just say that my Butterface was no longer angular and stick thin. She was nicely curved in all the right places and filled out her jeans with perfectly proportioned...assets.

I shook off her parents and stumbled to her side, feeling tongue-tied for the first time in her presence. "Wh-what's going on?" I asked taking her hands just to make sure she was real. "Who are you? What happened to you?"

She grinned even more widely and stepped into my embrace. She felt warm and soft and fit there absolutely...perfectly.

After a moment, the winged woman coughed and suggested we all take a seat.

This time I had no trouble with the suggestion. I sank onto the sofa and pulled Dawn down beside me.

"Prince Philip, I am Merridee, Princess Dawn's fairy godmother," the winged woman said. "When the princess heard of her father's treaty with Glencowrie, she came to me and begged a boon. I deemed it a reasonable request, and granted her wish."

I waited for her to continue, but the silence, now more embarrassed than tense, stretched.

"And?" I prompted.

Merridee stared meaningfully at Dawn, who squirmed in my arms and moved away from me. She was blushing to the roots of her curly dark hair.

"Do you remember that first night at dinner," she began, "when I asked you how you felt when you heard about the terms of our fathers' treaty?"

I nodded and caught her hand. I still needed reassurance of her reality.

"Well, I felt like you did," she continued. "Angry that Father would bind me to you without even asking what I thought. So I called upon Merridee and she found a solution."

"You see, young prince," Merridee said, "Dawn wanted to be sure that the man she married would love her for herself and not just as a prize who came with a kingdom. So we devised a twin for her. Either choice would bring the kingdom, but only choosing the uhm...ugly... sister would show true understanding of Dawn's worth."

"But what if I'd chosen Aurora?" I asked, confused. "She didn't exist. How would that have won me the kingdom?"

"It wouldn't," admitted Stefan. "I would have found a way to break both the engagement and the treaty rather than leave my people in unworthy hands."

My head was spinning. Granted, my own wish had come true in this twisted revelation, but still, I'd been used, made a pawn.

"One of you should've told me," I said to the king and queen.

"They couldn't," said Dawn, very quietly. "Merridee laid a geas on them. Trust me," she said, looking full into my eyes, "neither of them was the least bit happy about this scheme. If you're angry, and you've every right to be, you must be angry only with me."

I stared into her dark brown eyes and recognized my heart's desire.

"I do feel used," I said, "but I'll get over it. The question is, will you ever get over being called Butterface? Because that's who you'll always be to me."

She smiled through tear-filled eyes. "I'll get used to it," she whispered. "And just so we're straight, by the time we finished dinner that first night, I knew this ruse was unnecessary, but I'd set it in motion and had to let it play out."

She sank back into my embrace. "Thank you for choosing me."

I stroked her hair and kissed the top of her head, reveling in her scent of lavender and roses. She challenged me and made me think, was my equal in every way, and she was lovely both inside and out. How could I be angry?

I closed my eyes, not as a defense mechanism, but in order to savor the magic of the moment. "Thank you," I whispered, for her ears alone, "for making all my dreams come true."

ABOUT THE AUTHOR

Deb Logan writes children's, tween, and young adult fantasy. Her stories are light-hearted tales for the younger set—or ageless folk who remain young at heart. She's published 14 titles, including short stories, collections, and novels and has been featured in several anthologies. Author of the popular "Dani Erickson" series, Deb loves dragons and faeries and all things unexplained.

Find out more about Deb at:
debloganwrites.com

f facebook.com/deb.logan.750

g goodreads.com/deb_logan

BB bookbub.com/authors/deb-logan

CHANCE OF BUNNIES AND OCCASIONAL TOAD

ANNIE REED

T he house smelled dusty and abandoned.

Just like me, Cecily thought.

For a minute there, the old-fashioned lock, rusty with age, fought her. Cecily worried the real estate agent had given her the wrong key, but eventually the doorknob turned, and she pushed the door open.

Even though Cecily was a grown woman with a place of her own, it felt odd opening this door with a key that now belonged to her, just like the house itself now belonged to her. During all the summers when she'd been sent to live in this house with her aunt because her mother couldn't deal with having Cecily home from school for an entire three months, Cecily had never unlocked the door herself.

She could have. Cecily was one of a generation of "latch key" kids, a by-product of the feminist movement that saw women like her mother working nine-to-five jobs while their kids went to school from nine to three. Cecily had worn her house key on a lanyard around her neck, and for two and a half hours every afternoon, she sat by herself at the dining room table and did her homework in an empty house. Not because she wanted to, but because her mom would check Cecily's work first thing, even before starting dinner, and if Cecily couldn't show her mom two and a half hours' worth of work, she was grounded from watching television for the night.

Her aunt didn't place the same restrictions on Cecily as her mom had.

"Summer is a time for fun," her aunt used to say. "To read because you want to. Eat in the living room, have dinner for breakfast or breakfast for dinner. It's not a time for kids to worry about keys. Keys are for grownups."

The front door opened directly into the living room. Cecily stepped inside and shut the front door behind herself.

The room looked both smaller and larger than she remembered. Smaller, she supposed, because the last summer she spent here, she was only twelve years old. If she ever went back to her elementary school, it would probably look smaller, too. Perspective changed with age, and right now, Cecily felt every single one of her thirty-three years.

God, had it been that long since she'd visited her aunt?

All her aunt's furniture was gone, which made the room look larger. Cecily had handled those details over the phone. "Find a charity," she'd told her aunt's estate lawyer. "One that benefits abused women." She'd paused, remembering. "Or an animal rescue organization. I don't care about the write-off. Just make sure they can use my aunt's things, not just toss them away."

The real estate people had done a good job cleaning the inside of the house. Fresh, not-quite-white paint covered the walls. The old avocado-shaded nubby carpeting was spotless, if a little threadbare in places. She remembered stretching out on that carpet reading comic books, of all things. Her mom never let Cecily spend money on comics at home.

In place of her aunt's comfortable furniture, impersonal Pottery Barn knockoffs created a not quite lived-in look. A generic bookcase was centered on one wall, an uncomfortable, over-stuffed chair against another. Tasteful brochures from the realtor's office fanned out on a glass-topped coffee table. A silk flower arrangement crouched on the mantle over the brick fireplace, but the house felt empty. Unlived in.

The sight of it all made Cecily ache. Her aunt was really gone. Maybe coming here had been a bad idea, but Cecily had to know. The adult she'd grown into wouldn't let her say goodbye to this part of her life without knowing.

A framed print of a watercolor landscape centered just so on the wall opposite the front door reflected Cecily's silhouette back at her. Just for a minute, she could almost see her aunt in that reflection, not as Cecily had last seen her—a jovial, round woman of indeterminate middle age; ancient, really, to a twelve-year-old—but as she must have been in the last years of her life. A little bent with age, her hair gone frizzy white and thin, but still with that broad grin on her face, the one that said life was far more fun that Cecily's mom would ever know.

That grin—that attitude—was the thing that Cecily treasured

most about her Aunt Gin. It was the thing she didn't realize she would miss so badly after her aunt was gone.

"I could do all this for you," her mom had said. "Honestly, I don't know why Ginger wanted you to handle her estate. I'm her sister."

Cecily knew why, not that she could ever tell her mom. What could she say? "Because of the bunnies, Mom." Her mom would never understand.

Cecily was here for the bunnies.

Bunnies, and the occasional toad.

C ecily had been ten when Aunt Gin let her have a taste of beer one late summer afternoon.

They were sitting in lawn chairs in her aunt's big backyard beneath a tall maple tree, the wide, dense leaves keeping the sun off their skin. The air was hot and dusty dry without a whiff of breeze to cool things off, and Aunt Gin was fanning herself with a fancy fold-out fan she let Cecily play with sometimes.

Cecily thought the beer tasted gross, but because she knew it was something kids weren't supposed to have, she asked if she could have her own glass.

Aunt Gin laughed. "Oh, my, but you're going to get me in trouble with your mother. Viv will never forgive me for sending her daughter home with a taste for beer." Her eyes twinkling with amusement, she gave Cecily a long look. "You don't really like it, do you?"

Cecily scrunched up her nose. "No." She handed the beer back. "How come you do?"

"Can I tell you a secret?"

Cecily nodded. She was pretty good with keeping secrets. She didn't tell on Jimmy Cuthbert when he put an ice cube down Marilyn Skinner's dress because Marilyn Skinner had called Jimmy a turd. Of course, Cecily didn't like Marilyn Skinner either because she made fun of Cecily's name. But still, she knew she could keep one of Aunt Gin's secrets.

"The bunnies like it," Aunt Gin said.

"That's not a secret, that's just silly." Bunnies ate grass. They didn't drink beer.

"Occasionally the toads enjoy a nice cold beer on a hot day, too."

Aunt Gin was teasing her, she had to be. "Everyone knows toads eat flies," Cecily said. She hoped any toads that showed up in Aunt Gin's yard ate flies. A few persistent flies had been landing on her sweaty skin, and she'd grown tired of swatting at them. "Nasty old flies."

"They do eat flies," Aunt Gin said. "With a nice beer chaser. You ever taste a fly?"

Cecily shook her head.

"Well, compared to a fly, beer tastes pretty darn good."

Aunt Gin liked to tease, but not in a mean way like the kids at school. It was more like she enjoyed making things up. That's what Aunt Gin did for a living, her mom said. Made stuff up.

It wasn't until she was much older that Cecily realized her aunt was a writer. When she was ten, all she knew was that Aunt Gin would spend her nights typing in a little room off the hallway right behind the living room. Sometimes her aunt pounded the keys on her old typewriter so fast, it sounded like the *rat-a-tat-tat* of gunfire on a television show, interrupted often with the ring of a little bell and the ratcheting sound of the carriage return. Other times, Aunt Gin would sit in that room with the door half-closed, listening to music on her record player, and not type a word. But no matter how hard and fast her aunt typed or how late she stayed in that room each night, Aunt Gin always found time to spend with Cecily the next day.

Even if that meant all they did was sit outside beneath the maple tree while Cecily read a comic book and Aunt Gin sipped a beer.

Cecily's friends back home thought spending a summer this way was boring, but she loved it, and not just because she got to do things with Aunt Gin she didn't get to do at home. Aunt Gin had a huge backyard dominated by that big maple tree. The lawn wasn't much, but flowers grew along the fence in between bushy shrubs, and there was a little pond with a fountain in one corner in the back. Plastic statues and figurines, mostly of things like squirrels and chipmunks and birds and a silly-looking cat standing on his back legs, playing a violin, peeked out between the flowers and the shrubs. Cecily always had something to look at, and when she'd been little, things to play "let's pretend" with. She'd lost track of the number of times she'd whirled around in the yard, dancing to music the cat was playing just for her.

One side and the back of Aunt Gin's yard were closed off with a tall redwood fence, but the other side had only a little split-rail fence. On the other side of the split-rail fence was a field that seemed to go on forever.

"That's why I love this place," Aunt Gin had told her one time when they were sitting beneath the maple tree. "All that open space, as far as I care to see. There's magic in open spaces, you know. That's where imagination lives."

At ten, Cecily didn't know about magic, but she knew about the rabbits that lived in the fields. She saw them now and then, cute little brown bunnies with fluffy white tails. She told her aunt once that she wished she could hold one because it looked so soft and cuddly.

"You can't hold magic, Cici. If you try, it runs away. That's why adults can't see magic anymore. They want to own it. Control it. They've forgotten how to slow down and just let the magic happen."

Her aunt had been the only one who'd ever called her Cici. She'd liked it. Cici didn't sound nearly as odd as Cecily. Marilyn Skinner wouldn't make fun of a Cici.

It never occurred to Cecily back then that she could have decided she wanted everyone to call her Cici. Her mom told her Cecily was dignified, which was what a young lady should be. After she'd gone to law school, Cecily sounded more like what a lawyer should be called. Not Cici.

No, Cici had been the young girl who'd snuck out of her aunt's house in the middle of the night, beer in hand, to see if bunnies and toads really drank the bad-tasting stuff.

She'd poured the beer into a small bowl with short enough sides that she figured a bunny could reach. She wasn't sure about a toad, but she didn't really care about toads. It wasn't like she wanted to touch one. She really, *really* wanted to touch a bunny.

She'd sat in a lawn chair in her aunt's backyard all night, wrapped in a throw off her bed. Her aunt had the door to the typewriter room closed all the way, so it hadn't been that hard to sneak out. The stars filled the night sky. Cecily could hear the gentle burbling of the fountain and the buzzing of night insects. The yard was dark, but there was just enough light from the neighbors' house, where they kept their back door light on all night, it seemed, that Cecily could see the little bowl where she'd left the beer.

She wasn't trying to trap the bunnies. Really. She just wanted to see one up close, and she hoped that if she gave it the beer her aunt said it liked, it might let her touch it.

She thought she'd be able to stay awake all night. She hadn't been tired when she first went outside, but the throw was soft and thick and comfortable. She sometimes took naps in the lawn chair on a hot afternoon, and it really was a long night to just sit and wait. It wasn't surprising that before long she fell fast asleep.

When she woke up, the sky was just starting to get light with the first hint of dawn. Cecily hadn't meant to be outside all night long. Would her aunt be upset? Cecily's mom would be. Aunt Gin wasn't like her mom, but Cecily still didn't want to make her mad. Kids weren't supposed to sleep outside all night, especially not when they'd snuck out of the house to begin with.

Something rustled in the grass near the rail fence. Cecily held her breath as a rabbit hopped close to the bowl. The bunny was little more than a dark shape against the darker grass, but its fluffy white tail gave it away. The neighbors' back porch light made the bunny's dark eyes glisten.

The bunny hopped slowly, like Cecily knew bunnies did when they didn't feel threatened. She'd seen them freeze stock still in the field when they heard a dog or when they saw Cecily come out into the backyard. Then they'd hop away like crazy, their fluffy white tails bouncing along behind them.

The bunny got close to the bowl. Was it really going to drink the nasty old beer?

Something odd happened then. Something that Cici the ten-year-old thought might have been a dream, and something the adult Cecily thought was the result of straining too hard to see things in the dim light of early dawn and listening to too many of her aunt's stories.

A little pinprick of light fluttered out from one of the bushes near the back of Aunt Gin's yard. Another little light joined it, and then another and another until a whole group of little floating, fluttering light drifted toward the bunny.

Cecily had seen fireflies before. These little lights were too small to be fireflies. Whatever they were, some of them settled on the top of the bunny's head, and others settled on the rim of the bowl.

Soon so many of the little fluttering things ringed the bowl that they made it look like one of those glow-in-the-dark stars Cecily's friend Crystal had on the ceiling of her bedroom.

Then the toad came.

Like the bunny, the toad hopped slowly across the grass from beneath a shrub near the split-rail fence. Unlike the bunny, the toad had a much larger glowing thing riding on its back. Cecily thought it looked like a butterfly.

She blinked her eyes, trying to see clearly. That simple movement made everything freeze. The bunny went still, just like she'd seen the bunnies do in the field. The fluttery things ringing the bowl of beer stopped fluttering, and their glow dimmed. Even the little thing on the back of the toad quit moving its tiny wings.

"I won't hurt you, " Cecily whispered. "I brought you the beer. I wouldn't do that if I wanted to hurt you."

She was never quite sure what happened next. One moment she was sitting in the lawn chair watching something that couldn't be real, and the next her aunt was bending over her.

"Cici, honey?" her aunt said. "What in the world are you doing sleeping out here on the grass?"

And she *was* on the grass. She still had the throw wrapped

around her, but the lawn chair was empty beside her. The grass was damp and kind of scratchy beneath her, and the ground was hard. Overhead, the sky was pale blue and lavender and rose, and cloudless. The sun was almost up.

What had happened? Hadn't she fallen asleep in the chair?

Cecily sat up. "I think I had a dream," she said. "But I was in the chair."

Aunt Gin held out her hand. Cecily took it and got to her feet. She was stiff and cold, and she really had to go to the bathroom.

"What did you dream about?" her aunt asked.

"Bunnies." Cecily rubbed at her face with one cold hand. "And some little things that flew around and looked like fireflies, but not as big." She blinked as she remembered more of her dream. "And a toad! A big one, with a glowing butterfly on its back."

Aunt Gin's eyes widened a little, then she smiled. "So that's why my bowl is in the middle of the yard. You brought something out with you last night."

Cecily didn't want to lie to her aunt. Lying was wrong, her mom said, but more than that, it felt wrong to even think about lying to Aunt Gin. "Beer," Cecily said. "I brought them beer. You said bunnies and toads like beer, and I really wanted to pet a bunny."

Her aunt's face took on a strange expression. When Cecily thought about that morning now, she thought her aunt had looked wistful, but all ten-year-old Cici had cared about was that her aunt didn't get angry about the beer.

"That's fine," Aunt Gin had said. "But let's not do that again, shall we? I'll never hear the end of it if your mother finds out I let you stay outside all night long."

Cecily's mom didn't even like Cecily to go on sleepovers at a friend's house. Going to Aunt Gin's during the summer was the only sleepover Cecily ever had, and she didn't want to mess that up by disobeying her aunt over something Mom would ground her for.

"Okay," she said. "But I really want to touch a bunny. Do you think one will ever come in the yard for real and let me touch it?"

Aunt Gin put her arm around Cecily's shoulders and ushered her back into the house. "You never know," she said. "Around here, there's always a chance of bunnies, and occasionally even a toad."

C ecily didn't see any more bunnies in her aunt's backyard that summer. She did find the hole beneath the shrub that the toad had called home, although by the time Cecily found it beneath a bunch of dried leaves, all that was left was an empty hole in the dirt. The toad had moved on.

Three years later, so had Cecily's mom. Her job transferred her to a city far away, too far for her to send Cecily on a big Greyhound bus to Aunt Gin's for the summer.

Cecily had been thirteen then. She'd been disappointed, but there'd been Jason, a red-headed boy from school who played softball in the park during the summer. Instead of hanging around Aunt Gin's backyard, dreaming of touching a bunny, Cecily had hung out that summer with new friends at the park and watched Jason hit line drives over a low fence and flirt with other girls. Cecily forgot about bunnies and toads and her aunt, caught up as she was in the angst of her first unrequited teenage crush. Mom had said she was impossible to live with; looking back, Cecily tended to agree with her.

Years turned into a decade and then two, and Cecily never saw Aunt Gin again. Sure, she talked to her aunt on the phone whenever her mom said they could afford the call, and wrote her aunt letters when her mom said they couldn't. Aunt Gin sent Cecily a hundred dollar bill, the first hundred dollar bill Cecily had ever seen, when Cecily graduated high school. When she graduated college, Aunt Gin had sent Cecily two hundred dollars in twenties hidden in the pages of Aunt Gin's latest fantasy novel.

A novel about talking animals who lived in the same world as people, even though most people couldn't see them.

The book reminded Cecily of the bunny and toad she'd dreamed about. Aunt Gin must have told Cecily the stories that formed the basis for her novels. That's why she'd had the dream about bunnies and toads and tiny lights that ringed a bowl full of beer.

After college came law school, and after law school the horrible years when Cecily worked eighteen hours a day, seven days a week, trying to distinguish herself from the other young associates. Her mom was proud of her—she told Cecily that often enough, after all—not that Cecily was surprised. Her mom valued hard work. Now that she was grown up and living on her own, Cecily understood what her mom must have gone through after Cecily's dad left home when she was only two. Cecily had no memories of her father, but her life had never really felt incomplete without him. She'd grown up with two women, her mom and Aunt Gin, who were strong, independent women in their own ways. It was no wonder that Cecily was so driven to succeed.

But at what cost? Standing in her aunt's empty house, she felt like she'd lost a lot leaving Cici behind.

She hadn't brought any beer with her to Aunt Gin's house. She'd never acquired the taste. Even if she had, she would have been afraid to bring any here.

What if she had, and the magic wasn't real?

Or even worse, what if it was?

The real estate agent probably thought she was nuts. She hadn't cared about any of the furniture inside her aunt's house. She'd told the man to box up all her aunt's books and personal things—Cecily would look over them later, when the loss didn't seem so immediate—but the only furniture she told the man not to touch were the lawn chairs she knew her aunt would still have in her backyard.

The maple tree was bigger than Cecily remembered. Of course, it would be. Unlike the house, it had continued to grow in the twenty years since she'd been here. The lawn chairs were newer versions of the ones she'd sat in with Aunt Gin beneath the branches of the trees, both of them swatting lazily at flies. The lawn was neatly trimmed now, as were the bushes and the flowers. The real estate people had hired someone to come in and spruce up the landscaping. Houses, especially forty-year-old homes, were a hard sell in the current market. She'd authorized the expense as both executrix and primary beneficiary of her aunt's estate.

An estate, she was surprised to discover, that included not only the house and the lot on which it sat, but the three lots next door that made up the empty field.

Over the years, her aunt had purchased the land. To keep it undeveloped and wild? It was too late now for Cecily to ask.

That was the other purpose for coming here. She couldn't decide what to do with all the extra land. With houses going unsold, no one was clamoring for empty land to build on. Cecily had a job and obligations a thousand miles away. Cecily owned all of the property, or would as soon as the estate closed, but Aunt Gin's had been her summer vacation spot, not a place she intended to call home.

Cecily brushed off one of the lawn chairs and sat down. The sounds of suburbia surrounded her. A neighbor a block or so away was mowing his lawn. Down the street, a dog barked, a playful yip. Somewhere else, children were laughing. Birds flitted from tree to tree, chattering at each other. A sparrow hopped along the top rail of the wooden fence between her aunt's backyard—now Cecily's backyard—and the field next door.

She unfolded the fan her aunt had used all those years ago. The spokes were thin wood, the brightly patterned fabric red silk. Aunt Gin had sent it to Cecily as part of her Christmas present just last year. Cecily had sent her aunt a gift card for a local restaurant as a last minute present.

"When did we lose touch?" she asked the empty yard. "Why did I let you slip away?"

The slats in the lawn chair creaked beneath her weight. In the field, some insect started a persistent buzzing.

That long-ago morning after she'd fallen asleep in this yard, before Aunt Gin had walked her into the house, Cecily had caught a glimpse of the bowl she'd brought into the backyard. She'd walked carefully out of the kitchen with that bowl, careful not to spill a single drop. It had been tricky because she'd filled it with beer almost to the very top.

The bowl, still sitting in the grass, had been empty that morning.

Cecily wondered if her aunt thought Cecily had finished off the beer, and that's why she'd been asleep on the lawn. The dedication in the fantasy novel Aunt Gin had given her for a college graduation present had been "For Cici, and the empty bowl." Cecily's cheeks had reddened when she'd read that. She'd hoped her mom would never ask her what that meant. Only when her mom had called Cecily to tell her that Aunt Gin had died in her sleep in this very backyard had her mom admitted that she never read any of Aunt Gin's books.

Cecily shouldn't have been surprised. Her mom was much too grounded in the real world to believe in fantasy.

"Did I just dream that night?" Cecily asked the empty backyard. She must have. Things like beer-drinking bunnies and toads didn't exist. Not in this life.

The sun lowered in the western sky as Cecily sat in the lawn chair and thought about all the time she'd spent here. Aunt Gin's will had specified no funeral, no memorial. Cecily's mom had thought that was prudent. Cecily thought remembering her aunt in the place where she'd been the happiest was the best memorial of all, and she intended to take her time. She'd be going back to the real world of clients and deadlines and impossible hours soon enough.

The quiet yard and the warm day and the long hours on the plane caught up with her. She felt herself nodding off and thought for a moment that she should go inside and curl up on the little bed Aunt Gin had always kept for her in the small bedroom. Right about the time she remembered her aunt's furniture was gone, she heard a rustling in the grass.

She opened her eyes to see a rabbit sitting stock still on the lawn not three feet in front of her chair.

Cecily's breath caught in her throat. It couldn't be the same rabbit —bunnies didn't live that long—but it looked the same as the one she'd seen that early, early morning all those years ago. Soft brown coat, fluffy white tail, and dark, luminous eyes. Its ears were long and graceful. The only thing moving on the rabbit was its nose, tiny little twitches as it sniffed the air.

As it sniffed her.

Another movement caught her eye. There, at the edge of the field, was another rabbit. And another. And at the base of the fence, a brown toad, almost invisible against the dirt.

Had they all come to pay their respects to her aunt, like Cecily was doing?

But that meant they must have known that Aunt Gin was gone.

If she sat here long enough, would she see little pinpricks of light flutter out of the bushes in the back of the yard to light on the heads of the rabbits and the toad?

I'm too old for this, she told herself.

Or maybe she wasn't old enough. Aunt Gin had been in her forties when she moved into this house. Cecily had been a late-in-life child for her mother, and Aunt Gin was the older of the two sisters. Cecily had been surprised to learn that Aunt Gin was nearly eighty when she died.

Cecily made herself sit still. Soon the rabbits in the field joined the bunny in the yard. They all sat just out of her reach but close enough she could see their little noses twitch, all four of them.

The toad stayed by the fence.

"I loved her, too," Cecily said, her voice little more than a whisper.

She thought the rabbits might flee. Instead, one of them, the first one that had come into the yard, hopped slowly toward her. Nose twitching, ears cocked forward, it came toward her until it sat next to the right side of the lawn chair.

The one thing she had always wanted to do was touch one of the bunnies. Her mom would have been horrified. She would have reminded Cecily that rabbits carried rabies.

Her mom wasn't here. This had been Aunt Gin's home, a place where the magic was real no matter how old you were.

Cecily let her right arm drift slowly downward. She kept expecting the rabbit to run, but it sat there, watching her with its big, brown eyes.

She didn't try to touch it. She simply let her arm hang loosely at her side, her hand dangling in the air a few inches from where the bunny sat. The next move was up to it.

Starting with the rabbit next to her chair, they all touched Cecily's hand, one by one.

The first rabbit merely sniffed at it. Its nose was like a cat's, soft and rough all at once. She felt its breath on her skin, then it was gone.

The next rubbed its head against her fingers.

The third bunny butted her hand with its head, and as it passed by, her fingers trailed over the tips of its ears.

The last bunny sat next to her hand. Waiting.

Cecily moved her fingers until she could touch the fur on its back. The fur was incredibly soft and thick, like that throw from long ago. She could feel the rabbit vibrating, the nervous tension in its body making it seem almost like a purring cat.

Just about the time she wondered why it was so close to her if it was so nervous, the bunny sped away.

All four of them did, their fluffy white tails the only marker of their flight back into the field.

She hadn't seen the little lights again, but maybe she didn't need to. What had just happened with the rabbits was about as close to magic as a grownup was about to get.

Unless the grownup had been her Aunt Gin.

"What do you mean, you took the house off the market?" Cecily's mom's voice was strident even over a cell phone a thousand miles away.

"What are you going to do with that place? It's not like the market's going to get any better."

Cecily didn't know how to explain it to her mom. She couldn't explain it to herself. She had no idea what she intended to do with Aunt Gin's property. Maybe she'd keep it for a vacation home, or maybe she'd chuck the whole ladder-climbing, junior-associate-trying-to-be-partner career path and move here.

Aunt Gin had left Cecily more than the house. Cecily now owned Aunt Gin's literary estate, and Aunt Gin's books had done well. Cecily could live comfortably here while she studied for the bar in this state. When she passed the bar exam, she could figure out where to go from there.

She had time. She was only thirty-three. Aunt Gin had been in her forties when she'd bought this house, a little older when she bought the fields next door.

Cecily thought about her aunt's wide smile. The twinkle in her eyes. Her sense of fun. Had the magic in this place brought those qualities out in her aunt, or had her aunt's qualities attracted the magic that still lived here?

Either way, Cecily hoped that some of that magic, that good humor and enjoyment of life, would rub off on her.

Maybe, just maybe, she might even start calling herself Cici.

She thought her aunt would approve.

ABOUT THE AUTHOR

A frequent contributor to the *Fiction River* anthologies and *Pulphouse Fiction Magazine*, Annie Reed's recent work includes the urban fantasy mystery novels *Unbroken Familiar* and *Iris & Ivy*, and the near-future science fiction short novel *In Dreams*. Annie's also one of the founding members of the innovative Uncollected Anthology, a series of themed urban fantasy stories published three times a year written by some of the best writers working today.

Annie's full-length novels include the Abby Maxon private investigator novels *Pretty Little Horses* and *Paper Bullets*, the Jill Jordan mystery *A Death in Cumberland*, and the suspense novel *Shadow Life*, written under the name Kris Sparks, as well as numerous other projects she can't wait to get to.

Find out more about Annie at:
annie-reed.com

BB bookbub.com/authors/annie-reed

IF THE SHOE FITS

DAYLE A. DERMATIS

W hen I heard the royal family would be holding a ball to find suitable wife material for the prince and heir, my mind went into overdrive.

But not in the way anyone would expect.

I didn't have specific information about how a royal household was run; I didn't know the number and skill sets of the servants, or even how many people would be invited to this shindig. But within ten minutes I had a pretty good sense of how much it would cost per person, even factoring in peacock meat (which seemed like a waste to me, what with chickens being that much cheaper per pound, but I also understood the art of entertaining sometimes meant being flashy to impress certain guests).

Not, mind you, that it was any of my business. Party planning wasn't really where I wanted to end up, but I loved the idea of it. Just the way my brain works: a challenge, a puzzle. I can put together a fundraising dinner and auction for fifty people without breaking a sweat. The concept of overseeing a royal ball made me go squee (on the inside).

Actually going to the ball? Meh. Marrying royalty didn't interest me in the least, and besides, I had finals coming up.

My aunt, Sheila, thought differently.

"It would be a good networking opportunity for you," she'd said.

"I'm not in the market for a husband," I'd said.

She'd rapped my knuckles with her wooden spoon, not enough to hurt, but it got my attention. "Don't be an idiot," she said. "I'm talking about business networking. You're about to graduate with honors. All those other girls giggling around the prince? Their daddies will be there, and their daddies run corporations that have job openings for the right candidates."

Oh. Duh. I'd been so busy helping my sisters not lose their freaking minds over the ball that it hadn't even occurred to me that this could be all about the schmoozing. Bad future entrepreneur, no BMW.

There's a reason why Aunt Sheila runs a thriving chain of bakeries.

Around me, young women clumped together, giggling (just as Aunt Sheila had predicted) and craning their necks to get a glimpse of Rupert, Prince Royal and Most Eligible Bachelor. I, on the other hand, had handed out a fair number of business cards, and was feeling rather smug.

Everybody says I work too hard. But I just cannot abide a disorganized house. After my mother died, my father...well, he was grieving, plus he had his own business to run, so the household fell to me. I was still young, but I wasn't stupid. I could clip coupons and plan a week's worth of simple, nutritious meals.

When my dad remarried, bringing not only a new wife into the house but also two new stepsisters for me, I suggested a rota of chores. Seemed only fair. They all laughed and went on gadding about.

So I just went on managing things. Oh, it was a PITA, sure, but with more people in the house, somebody had to keep things running smoothly. Money was tight, but I was able to convince dad to let me hire a weekly cleaning lady so I had enough time to work on my degree in business management.

I was thinking about bailing and heading home to get some studying in when the crowd fell silent and parted, and there was Prince Rupert, handsome and dashing. He smiled, white teeth and dimples flashing, and the women around me gave a collective sigh.

Okay, he was a looker, I'll give him that. Piercing blue eyes, thick black hair, square jaw. Broad shoulders, slim hips. Almost a cliché.

He surveyed the people in this corner of the ballroom. I did my best to blend into the wallpaper. It would be the height of rudeness to sneak away, and I had a reputation to cultivate. With all the excitedly heaving bosoms around me, there was no way he'd notice...

Oh, crap. He was coming right for me.

He asked me to dance, and women who'd been mentally designing their wedding invitations glared daggers at me as we walked away.

"Your Highness," I said as soon as we were out of earshot of the crowd, "I'm honored by your interest, but I hope you'll allow me to speak plainly."

"Please," he said with a gracious nod of his head that struck me as a little too practiced.

Saying I'm not interested in you seemed a little blunt, so I explained that I didn't think I was princess material and that I had plans for a career and I was here largely to put those plans in motion. Only I said it much more politely and flowery.

"Well, I have to thank you for your honesty," he said. "When you first said you weren't princess material, it sounded like a line, but I think you really mean it. Believe me, that's refreshing. I've been desperate to talk to someone who has more on her mind than clinging to my every word and answering in a charming way that's designed to make me think she's The One."

It was quite a speech, let me tell you.

"If you want to find a potential wife tonight, you probably ought to be dancing with them, not me," I said.

"Protocol states I must give you the full dance," he said, "and I appreciate the chance to talk to someone interesting. Plus, I've been dying to ask you: Where did you get your shoes?"

My...huh? What?

Aunt Sheila had loaned them to me. She'd studied in Paris back in the day, and saved up her money for the one indulgence. I didn't know a shoe from a ship, but I knew these were exquisite, so-expensive-it-takes-your-breath-away pumps. They were, I knew, one of a kind, too—the burgundy silk and black lace were remnants, and no other pair had been made with the same fabrics.

I explained it all to Rupert (who was, I might mention, an incredibly good dancer).

"They really are fabulous," he said. "I wish I could get a better look at them. Would you like a drink?"

I blinked, recovered, and the next thing I knew we were in a private antechamber and I was drinking the best damn champagne on earth and he was turning one of my shoes over in his hands and examining the workmanship. He seemed to know what he was looking at.

He handed the pump back to me (I'd been afraid he'd gently replace it on my foot or something) and I slipped it on.

"You're so lucky," he said.

"Why?" I couldn't quite get that. He had the world at his fingertips, didn't he?

"You have choices," he said, "and the freedom to make those choices. My path is set: marry a suitable woman, produce heirs, be the figurehead for a kingdom that already has a perfectly well-running government. The end."

Well...I'd never thought about that. "But there's some much you can do, with your connections and power. What about creating charities?"

"My future wife is expected to do that," he said. "Don't get me wrong, though—I do see those benefits. It's just that I'd give anything to have the freedom to pursue my own passions, live my own life." He waved a hand. "Oh, never mind."

I wanted to tell him to just go do whatever he bloody well wanted, because really, who was really going to protest? Wasn't his decree practically law?

Then I thought about it. I could very well have moved out and left the chaos of my family home behind me, giving me tons more time to move ahead with my own plans. But I felt a responsibility to them—just as Rupert must feel towards the kingdom.

So we talked about that, and I have to say, he was pretty easy to talk to. I kinda liked him, in a "I've never had a brother" sort of way.

His counselor peeking in the door made us both realize how long ago we'd ditched the ball, and made me realize just how late it was.

Crap.

There'd been no way in hell I could have driven there; the traffic was beyond a gridlocked nightmare. There wouldn't be any cabs. So if I didn't catch the last train, which left Palace Station just after midnight, I'd be stranded.

"Reallynicetalkingtoyou, gottago."

I grabbed my stuff from the coat check, laced on my sneakers (there was no way in hell I was going to commute in those stilettos, either), and made a mad dash to the train station.

It was only after I was sitting in the car and catching my breath that I realized I'd dropped one of the shoes somewhere along the way.

I said a word that never would have been appropriate in front of royalty.

~

Thankfully Aunt Sheila was out of town, so I didn't have to break the loss to her just yet. I was eyeballs-deep in finals over the next few days, pulling all-nighters at the library and crashing on a friend's sofa closer to the university, so I didn't hear about the whole ruckus until I stumbled home.

"Where have you been; I've left messages," my stepmom said.

I pulled out my cell. Yep, there were messages. Who knew?

"The palace has been looking for you." She twisted her hands together. "We were hoping they were calling about Genna or Clara."

"It's just about my shoe," I said. "I dropped it when I was leaving. I'm sure they just want to return it."

But even I wondered why they couldn't have just popped it into the mail, you know?

So I called back, and was put on hold forever (royal Muzak is no better than your local bank's, believe me) before someone got back on the line and told me that Prince Rupert would like to return the shoe to me personally and was I free for a private dinner at the palace tomorrow?

That just didn't bode well. I'd caught up on the news and knew that the prince hadn't selected a prospective wife (or even a short list of candidates) since the ball. I couldn't imagine Rupert taking the time to hang out with me when he had bigger fish to fry...unless it was my fish he had an interest in.

Had I not made myself clear? Had he not made himself clear?

But I had to get that shoe back before Aunt Sheila got home.

I had a private audience with the prince in the "small" dining room, which was almost the size of my father's house. At least we weren't at opposite ends of the table that yawned the length of the room. If we had, we'd've needed walkie-talkies.

We made small talk through the soup course, and then he leaned forward and said, "Ella."

His tone of voice made me vaguely itchy. I doubted I'd like what he had to say. "Your Highness."

"I have a business proposition for you."

Oh. Well, then. I sat forward. "I'm always interested in that."

"I need a wife."

I sat back. "I don't—"

"Please, hear me out." He looked almost as unhappy as I felt, so I let him continue. "I've met many fine women, so many who would be appropriate for the role of princess. But I have some...special requirements, and I don't believe any of those women would understand or agree to them."

Great. He had a kinky streak.

"Those women are looking for a great romance, and that's something I can never give them," he continued.

Oh. A mistress, then, someone he could never put on the throne.

But no. He kept going. "You have other goals in life, ones that I can facilitate. I think we can both benefit from a joint venture."

He went on to detail what I'd get out of the deal, which included some pretty nifty corporate responsibilities. In return, I'd be his wife essentially in name only, and he'd be able to pursue his personal passions, as he'd called them.

The pre-nup included a confidentiality agreement, and when I read it, it was like a blinding light going off over my head. All of the signs had been there, but like everyone else, I just hadn't put them together.

His disinterest in the sea of heaving bosoms. His fascination with my fabulous shoes....

~

So there you have it. Rupert remains the country's figurehead, and designs shoes and handbags (and occasionally hats) under a fake name. He's quite good; his latest line got a huge write-up in Vogue. We pay a private physician handsomely to keep quiet about the artificial insemination to get me pregnant. (Yeah, I've always focused on getting a career, but I never said kids were out of the question.)

And me? I get to be CFO of Rupert's design firm and manage the royal finances, and for fun I throw elaborate, glittering dinner parties and fundraisers for up to a thousand people.

Squee.

ABOUT THE AUTHOR

Called "one of the best writers working today" by bestselling author Dean Wesley Smith, Dayle A. Dermatis is the author or coauthor of seven novels and more than a hundred short stories in multiple genres, including the first seven Uncollected Anthology anthologies and the forthcoming urban fantasy novel *Ghosted*. She is a founding member of the Uncollected Anthology project.

A recent transplant to the wild greenscapes of the Pacific Northwest, in her spare time she follows Styx around the country and travels the world, which inspires her writing.

Find out more about Dayle at:
dayledermatis.com

facebook.com/dayledermatis

twitter.com/dayledermatis

goodreads.com/DayleDermatis

bookbub.com/authors/dayle-a-dermatis

CITY OF NOWHERE IN THE WORLD

DIANA BENEDICT

Korshan Ilibasha walked down the muddy road on her way home from her auntie's house in Meluhha. Everything felt new: the road, the day, her worn skirt, the tassels of her shawl.

Even the mighty Tigris river roaring in its banks, thickly brown and frothing cream beside her, felt new, as if it were on the cusp of something. Korshan felt fresh and special.

Father Sun shone down brightly on her as her toes squished in the rich, dark mud. It felt good even if it smelled rotten.

She hopped and skipped to avoid a piece of dung, which is how she caught her toe on a rock the river god had left behind during the last flood.

She flung her arms out, trying to dance like the temple priestess had taught the girls, but she'd never been a good dancer. She flailed as she twirled. The river chuckled as she fell. She caught herself with her hands, so her knee-length cotton skirt only got mud along the front of the hem, but dark brown mud caked the soft fringe on her shawl.

When Korshan stood, she realized she had bloodied her right knee on a hidden rock. It stung, too, but any girl named for the sun wouldn't cry over a skinned knee. At least not much.

She limped over to the verge of the river and found a place where the water had pooled and the silt had sunk to the bottom. She washed her fringe, took her skirt off and scrubbed the mud out of the white woven cotton, and finally rinsed the mud off her knee. It wasn't too badly scraped, but knew she some salve would help it heal.

Korshan wrung the skirt out and swung it around her head six times, then put it on and tied it up on her scratched knee side, to keep it from getting bloody and giving men the wrong idea. She made her way home, using some grass to wipe away the blood as it flowed down her shin.

Soon, she reached the edge of the tiny village of Ishlikil, pausing only to let her neighbor herd his flock of goats across the road to drink from the river. Her mother worked in the garden behind the house.

"Mother, I am home," Korshan called, opening the sapling gate onto the rows of garlic and onions and lentils and cucumbers her mother grew for them to eat.

"And how was your auntie?" her mother asked, standing up with a basketful of weeds to feed the geese that lived on the other side of the house. She had her dark hair tied back and her pale skirt hitched up to keep it clean. The shawl, embroidered with blue wool, she had wrapped tightly around her breasts. The fringed ends wound over her shoulders and tucked away.

"Auntie Beshen sends her regards," Korshan said. "She said I should run in Ishtar's race around the temple.

Her mother smiled, her dark eyes twinkling in the bright sunlight. "You would do well as a temple initiate, but you are more, my sun; eager to travel and see the world." Then she noticed Korshan's skirt tied up and the dark smear of blood on her knee.

"Well, you can't run with a knee like that and you won't adventure far, either. What happened?"

"A rock Father Tigris left after the flood tried to dance with me, but I couldn't keep up. Do you have some salve to put on it?"

"No, but come with me." Korshan followed her mother around the back of the little lime-washed rubble house to the goose pen. Four geese honked agreeably at them as her mother spread the weeds out for them to eat. While they scrabbled in the greens, she hunted through the nests along the sun-warmed wall, pulling out two eggs.

She handed them to Korshan. "Take these to the shaman in Hichahich and ask him for salve for your knee."

"Thank you, Mother." Korshan walked down the road, dodging running children, patties of dung, and wagons heaped with produce, headed for Nippur. At last, she came to twenty wattle and daub huts sitting in a rough circle like grannies around a cookfire. Then she realized that, somehow, after passing a train of soft-eyed cattle and the crowd of people that walked alongside them, she no longer carried her eggs. She walked back, searching in the soft mud, even chasing the train and asking if they had seen her eggs.

The cows just lowed softly, and the steers snorted rudely.

"Ah, well, I was almost there," she said. "I won't return home empty-handed after she trusted me with the eggs. The gods may have an answer for me."

She turned and went back to Hichahich. When she reached the village she had to walk all the way through, since the shaman lived on the far side, past the midden.

His hut was small, just old, faded cowhides laid over bent saplings, with a goat skin flapping in wind across the door. Korshan saw the gate to his garden hung open. His goats were in the midst of it, feasting on the juicy cucumbers and sweet onions.

She shooed them out, chased them into their small corral behind the hut, and shut them in, tying the gate tight so they couldn't escape again. She turned back to the ravaged garden. They hadn't eaten much, but they had broken the gate.

Korshan had just finished fixing the hinge when an ancient man wearing a dirty, patched skirt with a frayed belt, knotted many times, tottered around the corner of the house, shaking a staff at her.

"Who steals from my garden?" he shouted, his matted hair falling over his milky eyes.

"The goats, grandfather," she said loudly. Everyone knew the shaman was hard of hearing. "But I, Korshan Ilibasha, daughter of Afelleh, have returned the naughty beasts to their pen and repaired the gate they have broken. And for that I only ask that you help me find my lost eggs."

"Lost eggs," the old shaman huffed and harrumphed. He squinted toward the goat pen. "Rascal demons," he said, shaking his staff at them.

He looked back at her, his milky eyes flashing in the sunlight. She swung the squeaky gate to and fro, proving it worked now, and smiled at him brightly.

"Come with me then, Sun Girl." He turned and made his way slowly around the hut.

She latched the gate and followed him. She paused when he disappeared into the dark and musty hovel. Everyone knew a shaman's house straddled the border between the mortal and spirit worlds. And crossing that border changed you.

He peeked out of the door. "You coming, girl?"

His milky eyes stared right at her and Korshan had the idea they saw something more. "I'm not waiting all day. Do you want to find your eggs or not?"

She considered just going home, but her knee stung fiercely, and eggs were worth something. And her mother had entrusted them to her. What kind of girl would lose her eggs and then not take up an offer of help from a powerful shaman?

Especially when she'd already done the favor that led to the offer.

Not she, Korshan decided. She wanted her eggs and she wasn't afraid of a blind, decrepit man who couldn't mind his own goats.

"I do, yes," Korshan said, and walked briskly to the door, back straight, head up, eyes forward. He held the skin for her and the let it drop when she passed over the threshold.

The air felt different, thicker, heavier, charged with something—possibility, Korshan thought as she looked around. All manner of herbs, which smelled fresh and sweet, hung from the ceiling, and white bones and skins, which smelled musty and sour, lined the walls.

It seemed much larger on the inside than it looked from the outside. He rummaged around in the back corner, clay jars clinking and clattering.

She thought she heard humming, but after a moment, decided it was just the old man breathing and harrumphing as he made his way to the far end of the hut.

When he turned back, he handed her a small red clay pot. "For your knee. You can't chase down lost eggs with a skinned knee."

"Thank you, Grandfather." Korshan smeared some of the golden, honey-smelling salve on her knee. It felt cool and soothed the sting.

"Now, wait outside."

All that just for a pot of salve, she thought. The sun outside seemed brighter and Father Sun seemed to twinkle just for a moment as she passed back over the threshold. Korshan stood in the yard, ignoring little boys who stuck their tongues out at her and then ran away. Farmers and merchants and skinny girls with jars on their heads stared at her as they went by. Korshan felt embarrassed to be standing in the shaman's yard, but she had asked a favor. And you couldn't complain if a shaman offered to help you. Even if it meant everyone stared at you and wondered why you stood in the middle of his yard.

Finally, the old man pushed the goat skin aside and stepped out of his hut.

He wore his shaman cloak, a great golden lion skin sewn with little shells, bits of bronze, bone buttons, and knuckle bones that clacked and sighed and murmured when he moved. His shaman mask was the black-maned head of the beast with fangs longer than her fingers. The eyes were carnelians and they stared down at her, glowing orange in Father Sun's bright light.

Korshan steeled herself to stand tall and not quake with the fear that rattled her legs and made her belly clench down tight. It was one thing to see an old man and call him a shaman. It was another to see him wearing his cloak and hear and see the magic in front of you. She looked away lest he see the terror in her eyes and think she wasn't worthy of his help, or shouldn't have been trusted with eggs in the first place.

"Come with me, little sun," he said, waving his staff at her.

She followed him around back of the hut, past the goat pen and the garden to the edge of the barley field, emerald against the dark mud.

"Fetch me a stick and a withy," he said. Korshan went and picked up a reed and found a long supple twig, and brought them to him.

He sang over them and waved his staff and danced a bit. The lion's eyes blazed like embers in a smithy's fire and the stick grew and split, grew and split, while the withy stretched like a long rope and wound around and around, the whole thing growing into a ladder that reached far up into the sky.

"Climb that and look for your eggs," the shaman commanded.

Korshan stared at the ladder standing straight up and reaching toward the sky. She looked back down the road where she had come, and then back at the ladder. How could this lead to her eggs?

But she wasn't going to ask when she had gone to all the effort to get the favor, and he had gone to the effort to help her out.

"Thank you, Grandfather," she said, and bowed a little.

He humphed and hrrrmed and flapped his cloak, waving her up with his staff.

Korshan mounted the ladder. The rungs were smooth and worn as if many hands had gripped them. It stayed firm, like a tree rooted in Mother Earth's bosom. She climbed and climbed until the clouds brushed against her cheek.

"I'd better stop now or I won't be able to see through the clouds," she said. She could see the whole of Mesopotamia laid out before her. The mighty Tigris and the Euphrates wound through the green land like lazy brown snakes. She peered, squinting against the Father Sun's brilliance, all the way to the desert that surrounded the River Land, and back to the sparkles the bright rays laid over the backs of the watery brown snakes.

Then she understood why he had made her a ladder and sent her up it. She saw her eggs! One had hatched and grown up into a fine goose that lived with an old woman along the eastern edge of the desert, who loved her and fed her corn and cooed over her.

Korshan looked again and saw the other egg had turned out to be a fine gander. They had him busy threshing corn in a village far away from Hichahich.

"First, I'll go and get that gander," she said, and she stepped off the ladder and strode strongly across the land in mile-long steps until she came to the small village on an island floating down a lazy tributary of the Tigris. She waded across the hip-deep current and, after she dried her legs with some grass, she let down her skirt, shook out her shawl, and walked right up to the village elders.

Standing straight, she said, "Give me my gander and his wages, for he's been working hard for you."

The village elders looked her square in the eye. One said, "He's a lazy steg, but I'll give you a measure of barley for walking across the river."

Korshan smiled and gestured to the corn. "Lazy enough to make a pile Ishtar would be proud to take in offering. I'll take two cow-loads of your crop for my fine gander's work."

An old man with sparse white hair and sparser beard invited her to his front door, and they sat. His eyes were barely visible in the deep leathered creases of his face, and he only had one tooth when he smiled. His wife, an old bent, white-haired granny with a pretty yellow fringed shawl, bowed low as she served them tea and bread and salt.

Then they got down to haggling. When Father Sun barely kissed Mother Earth, they settled on half a cow-load of barley, but, he said sadly, they had no bags for her to load the barley in.

"That's all right," Korshan said. She whistled and the village dogs came running. A likely honey-brown bitch came and licked her hand with a bright red tongue. Korshan took out the small knife her granny had given her on her name day. It had an obsidian blade and a handle made of a tusk from the King Bull of Syria. She ran her hand down the dog's back and captured a flea, which she killed and skinned with the knife. Then she whipped her fingers around the dog's fine fish hook tail, and pulled three hairs that she used to sew a fine bag out of the flea skin.

After Korshan loaded the barley in it, she strapped the half cow-load to the gander's back so she could take it to market, thanked the old man, and drove the gander across the river and on down the road. Two days later, she stopped at a halt for the evening and found the gander sore-backed from carrying the half cow-load of barley.

When the other travelers had stopped for their dinner, she found an old woman shelling chickpeas by the side of a wagon.

"My steg is sore-backed from hauling my half-cow load of barley to market," Korshan said. "Is there a remedy for it?"

The woman split a pod and dropped the peas into the fine woven basket and squinted up at Korshan. "Burn the kernel of a walnut and rub it on the raw spots, and he will get well."

"Thank you, Grandmother." She walked into the woods that lined the road and searched until she found a good sized walnut. She cracked it and set it into the embers along the edge of the fire. When it started to smoke, she fished it out with her finger and blew on it until she could carry it.

She held the gander down and rubbed the walnut over the raw marks along the goose's back and around his wings where the bag ties had rubbed him.

Father Sun went down to his home below Mother Earth, and Ishtar came out to gaze down from the heavens. Korshan laid her head on the bag of barley, watching the stars twinkle and dance in the vault of the heavens and listening to the travelers telling stories around the fire until she fell asleep.

She woke the next morning to shouting and laughing. Rubbing her eyes, she sat up and looked about her. A large walnut tree had sprung up out of the gander's back, and a band of unruly boys were throwing clods of dirt at the tree.

She chased them away and climbed up it. When she got up into the branches, she found the dirt had settled among the limbs and made a patch of soil about eight paces by eight paces.

Never one to lose an opportunity, she called down for a clod breaker to smooth the soil and a plow to till it. The earth was fit for melons, so she traded some barley for melon seed and planted a fine crop.

She so exhausted herself after that long day of labor, she could barely keep her hands about the branches as she climbed down. Then she fell right to sleep, her head resting on the bag of barley, never stirring until Father Sun peeked up over the eastern edge of Mother Earth.

After washing her face in a still pool along the river, Korshan climbed the tree and found that a fine crop of melons had sprung up. Her belly growled in hunger and she picked a fat watermelon, but when she cut into it, her knife got lost in the juicy meat.

"My granny gave me that knife," she said. "It has a sharp obsidian blade and a smooth handle of elephant ivory from the King Bull of Syria. I'm not going to lose it in a melon."

She slipped her skirt off and slung her shawl around her waist and dove deeply into the bowl of the melon to hunt for her knife.

She saw a city there, bigger than Nippur, surrounded by a grand wall carved with epic battles and splendid gods going about their business. The temple in the center of the city shone so brightly in the sun she had to shade her eyes, which watered from the smoke offerings rising toward heaven. Shouts and songs hung heavy over the tall bright white buildings, and Korshan thought the gods must just cock an ear to enjoy the fine music with their dinner of ambrosia and sweet wine.

When she reached the gate, she straightened her skirt, wrapped her shawl around her like a grand lady, and marched past the guards in their leather armor as they held their bronze swords at the ready.

She wandered the alleys and passed through a bazaar. At the far end, she found a cook shop and traded a handful of melon seeds for a little bowl of ragi. She scooped up fingerfuls of thick boiled wheat with bits of chopped mutton, flavored with cinnamon and honey. It was so good she ate it all down and then licked the bowl so hard she thought she heard it crack.

Then she saw a coarse black hair at the bottom of it. She grasped it to throw it away, thinking of the lazy boy who stirred the pot, but at the end of the hair, she found she grasped a lead rope and a train of seven camels came through the crack. They were all in a row, harnessed up with fine braided leather halters. And she saw, as they marched out, they all bore heavy bags of goods for market.

Then she saw her knife, the sharp one, with the handle of elephant ivory from the King Bull of Syria, tied to the tail of the last one. And she grabbed it and walked the camels all the way to market.

Korshan Ilibasha never went home, but traveled the world seated like a queen in a saddle draped in silks jingling with tiny golden bells on the back of a grand camel who spit out candy.

And the gander with the walnut tree on its back laid a magical golden

199

egg that a king used to buy a kingdom. A blind woodsman cut down the walnut tree and built a monastery for mute monks who wrote the days to come. And a one-legged woman with her one-armed husband picked up the bag of barley, and planted it. The crop saved the King's people from famine, and the monks wrote down this tale so that the future would read about Korshan Ilibasha and the City of Nowhere in the World.

ABOUT THE AUTHOR

Diana lives in a small suburban Colorado city a mile away from where she grew up. She loves studying magic and history and will take any opportunity to combine them into a good story. She once tried to work a spell inspired by a tale her great aunt told her and has always felt lucky that it only turned her fingers green for a week.

Find out more about Diana at:
dianabenedict.com

DOCTOR RUDOLFO MEETS HIS MATCH

DEANNA KNIPPLING

1. HOMEWORK AT THE HOSPITAL

The hospital always smelled. This was not a problem for me, but for my little brother Aiden it was an *issue*. He was sensitive to things in a way that had driven everyone up the walls when he was a baby. Pine cleaner, lemon cleaner, bug spray, toilet cleaner, anything with a strong smell would start him off crying. Garlic, onions, spices... It seemed like any little thing could set him off. I remember about a thousand times, our no-air conditioning house baking hot, when my mother told me, "Connor, run outside and tell me whether I can open the window." Shower cleaner was the worst. He would start throwing up for at least a good half-hour.

At home, we cleaned things with a lot of apple cider vinegar and then wiped it down with water, which was not too bad for him. And there were so many people with allergies that the stores had started making some cleaners that were okay. But, because Aiden was always a little shit, he never had to scrub a toilet, or wash dishes, or wipe down a mirror.

"I can't do it," he'd whine. I'd make him try, using vinegar or clean water. But he'd always screw it up and I'd end up doing it for him. I knew he was playing me. But the thought of Mom coming home from her work at the hospital with a wrecked house always got to me.

Don't get me wrong, I was never a saint. I used to threaten to throw out Aiden's toys and stuff if he didn't at least clean up after himself, and I always made him vacuum. I didn't care about what the carpet looked like, just that the dirt was off the floor. But Aiden always put perfect lines into the carpet. Edged everything, too. Mom always liked it.

All it took was a couple of threats and a bribe of ice cream. Since he was six years old I'd been making him vacuum the carpet, and now he was almost eight to my nineteen. He could dust, too. He left his own stuff all over the place. But watch out if a knickknack on the shelf was a millimeter out of line. Somehow we all made it work. I love my brother. It's just that sometimes it feels like navigating a maze to get to the treasure inside.

I think I've explained Aiden's reasons for hating the hospital pretty well. The smells were the worst. But he also hated the bright lights and all the beeping sounds.

Me, I didn't care for all the ghosts.

I've been able to see them since I can remember. I know that Aiden can see at least one ghost, Dad's. But he's never said anything about any of the others.

The hospital was thick with them. I don't mind a ghost or two as long as I don't know them personally, but the number of ghosts at Mom's hospital was real bad. Being around ghosts is a little bit like being carsick. A little bit of carsick is bearable. But driving too fast over a road covered with potholes, bumping and swerving around, the car speeding up and slowing down all the time, there's only so long you can take it.

I had to drop Aiden off with Mom so I could go to work at the fried chicken place, but her shift was running long, and I was starting to feel edgy about the number of times that I'd had to miss one of my shifts because someone needed to watch Aiden. Sometimes there's just no one. Mom's a nurse. It's not like she can just walk away from the middle of an emergency. I'd missed enough work, and I'd been late enough times, that I was thinking it was about fifty-fifty that I was going to get fired. All I do is fry chicken, it's not like the world was going to end, but that stuff ends up on your employment history. It's a small world. Everyone knows everyone else, and if you think they don't talk about how you put your family over your job behind your back, you have another think coming.

In short, I was distracted.

But then something undistracted me.

Aiden was lying on his stomach on the floor in the waiting room, doing his homework. Homework was always a struggle with him. He would chase the answer to the question "why" all the way down to nonsense. Every time. "Why is the sky blue?" The answer would be a week's worth of research on optics, Isaac Newton, and the energy spectrum.

"Because I said so" was not an option.

It probably didn't help that I had given up trying to make the world make sense to Aiden in a way that Mom wouldn't complain about. "You're making him too cynical," she would say. I would give her a look. "You don't think he's gonna get cynical?" And then she would sigh.

As Aiden colored in fractions with a packet of crayons, we went on another round of his endless game of *why*. This time, it was about his lame-ass homework. The kid was tearing through calculus and here he was, coloring in circles with crayons. He had my sympathy.

"Why do I have to do homework?"

"Because your job, your employment at this time, which you are not going to get paid for but that you will surely be held accountable to by Mom, your *responsibility*, is to get good grades at school."

"Why?"

"Because there are hundreds of millions of people on this earth. And because there has to be some way to measure them that fits into numbers. Not because this is the right way, but because there are some real shitheads in charge who don't know how to understand people, but only numbers."

"So I have to be turned into a number?"

"You have to have a number associated with you. You do not have to be a number. You can be a dog, or a type of dinosaur, or a ballet dancer if you want, as far as I am concerned. But you do have to do your job, which is currently getting good grades at school."

"Why?"

"Because if you can learn to do what you're told and how to sit still, then the people who only understand numbers will forget that you're anything more than a number. And sometimes it can be real helpful to be invisible like that. It's a life skill, Aiden, useful in a number of craptacular situations."

A pause. "I like numbers."

I glanced at him. He was clutching a red crayon in his fist hard enough that I thought he would snap it.

"I know, Aiden. That doesn't make you a bad person, unless you forget that people and numbers are different things. If you grew up and you were like, 'I can use numbers to make a spaceship that saved humanity from an asteroid strike,' that would be a great use of numbers. But if you were like, 'The number of people who get shot by the police is down this year, so we don't need to do anything else about the situation, all good,' then that would be a bad use of numbers."

Another pause. "I won't do that."

"Good."

"Why do I have to put up with it, then? If it's bad?"

"Because the world is not just, and you have to pick your battles."

"Why? Why can't you fight evil all the time?"

"Most of us get tired, Aiden." I checked my watch, then got up and walked over to the nurse's station. "How long before Mom gets out?"

The aide at the desk was a thirty-year-old, solid-looking white lady named Ellen.

She shook her head.

You don't know how I was tempted to ditch Aiden in the waiting room for Mom to deal with when she got off her shift. Instead I called work and told them the situation. The manager said, "I guess that means you're turning in your resignation, then."

I said, "Is that official?"

She snorted and hung up. I'd talk to the head manager later.

Frank was all right; he had grown up with a single mom, too, and had two little sisters who were now full-grown. But I'd been pushing it a lot lately. I might be done there.

Mom was working hard to try to save up money for us for college. The thing was, Aiden was going to get a full-ride scholarship to MIT or something. And I knew I wasn't college material. What was I going to *do* with my life? Mom was always asking me. In my heart of hearts, I knew the answer.

I'd take care of Aiden. There was nobody else to do it.

2. THE ANTIQUE SHOP

Ｗe left the hospital. It had been getting on both our nerves. When we stepped out into that bright blue light that you only get in Colorado, Aiden walked up to the first window he spotted and started banging against it with his hands. It was loud. Fortunately, we weren't anywhere near the smoking area, and the guard at the front desk had recognized us and gave me an *it's okay* wave. I let Aiden run himself down until he was calm again. He used to hit the bricks instead of the windows, but they tore up his hands, so I made him switch over to the glass. It was thick enough not to break.

"You all right, buddy?"

He moaned, shaking his head.

"Good job keeping it together in there," I told him.

"Ice cream," he said. He was nuts about the stuff.

I said, "The good place or the close place?"

He chewed hard enough on his lip to worry me. "The other place."

"Where's that?"

He closed his eyes and tipped his head back. "Gimme your phone."

I did, and in half a minute he had pulled up an address for a place I'd never heard of.

"I don't know if they'll have the kind you like," I said, but he was already walking. In the wrong direction.

I got him turned around. A block and a half later, it was like being in a different country. The hospital is kind of between places. On the west side of the hospital, the grass is mowed and the cement isn't cracked. Everything's clean and polished. On the east side, though, it's all apartment buildings and weeds. You have to watch where you walk. But it's set up so some of the houses have been turned into restaurants, and some of the older apartment buildings are getting torn down and replaced with condos that have boutiques on the ground floor. It's not my neighborhood, though, so I guess—whatever. Not my battle.

Aiden stopped.

"What's that?"

On the sidewalk in front of him was a message written in chalk. An advertisement. *ANTIQUES – ART – CURIOSITIES – FORTUNES TOLD! AFTERLIFE ANTIQUES, 2 BLOCKS AHEAD!!!*

Now *that* was a name for an antique store, I thought to myself. Both realistic and gruesome, considering that antiques are just a dead person's old recycled furniture.

"I want to go there," Aiden said.

"What, and get your fortune told?"

He gave me a dirty look. I had a knack for telling fortunes. My genuine talent for seeing ghosts was one thing, but with fortunes it felt like a lot of b.s. that just happened to always come true. In the summer tourist season and over Christmas break, I sometimes worked as a "free prize with every fortune!" teller at a local game shop, Epic Toys & Games.

"Fortunes are fake," he said.

"So...why there? Don't you want ice cream?"

"I want both there and ice cream."

"Which one first?"

He glared at the universe. "The one that is first."

"Lead on."

We walked down the sidewalk.

"On your left!" someone shouted, and we both stepped off the sidewalk onto the grass automatically. A little white girl in a pink helmet and on a bicycle with streamers sped by, pedaling furiously. As we watched, she jerked a water bottle off the bike frame and drank from it, then shoved it back into its holder. We both laughed. She was so intense. I looked back to make sure she didn't have any company.

The chalk marks on the sidewalk behind us? Were gone.

I failed to mention this to Aiden. When I looked forward again, the air had a hazy shimmer to it.

When I see ghosts, they *look* like they're really there. Solid and three-dimensional. I try not to walk through them. That's just basic etiquette, right? You don't step through someone else's avatar online; I try to extend the same courtesy to ghosts. But there's something kind of off-putting almost-humanness about them. And if you look *real* close, although why would you want to, you can tell by the insides of their noses, because nobody gets noses right. Real noses have hair, red spots, boogers. Ghost noses are kind of plastic looking. You can also tell by their shadows, which are never quite right.

The air that day, it kind of felt like a ghost waiting to happen. The houses looked a little bit *too* good, a little bit too much like something you'd find in a video game. They repeated the same pattern of house about every five or six houses, although each one of them was a little bit different. That doesn't necessarily mean anything. The suburbs are like that.

But this wasn't the suburbs, it was the east side of the hospital.

We kept walking. Aiden said, "Almost there."

Then he stopped again. A big chalk arrow on the sidewalk indicated that we needed to take a right turn toward the *AMAZING DEALS FOR EVERYONE! AFTERLIFE ANTIQUES TWO BLOCKS AHEAD!!!*

Aiden's feet followed that arrow like magic.

"Uh, Aiden," I said. "I don't know if you should go that way."

"I should go this way," he said confidently.

"This place feels weird."

The arrow should have taken us in the direction of the hospital. It was a big place that took up more than one block. We should have seen it.

We didn't.

Aiden hesitated. "Ghost stuff?"

"Something wrong," I said. "Where's the hospital?"

He shook all over and his eyes widened. Sometimes I forget he's only eight. He jerked his feet off the sidewalk arrow, one at a time, like he had to rip them away. He ran behind me, grabbing onto my shirt with both hands.

"I don't like it!" he said. "It tricked me!"

"So...let's go get some ice cream," I said. "Let's just forget about this place, okay?"

"Okay."

We ignored the arrow and went straight, which should have taken us to the ice cream shop.

It didn't.

The houses got nicer and nicer, turning into Victorian-style places with yards full of bushes and flowers and cement lions and stuff like that. The hair on the back of my neck was standing up.

DID YOU GET LOST? TURN HERE FOR AFTERLIFE ANTIQUES!

The chalk appeared in the middle of the block, stretching from one side of the sidewalk to the other. There was no place to turn, not even an alleyway.

Just a house.

With a small, discreet sign in the window. *OPEN – YOU'VE FOUND US!*

Aiden took a deep breath. "It smells like old things," he said.

I took a whiff. It did. *Fancy* old things.

"Should we go in?" I asked.

He shook his head.

"Okay, let's keep going." I tried to walk past the chalk on the ground. One foot up in the air, and...a lurch in my stomach. I threw up in my mouth a little. I was facing the house, one foot on the first step.

Aiden whimpered, an animal sound.

I held out my hand. Aiden's not a big hand holder. He's not big on physical contact, period. He'll grab my shirt if he's scared, but that's about it. But that time, he took my hand without a word.

I turned back the way we came. "One...two...three!"

Both of us stepped forward.

The door was shut behind us but the bell jingled anyway. Aiden's hand was shaking in mine. Mine was probably shaking in his.

We were inside the antique shop. Something had picked us up and put us inside it, like a hand moving dolls inside a dollhouse.

The inside of the building...man. I don't know how to describe it. It had smelled like fancy old stuff all the way out to the sidewalk because the inside was *full* of fancy old stuff, top to bottom. Like, there was no way to tell what colors the walls were. Every surface was covered with *something*, even the ceilings. There were so many things to see, all of them interesting, all at once, that you couldn't actually see anything. You kept interrupting yourself by jerking your eyes all over the place.

"Don't touch anything," I said.

Aiden was still whimpering. Slowly, the two of us backed up. With my spare hand, I reached for the doorknob.

And got a handful of slime. I jerked my hand away.

A high-pitched voice giggled. My eyes snapped in that direction, but my head seemed frozen.

"Welcome, welcome!" The voice belonged to someone that wasn't human. He looked like one of the goblins out of the Harry Potter movies, only not quite so sharp-looking? More like he had been clay-mation at one point before being brought to life. I tried to remember the name of the creepy old guy who sold Harry his wand at the wand shop. My mind was a blank.

"Hi," I said. "Sorry about that. We didn't mean to come in here. Like, at all."

The guy snorted. It was so high-pitched it was almost cute. "The shop has very *distinct* opinions," he said. He was sitting behind a tall wood booth that looked really fancy. A bronze sign hung over the top of the booth: *POST OFFICE*. An old-fashioned cash register with about a thousand brass buttons on stilts sat beside him, along with a thick ledger and a fountain pen. He had a stack of manga magazines next to him, the covers all dog-eared around the corners.

"So, uh, the shop brought us?" I said. "What are we supposed to do? I don't have any money. I mean, I do, but not enough for this stuff." I waved my hand toward a carousel mermaid whose tail looked like it was made out of cloisonné and who was wearing a pearl tiara.

"I haven't the slightest idea. My name is Angela Lansbury, by the way."

I squinted at him. "Come on, you're just messing with me. That's the old lady who murders everyone in her small town, then pretends to investigate it, right?"

This got him laughing so hard that he started wheezing. "Quite, quite! Well, then, call me Balthazar."

That name sounded sort of fake, but I let it go. Aiden was starting to panic. And that could be bad for all of us.

"So, hey, Balthazar," I said. "My little brother is scared, and we need to get out of here before he loses it. Why don't you just let us out? I don't want to cause trouble."

Balthazar shrugged. "Do what you want. It's not my store."

"It's not?"

He grimaced. "I just walked in here one day and never walked out again."

"You're trapped here?"

He shrugged again.

Aiden was panting and making a keening noise in the back of his throat. He was looking around in a panic. Out. He had to get out. He grabbed onto the back of my shirt, flinching away from a ghost-white bicycle frame next to him.

I tried the door again. This time the handle burnt against my palm. No go. I crouched down and said, "Get on, Aiden."

He didn't like piggyback rides. He didn't like to touch people. But he wrapped both arms around my neck so tight I couldn't breathe. I stood up, holding my breath, then hiked him up so his weight was a little easier to carry. I moved his arms so I could breathe again. "Come on, Aiden. There has to be a back door to this place somewhere."

Hunched forward, I lurched deeper into the store.

So in the hospital I had seen some ghosts. Okay, no problem, a bit stomach-churning but otherwise fine. And a couple on the street when we had first come outside. Sometimes the dead refuse to go away. They're kind of like feral cats. They go where they want, do what they want. Some people leave food out for them. But I hadn't seen any since we had seen the first chalk drawing.

"I don't think this place is real, buddy," I told Aiden.

He whimpered. I decided that what he meant was "why?"

"No ghosts."

I felt his head turn. He was at least looking around, although he was still making a horrible animal noise in the back of his throat that set my teeth on edge. It was both guttural and piercing.

"Now, with a name like Afterlife Antiques," I continued, "you'd expect that we'd be dead, right? Like we got hit by a car coming out of the hospital, both died instantly, and now we're walking through the afterlife, which is an antique shop, where we will become a couple of antiques."

I felt, more than heard, him snort in a sarcastic, disbelieving manner. And he quit making *that sound*, for which I was profoundly grateful.

"But then again, this doesn't feel like an episode of *Twilight Zone*, does it? Or *Black Mirror*, or *Alfred Hitchcock Presents*. What does it feel like..."

Aiden started wriggling, then dropped his legs, choked me briefly, and let himself down. I patted my neck while making cat-barf noises, to make sure he hadn't crushed my windpipe. Aiden gave me a disgusted look—he knew I was faking—and then he was off, eeling through a crack between two ancient, silver-backed mirrors. The one facing him, I noticed, didn't show his reflection.

"Aiden! Come back here!"

The mirror reflected me, though. Whether that meant Aiden was special or I was, I had no idea.

3. QUERCUS POTESTATEM

I started searching in the direction that Aiden had gone. I heard a snatch of organ music and turned toward that. Something brushed against my face—a piece of gauze stained by what looked like cockroaches. I ducked, twisted, turned...a ukulele being played by a bronze, round-bellied robot...about a hundred red glass hummingbird feeders dangling from the ceiling, all empty...an old-fashioned streetlight...a set of encyclopedias that were about four inches wide and seven feet tall, bound in leather...the front end, including headlights, of a car completely covered in chrome...a fairy garden in a pot with a dead bonsai tree...a glass case full of bees pinned to a piece of silk...a poster for Carter the Great, one of the classic stage magicians...a stack of old dirty magazines with cat women on the covers...a Christmas tree covered with plastic apples, wax candles, and silver spoons...those big wax-covered wheels of cheese, only made of plastic...glass fishing floats dangling from an old upside-down canoe...a stuffed leopard pouncing on a group of stuffed mice in top hats and tail coats...it went on and on and on.

No Aiden.

Then, thump, I literally came face-to-face with one of those old fortune-telling machines, the kind with the guy in the purple turban behind the glass. I didn't have a quarter in my pocket, so I kind of tapped the glass. "Hey, mister," I said. "Have you seen a little kid go past?"

The automaton in the box gave a little jerk. Then his "crystal ball" started to glow and his hands moved over it. A mechanical voice said, "The future...is never clear...but Doctor Rudolfo knows all!"

Ha ha. That was my fake fortune teller name. The machine started to rumble and buzz, and a card dropped into the slot below. If it said "believe in yourself" I was going to kick the machine.

It said, *HAVE A LITTLE FAITH – AFTERLIFE ANTIQUES!*

I turned it over. There was an arrow pointing to the right. I turned the card in a half-circle.

The arrow still pointed to the right.

Look. Maybe what *you* want out of life is for magic and enchantment to fill your days.

What I wanted was to find my brother.

I started following the arrow through the shop. A chandelier made out of real bones and plastic candles...a hundred tambourines stacked on a fire pole...an indoor koi pond...a horse-drawn carriage stuffed completely full with chopped-up mannikins that I was afraid to touch, they were so lifelike...a bunch of old pistols with like eight or ten or twenty barrels all strapped together, leaking something green onto a red velvet chair...a miniature version of the Trojan Horse in a dirty old fish tank, surrounded by tiny plastic velociraptors...a magician's trick box, the kind where you put the pretty lady inside and start shoving swords at her...a row of six big dusty plastic bags marked *MERMAID SCALES – ETHICALLY HARVESTED – SPRING RUN 2023*...a peacock made out of horseshoes and barbed wire...a bronze bull so big you could walk underneath it, and I would have, but there were char marks and ugly stains on the bottom that turned my stomach.

Then I came to a curved staircase, not quite spiral but clinging to the inside of a small square area, and followed the arrow upward.

"Aiden?"

I heard him grunt. I followed the arrow around a tree made

completely of—I'm not lying—stuffed snakes. Big ones that made my skin creep. And then there was Aiden, sitting on the floor surrounded by a semi-circle of comic books. They weren't anything I recognized, titles like *Creepy Claustrophobia Comics* and *The Adventures of Exclamation the Dog!* He was nose-deep in one called *Feynman's Jetpack*, whose cover featured a T-Rex in a smoking jacket, holding a cup of tea with one delicate foreclaw.

"Buddy, you better put those back," I said. "We can't buy 'em."

"The shop wants me to have them," he said. Then he reached into his pocket and pulled something out. At first I thought it was a skull, a mouse skull or something. Then I looked again. It was some kind of seed. "As payment for planting this."

"And you found all this out how?"

He dug around in the piles of comics until he pulled out a cardboard card.

PLANT ME 12" DEEP IN FULL SUNLIGHT AWAY FROM HOUSE FOUNDATIONS AND POWER LINES – KEEP SOIL WET UNTIL WELL ESTABLISHED – REACHES ABOUT 25' HEIGHT, 25' WIDTH – GROWS RAPIDLY UNTIL FULL SIZE – QUERCUS POTESTATEM. I flipped it over. *TAKE THE COMICS TOO, AIDEN, I THINK YOU'LL LIKE THEM.*

I sighed and looked back down the stairs.

The way looked clearer. I edged around the snake tree and looked over the rail.

Below us was a clear path through all the treasures and junk. After traveling what had seemed like half an hour to get to Aiden, it seemed like a freaking miracle. I could even see the front door, as well as the weird booth thing that Balthazar was sitting in. He waved, grinning.

I raised one hand. "You're sure you want to do this? Plant the seed, I mean? In our yard? Without asking Mom first?"

He gave me a classic *duh* look.

"Get everything packed up in your backpack. Let's try to get out of here."

"Ice cream."

"If I still have money when we get out of here, and *if* we get out of here and can find the ice cream place."

"Okay."

Two minutes later, we walked out of the front door, the sound of Balthazar's giggling still ringing in my ears like a maniacal door chime.

~

That night—the new ice cream place had been okay but not great, by the way—Aiden surveyed the yard like Michelangelo viewing a block of marble, circling here and there with one hip jutting out and his hand on his chin. He was taking the whole seed thing seriously. Finally he selected the location.

Our house is a tiny two-story brown house with a chain-link fence, weeds growing up in the grass cut down enough to look mostly okay, a porch with a wood lattice to help give some shade, a narrow side yard with a gravel path in the middle that's a pain to mow around, and a back yard with a tiny, creaking swing set that I'm too big to use. Literally. The top of the swings come up to my shoulder.

And in the back corner away from a tiny metal shed full of rust, lawn crap, and spiders, is an old sandbox. Aiden refused to use it. The local cats used it as a litterbox.

That's right. He decided to plant the weird seed right in the middle of the sandbox.

"Uh, Aiden," I said as he was digging the hole, "I don't think that's a good idea. All that sand isn't good for plants. And there's a plastic liner under the sandbox to keep anything from growing up through it."

He gave me another *duh* look, and I realized how dumb I sounded.

"Okay, but at least dig down deep enough to hit the real dirt."

"I know what I'm doing."

Good thing one of us did. I had called in to work to talk to Frank. "Sorry, Connor," he said. "You've missed too many days of work. People are complaining that I'm treating you different than everyone else. If I let you stay, I'm going to have a riot on my hands."

Mom said she was sorry. Someone had coded on her shift. Died. And she had been the one left talking to the family afterwards.

I started calling around to see if anyone had any openings, sick to my stomach. What else could any of us do?

The next morning, still jobless and interviewless, I woke up like *that*, sitting bolt upright in my bunk, hands automatically coming up to protect my face from the bottom of Aiden's bunk above me. My heart was racing, my whole body twitching.

I could have sworn Aiden had called me. I jumped out of bed. He wasn't in his. The window was open and the screen pulled out.

"Aiden!" I leaned out the window. He was in the tree in the back yard. Oh, sure. Fine. The tree that hadn't been there yesterday, which he had planted from that seed. The trunk was kind of cocked from side to side and covered with scars and lumps, like a tree that had been growing so long that it had survived just about everything. The roots had busted up the wood of the sandbox walls, they were so huge. I shouted, "Aiden! Get down from there before you break your fool neck!"

I ran downstairs. Dad's ghost sat in the living room in his old chair, same as always. Mom was always trying to get me to sit there, but I wouldn't. Aiden would, but only rarely. He wasn't a kid to go sitting in grownups' laps most of the time.

Dad's ghost seemed like he was trying to get my attention, but I didn't have time for it. I ran out the front door with my shoes in my hand.

"Aiden!"

I stopped myself from asking a bunch of stupid questions, like *where did that tree come from?* or *what are you doing up there?* or *you know Mom's going to kill you when she sees that tree, right?* As far as

Aiden was concerned, I would just be flapping my mouth and making noise. He wouldn't even bother answering me.

He was about twenty feet off the ground, climbing up toward something glittering in the branches.

"What is that?" I asked.

"Stuff," he said.

Out of the blue, I asked, "Why did that damned shop pick you, anyhow?"

His face turned toward me, a small oval from between the slivery, slim leaves and the cockeyed branches. He snorted, then went back to climbing upward. One branch led, like a tightrope or an invitation, to his window.

Aiden reached the glittering thing and shouted "catch!" Then it was dive-bomb city, with my arms stretched out in case Aiden himself decided to jump.

Something solid yet soft landed in my arms. I juggled it for a couple of seconds, but the outer fabric was all slithery, and I lost it on the scruffy grass underfoot.

I cursed. Aiden lowered himself out of the tree with all the confidence of a squirrel, using his tennis shoes to slide down the peelings strips of bark. He walked over to the bundle on the ground and flipped it open.

Inside was an ivory-colored plastic doodad, an off-brand Speak and Spell. Aiden had got one of those from a thrift shop when he was, I don't know, like two. He dragged it around until he discovered the hard way that chocolate pudding was no good for electronics. He didn't cry after he wrecked it, but you could tell he was disappointed. Not in himself so much as reality. Anyway, it had rows of plastic keys marked with letters and numbers and a tiny, old-fashioned LED screen.

Aiden grabbed it and slung the strap (it had strap built into the case, which, duh, they should have done with the original ones) over his shoulder. Then he dashed into the house.

I bent down over the rest of what was on the ground, which was a cheap purple and gold costume, compete with cummerbund and vest, a cheap gold turban with plastic jewels and beads, and a plastic "crystal" ball.

Clearly, those were meant for me.

I felt my throat tighten. It was all cheap stuff from a dollar store.

"What are you trying to do to us?" I asked it, my voice breaking. "What is this gonna fix? How is this gonna help anybody? How is this gonna help my mom get off her shift on time? How is this gonna make Aiden able to cope with the world without using me as a crutch? How is this gonna make me into something more than a..."

I broke off and ran toward the house, running past my dad's ghost, still sitting in his recliner. I couldn't see him for all the tears I was trying to hide.

It felt like all that magic had happened just to be cruel.

After Dad died, I grew up believing that the world was out to get me. It kind of was. I fought Mom about it for a while. None of the things holding me back were fair, or right, or just. I was going to stand up for myself. I would fight the whole world.

Finally, one day when we were over at one of Mom's friends' houses, the temporary man of the house, who was Mom's friend's boyfriend at the time, took me out to the park to play some basketball. Aiden had been acting up a lot then, and I cut loose with a flood of complaints as we played.

He heard me out. Then, as I started complaining about Mom, he said, "I get that you're mad at Aiden. But you got to leave your Ma out of this."

"Why?"

And then he gave me the Talk. I was fourteen. How I lived that long without it, I don't know. The Talk isn't about S-E-X. Mom, being a nurse, had given me that one a long time ago. This was the one that all black kids, especially boys, get. How the world ain't fair, and your job—your *only* real goddamned job in this life—is not to get killed.

"It gets worse for you," he added. "You have to make sure that Aiden doesn't get killed, either."

I stopped dead right where I was. The basketball rebounded off the backboard and hit me in the head. The boyfriend caught it before it could get away.

I suddenly saw that there was no hope for anything in this life for me but taking care of Aiden. I'd always loved my little brother, but it was that moment that turned him into a job. My dad had died only a few months before that, but it wasn't until then that my childhood ended.

I remember having had big dreams before then. Now I can't remember what they were. Like, at all.

I'm afraid to ask Mom what they were. Probably something dumb, like becoming Michael Jordan from *Space Jam* or something.

4. IN THE GARBAGE

I stuck my head into Aiden's room. He was playing with the plastic toy machine. I could hear it talking to him in that precise yet stilted way that machines have. I rolled my eyes and went into my room. Finally, Aiden had found someone to talk to that didn't use any of that stupid human nuance that he always hated so much.

I felt mean, and bitter, and angry. I closed the door and threw the stuff the tree had left for me in the trash on top of all the wadded-up pieces of paper that I threw in it, notebook pages that I wrote on, then crumpled up and threw away. Thoughts, feelings, dreams. I knew where that stuff belonged.

I hated on Aiden, I hated on my mom, I even hated on my dead dad, both for dying and for becoming a useless ghost constantly sitting in his chair downstairs. For leaving us alone to deal with life without him, but not really leaving. Just hanging around to make me feel guilty, I guess.

It wasn't fair. Life was not far. And I was gonna start being not-fair back to life.

Starting with my old job.

I was burning with hate over getting fired for—what?—taking

care of my family. What kind of job forces you to not take care of your family?

What kind of monsters were they?

I tossed some stuff in my backpack. I thought about throwing in some of the papers from the trash. But what if they didn't burn up completely? What if they tracked it back to me, based on my handwriting?

I knew where the key to the back door was, and I knew where the cameras were: covering the register. There *was* a camera watching the back door, but it was busted. The grease in the fryers, that would be easy enough to start on fire. Pour some rubbing alcohol from the first-aid kit on it, toss in a match.

Maybe the whole store would burn down. Maybe the fire alarms would go off and it would all get put out before anything too bad happened. I didn't care. Do you know what it feels like, when your heart is on fire with rage? My heart was like fryer oil with the temperature cranked all the way up. That stupid tree had added insult to injury. It had thrown down a match.

I packed up the costume along with a fake mustache that I had lying around from Christmas. If I was stopped, I could say that I was going to a party. Anyone who saw me would probably remember the costume. Afterwards, I'd pack it back in my backpack and walk home, minding my own business. I put some of Mom's blue nitrile gloves in a side pocket. No sense leaving fingerprints.

It was only about fifteen minutes' walk. I circled around the store, put on the costume, and walked the rest of the way to the building via the main road, in other words, *not* from the direction of my house.

The back door opened easy and I put the key back. I had my gloves on. Nobody could see me. The camera was still busted.

The hot anger I had felt earlier had gone cold. Not with fear, but with calculation. This situation was an algebra problem. I could see the formula; with a little effort, I could solve the variables.

Costume off. Gloves still on. Hairnet on in place of the turban. Mustache still on—then it was off and safely stowed in the backpack.

I took the bottle of rubbing alcohol out of my backpack and set the matches beside it. I took off the cap on the bottle, then froze. The room didn't smell like it was supposed to. I screwed the cap back on.

Turning around in a slow circle, I smelled the kitchen. Whoever had closed for the night had done a shitty job. You could see grease streaks on the floor from where it had been mopped badly. The dishwasher was still shut, which meant the last load of dishes was still inside. The trash hadn't been taken out...

...and the fryers were still on.

I reached a hand toward them, bile rising up in my throat. You can't leave the fryers on like that.

It's dangerous.

I thought, *You wouldn't even need to use the rubbing alcohol. Just toss in a match. You wouldn't even have to do that. Just walk away. Turn around and go home. And this place will burn down all on its own.*

It would have been easy to do the wrong thing. It would have been easy to do the right thing, for that matter.

Instead, I did the stupid thing.

I lit a match, then leaned over the hot oil. The match burned down almost to my fingers, and I almost dropped it.

I didn't. I let the match burn me, rather than drop it.

I didn't know what that meant. But I put the rubbing alcohol away. I turned off the fryers.

And then I cleaned the store.

And went home.

It was after midnight and Mom wasn't home yet; she was only supposed to work a three-to-eleven, but you know how it goes, at least how it goes for our family. Aiden was still awake in his room. The door was closed but I could hear the mechanical voice still talking to him. I tapped on the door.

"Aiden. Time for bed."

"'Kay."

The speaking didn't stop; it just became muffled as he shoved the toy under his pillow. I went into my room and closed the door. Then I came back out and went into the bathroom and started the shower. I smelled like grease and lemon cleaner. Not as bad as if I'd actually gone to work, but still enough to give me away. Aiden would smell it.

As the shower heated up, I stared at myself in the mirror, looking over my shoes and my clothes. I didn't *think* I'd left any traces behind. I went through the backpack. It was all still there, turban, vest, cummerbund, mustache.

I put the turban on my head and looked at myself, then added the mustache. Steam was filling up the top third of the room. I watched myself swirling in the mist for a second, then turned on the vent fan.

Tomorrow would be laundry day.

As I took off the turban, something rustled. A piece of paperboard had been tucked into the folds.

NEVER FEAR, the paper said. AFTERLIFE ANTIQUES NEVER GIVES CLIENTS AWAY.

I turned the paper over.

≈

The next morning, Aiden had left a note on his door.
I DID ALL MY HOMEWORK
I MADE BREAKFAST FOR YOU
MOM IS SLEEPING SHHHH

≈

Breakfast was soggy cereal that had been sitting in milk for at least five minutes. Sludge, in other words. Aiden had one hand on his chin and his head tilted to the side, staring at it.

"Cereal grains are porous," he said.

"Yes," I said. "But hey. Thanks." I sat down and started to eat.

He made a face. "You can just make yourself some fresh cereal."

I chewed with my mouth open, which he always thinks is disgusting. That morning was no exception.

"Don't do that."

"Ready for school?"

He had one hand held up in front of his face so he didn't have to look at me. "Yes. I am wearing my clothes in an appropriate fashion, my shoes are on, my teeth are brushed, I contemplated brushing my hair but decided that I would not and don't fight me on that one."

"Okay."

"My homework, as previously stated, is completed, and will earn me a nearly perfect grade."

"Not a perfect grade?"

"I thought about it. People treat perfection as freakish, but things that are nearly perfect are assumed to be the work of a brown-nosing overachiever."

"You're not wrong," I said, shoveling in more of the disgusting sludge.

"Coffee?"

"Please."

The coffee was bad, too. I drank it.

"What made you...?" I didn't know how to ask.

"The machine told me a few things I needed to hear," Aiden said.

"Like what?"

"Like..." He stared into space, looking adorably thoughtful. I thought about how mad I had been at him the night before, and my eyes burned with shame. Finally, he shook his head.

"It talks to you?" I asked.

He gave me a *duh* look, which was still going to be one of his primary modes of communication, apparently. "It's magic? From a magic tree? From a magic antique shop?"

"It's not telling you how to do anything dangerous, is it?" I asked, joking around. What was I gonna do? Take it away? Sabotage it?

"It is," he said. "But it's also telling me how not to."

I had clipped off a piece of turban, a shiny bit of gold fabric, and stuck it in my pocket. I put my hand in my pocket and touched it.

Yeah.

Well.

I nodded. "You still need help to go to school?"

"Yes, please. There will be bullies."

Darkly, I said, "There will *always* be bullies."

Aiden pulled on his jacket and backpack, then stood by the door as I loaded the dishwasher and wiped down the counters. He had a thoughtful look on his face.

Then he said something to me, something that made me twitch, because it had been on the back of that card, too.

"Sometimes the worst thing you can do is fight back," he said.

Nothing ever happened to me because of my breaking into the restaurant. Nothing good, nothing bad. I washed my uniform and turned it in to Frank; he gave me my last check. He told me he was sorry, but I could tell he was kind of relieved to have me gone, too. It would have been nice if he had somehow known what I had done and offered me my job back, gave me a bonus, or at least steered me toward another restaurant job somewhere.

But he didn't, and I couldn't help but think it was his loss. I looked around the kitchen and said, "I'm gonna miss this place."

He didn't answer. I left.

I felt clean in a way that I hadn't felt, the night before. Working there was already a memory. I laughed about what I'd done on the way home. A knot in my guts had been cut loose.

In a strange kind of way, I felt free.

ABOUT THE AUTHOR

DeAnna Knippling is always tempted to lie on her bios. Her favorite musician is Tom Waits, and her favorite author is Lewis Carroll. Her favorite monster is zombies. Her life goal is to remake her house in the image of the House on the Rock, or at least Ripley's Believe It Or Not. You should buy her books. She promises that she'll use the money wisely on bookshelves and secret doors. She lives in Colorado and is the author of the A Fairy's Tale horror series which starts with *By Dawn's Bloody Light*, and other books like *The Clockwork Alice, A Murder of Crows: Seventeen Tales of Monsters & the Macabre*, and more.

As always, this story is dedicated to Lee and Ray,
without whose love none of this would be possible.

Find out more about DeAnna at:
WonderlandPress.com

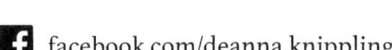 facebook.com/deanna.knippling

twitter.com/dknippling

 bookbub.com/authors/deanna-knippling

LIKE WIND OVER WATER

KAREN L. ABRAHAMSON

The fog had blown in like a mask over the water. Weak sunlight placed a steel-edged glare on the placid waves. The big ferry's diesel engines chewed up the silence and placed a sour tang on the air as the vessel chugged up the miles. The Borealis Queen was on its regular three-day journey to the northern port of Prince Rupert, but even with the white ship's movement there was only the barest of wind. It was a lie, given the weather reports were of a storm coming in from the Bering Sea.

The ship's horn sounded, crying through the pillowing fog like a dying beast, but really it was the call of one lonely beast to another. At least to crewman Romy Spencer. She stood on the prow with the mist coiled around her and the glassy waves hissing past below. Her gaze strained as she sought to see or hear anything that might signal the danger of a shore line, shoals or another vessel.

In a January fog, her breath didn't show in the cold. The moisture that beaded her long hair and knit cap didn't bother her, either. Instead it was the lack of pressure on her skin that, even after all these years and fully clothed, left her with a tingling in her flesh and feeling uncomfortably exposed. She hugged herself a moment and swallowed back the discomfort she'd traded for youthful adventure amongst men. Now she wasn't as certain of her decision. Five years without a tail was entirely too long, but she wasn't about to return home with her tail figuratively between legs she didn't have. She had to find Matthew.

Something ruffled the smoothness of fog and her preternaturally keen hearing went on alert. It was why she often found herself on this duty. At least that was what she told herself. It had nothing to do with being the first female crewman, and this being the coldest post on the ship. Or the fact that she'd turned away the advances of the Chief Crewman.

A muffled cry? An engine sound? She craned over the white rail and looked back at the pilot's windows. Garet would be watching her for any indication of a problem, but the fog was so thick at this point of the northern inside passage that the Borealis Queen was travelling by radar and the chances of seeing her from the bridge were iffy.

Another sound and she held her breath trying to hear over the engines and the water hiss. A gull cried. From the upper decks came the sound of tourist voices delighting in the fog.

There it was again: a cry and the thunk of something hollow.

She grabbed the radio at her hip. "Bridge from the bow. Bridge from the bow. I'm getting something about thirty degrees starboard. Sound only, no visual."

"Copy that bow. Keep watch." She turned her attention starboard and heard/felt the change in the ship's diesels as the engines slowed. At the rear of the huge ferry the propellers would slow, but momentum would carry them along. The ship shuddered under her, its heading changed, and she swayed a little. Passengers on board wouldn't like this. There'd be complaints and maybe a few bruises from landlubbers staggering against bulkheads.

She hoped whoever or whatever was out there could stay out of the ferry's path.

A slight wind lifted the ends of her pale blonde hair and stirred the fog, thickening it in spots and leaving other portions of the water's surface bare. A shadow moved upon the waves, not thirty degrees starboard. Not ten degrees. Instead it rose and fell with the water—about the length of two lifeboats—right in front of the Queen.

Through a curtain of fog, she saw the mast of the sailboat, half of it dangling in the water. Was that a lone figure waving on deck as the powerless craft drifted right toward the prow?

Romy grabbed the radio. "Bow to Bridge. Bow to Bridge. We've got a sailboat adrift dead ahead about a quarter mile."

A quarter mile was too close to turn the huge ferry. A quarter nautical mile was a bare fifteen hundred feet. There was no way they were going to miss the man—or his boat.

Ship's horns sounded. She could imagine the frantic actions on the ship's bridge. The diesels groaned and the hull shuddered futilely as the engines dropped into reverse. The deck convulsed under her feet, but the huge screws that drove the ship forward couldn't reverse their momentum that quickly.

Ahead, the man aboard the sailboat waved his arms and yelled as if waving his arms could wave them away. The Borealis Queen churned closer. Closer until Romy swore she could look down into the surely-soon-to-be-dead man's eyes.

Blue, she realized. The color of light through tropical waves. Once upon a time she'd known a man with such color eyes. He'd carried the scent of land and grass fields. She had met him on a rocky shore and in that distant time she thought she might have fallen in what the humans called love. But her man had returned to the land and she couldn't bear losing the sea.

She had never seen him again even though longing had led to her trading away her tail soon after in hopes of finding him again. All she'd known was that he liked to walk by the sea and that he lived in a place called the Sunshine Coast of British Columbia. Not much to go on.

Or maybe it was.

After five long years, it could not be, but a breeze stirred the wind and brought with it an unforgettable scent. Male musk, green grass, and something sweet that Romy had since learned was called 'Old Spice'.

Matthew's scent.

Could it be?

She inhaled deeply, and there it was, stronger now. As if he stood on the Queen's deck.

But Matthew was never a mariner, in fact he was suspicious of the sea. "Too much unfathomable darkness," he'd always said. Too many secrets to weigh you down—as if secrets were worn like the lead belts divers wore. Sometimes secrets were simply too precious for sharing until you were sure of a person. Her people had long had proof that the secret of their existence was not something humans were fit to know.

The sailboat slipped closer to its destruction as the fog closed in around the ship. Chief Crewman Chad Avery ran up beside her. He had his radio out as his gaze slithered up over her to her face. "Where? Where is it?"

"There!" Ignoring his gaze, she pointed in the direction of her sighting, but the fog had turned a glistening silver that refracted light into their eyes. The water was invisible and so was what it carried.

He glanced at her. "You sure?"

She nodded.

He put the radio to his lips. "Get ready for impact." He turned to her. "Spenser, a hand here."

He ran to one of the life rafts held in thick fiberglass barrels and started to undo the locks that held the barrel on deck. The barrel clicked free and she ran to the rail, opening the space that allowed the barrel to roll free. Chad kicked the barrel over on its side and the case rolled past Romy and off the deck. It split in two on impact and the thick rubber life boat self-inflated—a refuge for any survivors.

Romy and Chad ran to the prow again.

Through the fog, the disabled sailboat was barely visible right below them and the lone sailor looked up. A shiver ran through her body and her skin burned...

Silver strands of fog threaded between them and then cleared to expose dark water.

Not a sailboat. Not a boat at all and no one was aboard. Instead, three large logs spun in the water—probably tethered together before being lost from a log boom along the coast.

Romy blinked and fell back from the rail, the strange sensation passing. That had to be wrong. She rubbed her eyes and peered down again.

"What the hell." Chad swore beside her. "Where's this boat of yours?"

She scanned the black ripples that were torn apart by the ship's prow.

"I—I don't know. I was sure..." She looked up at his angry face. Chad was tall—almost six foot three—and towered over her, his hulking shoulders made broader by the thick, blue ferry-issued parka he wore. A navy toque was pulled low over his ears and his brown gaze glared out at her.

"Jesus!" He turned away and brought the radio to his lips. "False alarm. Crew*person* Spenser apparently jumped the gun."

He gave her a disparaging glance and stalked away.

"But..." she said to his retreating form. She *had* seen something. She had *smelled* Matthew and scent never lied. She craned over the prow of the ship, but there was nothing but smooth water through the fog.

~

S he stayed on the prow until Randy Baker arrived. He, like all the male crewmen, looked like a hulking bear in his waterproof parka. His blonde curls, damp with fog, stuck out from the edge of his fisherman's toque, but his moss-brown gaze wouldn't meet hers.

"Cap'n wants to see you," he said. He hitched his head toward the ship's bridge. The dark glass peered down at them.

Romy nodded and felt Randy's gaze follow her as she headed across the deck. Inside, in the narrow metal passageway out of the cold damp, she leaned back against the bulkhead hatch and inhaled to clear her mind. Just what had she seen? She'd been so sure? And the scent... Even now, her cells were certain Matthew was here and had been lost when the ship ran his boat under.

But it hadn't happened like that, had it? Something was wrong— with her. She checked her watch and figured she had time to go down to her cabin while she cleared her head. In the narrow passage below the car deck, in crew quarter country, Chief Crewman Chad Avery caught up to her.

He caught her arm and pulled her around. The crew passageway was barely wide enough for his shoulders and now he loomed over her and pressed her back to the wall.

His scent of musk and male sweat soured in her nose. "What the hell did you think you were doing? Someone could have been hurt doing something dramatic like stopping the ship. Was this your way of trying to get my attention?"

He leered down at her.

Romy went to duck away but he blocked her with his arm.

"Your attention was about the last thing on my mind," she said and felt exhaustion weigh her down. She'd spent too much time aboard avoiding exactly this kind of too-close interaction with one Chad Avery.

She sighed and met his gaze. His face was too close. There was anger there and concern—or was it hunger.

"Listen. I'm cold and tired. I have to see the captain and I'd like two minutes alone to clear my head. Is that okay by you?"

He hesitated. Then with a shake of his head, he dropped his arm and straightened, the absence of his body heat leaving her momentarily breathless. With a nod she turned and walked away, let herself into the room she shared with three of the female catering staff and closed the door behind her. She leaned against the barrier, still feeling Chad's presence, still scenting his sour musk. Her hands were shaking.

Just what was that? Was he concerned or angry? The two emotions didn't seem to go hand in hand, but then she wasn't adroit at interpreting human emotion. Hands still shaking, she stripped off her heavy boots and the extra layer of socks—and stopped. A pale nacreous glow seeped through her thin wool socks.

What the...?

She yanked the socks off. The glow covered her skin and darkened down to clearly green toes.

She yanked down her trousers and long underwear. The green spread up over her ankles half way up her calves.

"No. No. No. No. This can't be happening!" She rushed to her bunk and brought her knees up to examine her toes. Not just green, but a fine frill of webbing had grown to join them. She'd been careful. She stayed out of the water these past five years to avoid just such a thing happening. It *should be* that her human body was becoming more permanent—after all, she'd been in this form for five years... But then none of her kind had tried to be human for this long before.

She closed her eyes and willed the change to reverse, but there was no tingle, no shimmer of pain across her skin. Instead, a chill crept up her back and seeped deep into her bones. A change like this —it was the sort of autonomic change that occurred when one of her kind was in danger.

But there hadn't been any danger and she hadn't *done* anything... Not even dipped a toe into the water.

She stood in front of the small mirror to examine her face. Perhaps her jaw and brow had narrowed as was the case with her kind. Perhaps her eyes and had widened the slightest bit, too. But her hair was still blonde. Her shoulders were pale. If she dressed for her shifts in the early morning, none of her roommates would know. There was that at least. She could hide what had happened and keep searching for Matthew.

But now her task was to face the captain's inquisition. Fighting back shivers, she pulled on dry tan pants and a brown, long-sleeved sweater over her shirt. Her hair she combed back and pulled into a ponytail. She pinched her cheeks for color and headed out into the gangway.

Thankfully, Chad had left.

Her booted feet clanged on the narrow steel ladder past the passenger cabin deck to the vehicle deck, and then up and up on the crew's ladders away from the broad stairwells that would bring her under ferry passenger eyes.

At bridge level she turned forward on the wood paneled gangway and knocked smartly on the bridge door, then entered. The room was dimly lit, the better to highlight the glow of the helm and radar. The large glass windows were tinted against the fog's glare. The First Officer stood by the forward window gazing into the fog that was thickening with the fading daylight. The Third Officer stood at the helm, his gaze on the panel of navigational instruments. When he noticed Romy he shook his head and nodded at the door she had just entered.

The First Officer must have noticed the motion, for he turned around.

"Well if it isn't our little wanna-be heroine. The radio phones are buzzing with management demanding to know what happened."

Romy went still. "Management? I'm here because the Captain wanted to speak to me."

"The captain's in his cabin," the Third Officer said.

She nodded thanks and stepped back into the gangway, closing the door softly behind her. Management had called the ship? How could they know already? If they did know, it probably wasn't going to be good for her. She'd learned that ferry schedules were everything, but the ship's evasive maneuvers couldn't have put them much behind...

She turned back to the captain's cabin and stopped, then smoothed her palms over her neck to make certain the weird change in her body hadn't opened her gills. Satisfied, she knocked once.

"Come," came the rough bark from inside.

She swallowed back her nerves, pushed the door open and stepped inside. On a ship like the Queen, all the staterooms were below the vehicle deck except for the captain's. His was small, like the others, but the difference was that instead of four women sharing a cabin where the rumble of the engines drilled into your bones every minute, here the space was occupied by one man and a desk. The rarest of crew luxuries, a window, was covered in condensation but gave onto the growing foggy darkness of the afternoon.

"Captain. Sir. You wished to see me." She stood at attention trying to wring as much height as possible out of her five-foot-four frame.

He looked up from reading a file, his pince nez glasses sitting low on his nose. Captain Salter was a big man with broad shoulders and gray hair. Though he had to be in his sixties, he still cut a trim figure, like most of the males of Romy's species—after all, a fat merman would be slow and far easier prey. Captain Slater wore black uniform trousers and a white shirt with gold epaulettes gleaming on his shoulders. His jacket with the four bands around the cuffs was hung on the back of his chair.

He left her standing while he looked her over. Then he sighed and removed his glasses.

"Have you gone blind, Spenser? You can't tell the difference between a sail boat and stray logs? What the hell were you thinking sounding the alarm before you were certain? The fog already had us late, without bloody course deviations."

Romy stayed silent. There was nothing she could say except her mind had been on the man she'd been searching for these past long years, and *that* would not go over well.

Salter squeezed the bridge of his nose and looked back at her. "So, what have you got to say for yourself?"

She met his gaze. "Sir. I've been a good crewman. I haven't caused any problems." Even though she could have complained many times about the treatment she received at the hands of her crewmates. "I was keeping watch and was sure I saw a boat." She shook her head. "Other than that, I can't explain it."

Salter's gaze twitched across her face as if searching for something. Maybe guilt? Then he shook his head and replaced his glasses.

"You leave me no choice but to write you up for failure to confirm your observation before sounding the alarm. Sudden changes of speed and evasive maneuvers place the ship under stress and the passengers in jeopardy. Someone could have fallen overboard. You'll be relieved of duty until a full assessment of your competence can be completed."

"But Captain! The ship's already shorthanded what with the flu that's cutting through the crew. You need me."

"We're only a day out from Rupert. We'll manage."He hiked his head at the cabin door.

Romy hesitated, but protesting about the unfairness wasn't going to get her anywhere. She turned on her heel and left.

She felt like storming off the ship. Let her stand on the prow and transform in front of them and then dive into the water while they were all trying to figure out what the hell was happening. Leave them with a mystery they could never solve.

But that would break all her vows to hide her people's existence. Given what she knew of humans she knew the vows were wise. She headed down the crew ladder, turned the corner and almost tripped over a small girl curled up behind a door that led to the passenger saloon.

"Well hello," Romy said, for a moment not sure what to do.

The child looked maybe four or five and had blue eyes the color of sunlit water. She gave off an almost familiar scent of talc, green grass and apple orchards and had hazel curls that fell loose over her shoulders. She wore jeans, a deep green sweat shirt and red sneakers.

"Shh." The girl held her finger to her lips and then pointed at the door.

"Is there a reason we have to be quiet," Romy whispered.

"I'm hiding. There's a bad man on the ship."

"A bad man? Really?" Romy looked at the door. "But you can't stay here. You're not allowed. Where's your mom?"

The child just looked worried. "I—I'm not sure." She looked up at Romy with her eyes full of tears. "I'm scared."

"Oh, sweetie, you're safe on this ship. Nothing's going to happen to you. I promise. Now what's your name and I'll help you find your mom."

"I'm Sarah with an 'h'. Sarah Woodman."

"Well, Sarah with an 'h', I'm Romy. At least that's what my friends call me. Why don't you come with me and we'll go find your mom?"She held out a hand and Sarah stood and caught hold. Small warm hand in larger one. Romy felt a tingle in her skin at the contact —the first time she had touched a human child palm to palm. The touch was one of the most intimate amongst her people, a touch she rarely shared with anyone and with no one since Matthew.

Romy almost recoiled, but young Sarah held on tight. It was many years since she'd had anything to do with a youngling, though once she'd thought she'd have her own brood of hatchlings. That had been before Matthew and the impossible love between them.

Romy opened the door to the passenger saloon a few inches and peered out. Two young women sat chatting at a table in the café. Otherwise, the area was empty.

"Looks safe to me." She glanced down at Sarah who then peeked around the doorframe.

A huge sigh escaped Sarah. "He's gone."

Romy pulled the door farther open and stepped through. "Coming?"

Cautiously, Sarah stepped out beside her, her shoulder brushing Romy's thigh. The child was a slight little thing, all sinew, bone and muscle. It explained her thin face. But weren't children supposed to be rounder?

Sarah's brow crinkled. "He's not here, but neither's my mom."

"Well, let's see if we can find her, shall we. We have a list of everyone aboard. What's your mom's name?"

Sarah looked up at her. "Meghan."

Romy smiled encouragement at her. "That's a pretty name. Almost as pretty as Sarah-with-an-'h'."

She led Sarah away from the stairway door and the broad passage to the Chief Steward's office. She knocked once and stepped inside, not waiting for an answer.

"Sorry to bother you, Sir." She said as the Chief Steward looked up. He was a small, balding man with an ample belly and a pencil-thin moustache that made his face look soft. "I found Sarah, here, in the forward crew interdeck stairwell. She says that there's a bad man aboard and that she doesn't know where her mom is." She looked down at Sarah. "Have I got that right?"

Sarah nodded. She stood half-hidden behind Romy's leg, a fist and thumb having found its way to her mouth.

Romy knelt beside her. "It's okay, Sarah. We'll find your mom."

She looked back at Chief Steward Pierce. "Her mom's name is Meghan Woodman, right Sarah? Do you know what the bad man's name is?"

But Sarah swallowed, before shaking her head. Then her gaze dropped to her running shoes and her shoulders slumped. "He's not really a bad man. He's my daddy, but he made my mommy cry."

Confused, Romy glanced from Sarah to Chief Steward Pierce.

Pierce's narrowed gaze slid down a passenger list he'd pulled out of his desk. His finger followed his gaze and stopped. "Woodman. There's a Meghan Woodman and Sarah Woodman-Wilson sharing a room with a Matthew Wilson. Cabin forty-seven. I'll call down for them to come and get her. They're undoubtedly looking."

Matthew Wilson. Matthew? Her Matthew? This was his child? Her skin went cold and for a moment she couldn't breathe.

It couldn't be true. Wilson had to be a common name. But still... she needed to know... Romy squeezed Sarah's shoulders.

"I can take her down to them, if you like," Romy offered.

"You're ship's crew, Spencer, and from what I hear, not even that. Leave it to my inside staff." He stood up and held out his hand. "Come on, Sarah. You can wait with me until we find your mommy and daddy."

Sarah clung to Romy's hand, but the expression on Pierce's face said he wasn't going to change his mind.

"Sarah, you'll be safe here with Chief Steward Pierce. He'll take care of you until you find your mom and dad."

"But I want to stay with you..." Sarah looked up at her with pleading eyes.

"I'm sorry, Sarah. You can't. Crewman Spencer has other places to go."

Romy hesitated, but then sighed and loosed her hand from Sarah's grasp. "It will be okay."

Pierce caught Sarah's hand. "You can go," he said. Sarah started to cry.

All the way down to her quarters Romy told herself that Sarah's father couldn't possibly be her Matthew. Matthew had been single when they'd met on the east coast shoreline. But that couldn't have been the case if Sarah was his daughter. The timing just didn't add up.

No, it simply could not be her Matthew.

But there had been his scent when she stood on the ship's prow...

Had she scented him from elsewhere on the ship? Was that what had her senses so confused that her body had thought she was in danger and started to transition?

Impossible.

At least that was what she told herself.

Back in her room, on her narrow bunk, staring at the ceiling barely two feet above her, it didn't feel so impossible. Even now she imagined she could inhale Matthew's scent. Either something was seriously wrong with her so her transformation came undone, or Matthew was on this ship. But then maybe something *was* wrong with her. Long years surviving in the depths had taught her to listen to her feelings. In the darkness of the depths it was feelings that kept you from the mouth of a feeding shark, from the silent death of a jelly fish's tentacles, or from the clutches of a giant squid. It was feelings that first told you about vibrations in the water that telegraphed new volcanic activity. It was feelings that warned you about approaching human ships.

She closed her eyes. Life had been so simple before that fateful night along the shore when she'd first seen Matthew. In truth she'd been cruising the shore for many days, drawn by curiosity about humans. Then she'd seen Matthew along the shore. Tall and with a swimmer's torso, slim-hipped as the fastest of her kind were. He was running barefoot in the damp sand along the ocean's edge, the gentle waves running over the sand to cover his feet. She could hear his breathing, could hear the thump and splash of his feet and smell the suntanned human smell in the water. She'd imagined she could hear his heart beating like a match of hers. That was how her kind knew they'd found their mate.

She'd watched him the next morning and the next and then, the next morning, she'd lost her tail and walked up out of the water to meet him as he ran.

That had felt right, but now everything felt wrong, even if Matthew was here on the ship. She had to know if it was really him.

She swung her legs off her bunk and slipped onto the floor. Simply head to Sarah's cabin forty-seven? But if she was discovered venturing into passenger territory without permission there was an even better chance that she'd lose her job. She needed to show she was responsible and not a wild card and that meant going up to the captain and seeking his permission. Surely, he could allow her to check on Sarah given she had no duties to perform.

Squaring her shoulders, she headed out of her quarters and up the narrow ladder toward the bridge. When she arrived on the top deck, she stepped out and down the short corridor to the captain's office and knocked on the closed bulkhead door.

"He's not there." Chad's voice made her freeze. She didn't need Chad lording her circumstances over her.

When she turned, he stood framed in the bridge doorway, the corridor lights placing a greenish pall on his skin.

"Where is he?" she asked and looked back at the door.

"Gone for dinner, probably." Chad shrugged.

Dinner meant Captain Salter could be an hour or more. Go back to her cabin? Simply go to cabin 47 without permission?

"Why don't you come give me a hand on the bridge? You can wait for him there." He grinned and she wasn't sure whether it was born of comradery or something darker.

But if she went back to her cabin now, she might never have the nerve to return. She gave a single nod and stepped past Chad as he held the door open for her.

When he shut the door behind her, the bridge was cast in darkness. The afternoon had passed and evening had allowed the coastal fog to close in around the ship. The lights of the ship's navigation console placed an eerie yellow-green glow on the bridge. Radar and GPS indicated that they were plying one of the narrow channels in the coastal inside passage. The ship's heading was set to automatic which meant the watch officer—Chad—was left with limited tasks to perform, other than taking calls from the crewman keeping watch on the prow and adjusting headings based on watch information. Given the fog, the engines were set to slow.

She turned back to Chad and found he now stood close beside her.

"You really made a mess of your job, you know," he said.

Swallowing, she looked back toward the darkness beyond the bridge windows. "It wasn't intentional. I thought I saw a sailboat."

"One of them logs pointed straight up as they turned... I might think the same thing."

She turned around to look at him and found him eyeing her.

"You saw the logs?"

He shrugged.

"But you didn't tell anyone?"

Another shrug.

"But that would clear me! Show it was an honest mistake!"

"I guess it would." He studied her appraisingly, but he stood too close.

Close enough she had to crane her head back to look him in the eye. A part of her went cold.

"What do you want, Chad?"

That annoying shrug again, but he caught her shoulders with too strong hands and looked down at her.

"Seems to me that me telling the Cap'n what I saw could really help you out. Seems to me that kind of help has got to be worth something..."

He leaned down to her, just as he had in the crew quarter gangway and just as before she went to duck away.

This time his arm didn't shift out of the way. This time his grip on her shoulders strengthened. He dipped his head and his lips found hers, forced hers open and she was gasping for breath. Gasping to rid herself of Chad's sour breath and the taste of old fish that he'd eaten for dinner.

She struggled in his grip and got her hands in between them. Shoved, and he staggered back a pace.

Romy put the navigation console between them. "I don't need your help that badly."

"Good to hear, because hell'll freeze over before I help you." He started around the console after her and she ducked away. She ran for the door, but he'd locked the damn thing upon their entry.

Her fingers shook so badly she couldn't get the darn thing unlocked.

He was on her before she could dart away. Had her pressed against the door, his hand snaking around her, up under her sweater and inside her shirt as she fought to get free. His face came in beside hers, his breath hot and fetid on her cheek as seeking fingers pinched her breasts.

"No!" She squirmed around and caught him with her knee. Shoved past him as he sagged and ran for the bridge phone.

Doubled over, his long reach snagged her as she ran by. He shoved her back and back and back into the navigation console, grabbed her sweater and hauled it up over her head. Her arms were trapped, her protests muffled.

He ripped open her shirt and his hot breath found her breasts. Then he hiked her hips up onto the console, ripping the fly open, his hands seeking inside her panties. Hauling at her waistband.

"No!" She tried to bite him through the sweater. Tried to pull the sweater off, but her squirming didn't help, and her trousers were almost off. "Help!"

A claxon answered her, alarms filling the bridge. Lights flashed through her sweater and suddenly Chad released her.

She crumped, sobbing, to the floor, fumbled her sweater down, her trousers up and stumbled to her feet. Through her tears Chad's hands were rushing across the consoles. The bridge radio was squawking. The ship's engines grumbled and the hull groaned and then shuddered—a long, horrible, squeal that vibrated through the bulkheads and the Queen shuddered further, the bow lifting unnaturally and canting to starboard.

The ship's huge screws continued churning, but the Queen only trembled like a whale beached on the shore.

"Jeesus. Jeesus. Jeesus." Chad's voice rose and became part of the claxon. "We knocked the Queen's navigation off course!"

Through the noise, the vibration shuddering up through her feet, Romy found herself suddenly calm.

"We've run aground," she said.

"You think I don't know that, you stupid bitch," he snarled.

"We ran aground on your watch." From far below, she felt the shift of water rushing into the Queen's broken hull and the greedy depth tugging the Queen under. She smiled bitterly at Chad for he had wrecked everything better than she ever had, but she was sure the blame for this disaster would come her way. "You better hope we don't start taking on water, but just so you know, we already are." She strode to the door again. This time shaking fingers didn't deny her escape.

In the corridor, she met the captain and first mate running for the bridge. They pushed past her as if she wasn't there. Captain Salter's shouts followed her down the corridor. She needed to get to her lifeboat muster station. The rate the water was pouring into the hull, the Queen had no hope at all of surviving.

She pushed outside onto the deck. The weather had changed. The fog had blown away on the predicted storm wind that had brought heavy seas and pouring rain. Far out across the water a faint light spoke of one of the small fishing villages along the coast. Most were small enclaves of First Nations fishermen. Most had no land-ward access and depended on the small steamers and barges that brought goods to them. By Romy's estimation, they must be nearing Smoky Point, named after the cannery that once stained the sky with its smoke stacks.

Through the driving rain she clung to the rail and descended the slippery stairs to the passenger viewing deck and down again, to where the lifeboats hung covered and ready to be deployed when the captain gave orders. The ship groaned under her and the list increased. From elsewhere onboard came passengers' screams.

The first passengers huddled in a daze by the lockers where the emergency life vests were kept. Most had forgotten the vests that they'd been issued in their rooms. A man grabbed her arm.

He was tall and thin and clad in fleece and Gortex like most of the outdoorsmen headed north.

"What's going on? What's happening?" he asked with an American twang so he was likely Alaska bound.

She looked up and forward to the bridge. What was taking so long? Captain Salter should have sounded the alarm. She shook her head.

"I can't rightly say, sir, but I think it's a good thing to be here and ready." She couldn't take a chance on panicking passengers.

Overhead, the ship's loudspeakers clicked on and Captain Salter's voice boomed out and was lost in the gale of wind. She could barely pick out the words "aground" and "lifeboat stations", before the loudspeaker clicked off and the ship's alarms took over. The rain whipped over them.

"Can you give me a hand? We have to get the lifeboat ready." She asked of the tall man. Chad, who was her partner at this station, was nowhere to be seen. It was good and bad both at the same time, for loading and lowering one of the lifeboats wasn't easy at the best of times, and the ship's list was going to make it more dangerous moment to moment.

She started to release the canvas cover, the American starting from the other end, when Chad arrived.

"Hey, what's going on? You shouldn't be doing that." He shoved the American out of the way and started doing his job. When he finished he leaned down to Romy.

"Just so you know, this is all your fucking fault. You and all your hard-to-get."

She looked up at him, too shocked to move, the rain pummeling her face. By his expression, she knew that was going to be his story. He probably even told them she'd come to the bridge purposely to meet him and lead him on.

The injustice of it filled her with fury. She swallowed it back and went to turn away and then spun around, landing a punch on his nose so hard she felt something break in her hand.

Chad staggered back and his nose started to bleed. Romy turned to the passengers crowding the station. They were flooding out of the passenger deck lounges, pressing toward the first boats they could see and impeding the crew who were trying to help them. "Stand back, please. I need to lower the boat."

Thankfully, the American and two others helped push the terrified passengers back.

Romy ignored the pain in her hand as she hit the lever that lowered the lifeboat to loading position. As the boat rolled down a hand fell onto her shoulder. Chad. Again.

She ripped away.

"You're going to pay. I'll make sure of it."

She ignored him.

"Women and children first," she called. They began to load. The ship lurched, the list increasing and the lifeboat thudded against the side of the hull. The lifeboat passengers screamed. The passengers on the deck surged toward the lifeboats. Through the screams and cries caught in the howling wind a distant wail of terror caught Romy's ear.

She froze, looking around. No one else seemed to have heard it, but she certainly had and she knew what, and who, it was.

Sarah with an 'H'. By the sound the child was somewhere far below in the ship and something was horribly, horribly wrong.

"Chad!" she yelled. She pushed through the crowd to where he helped passengers aboard the lifeboat. She caught his arm. "You can manage, right? There's—there's someone in trouble and I have to help them." Gods, how could she explain what she knew?

"No, I can't manage. Look at these people. They're barely listening to instructions at all."

He *was* right about that. Men were jostling women and children out of position. Instead of heading to their own lifeboat stations, too many people were waiting to board the first lifeboat they saw.

She turned from him and once more called on the American. "Help him. And get one of your friends to meet people at the door. If they aren't assigned to this lifeboat, tell them to move on down the deck, or better yet, help them check the lifeboat diagram by the door so they get where they need to be."

She turned back to Chad. "I'll be back, but if I'm not here when you're loaded, don't wait for me."

"I won't," he snarled.

She turned to go, but could barely move through the press of passengers. They jammed the external stairwells. There was no way she could get down below from the exterior of the ship. She managed to shove past passengers trying to get outside and almost fell into the interior passenger lounge with its cushioned chairs and card tables and the dark-stained, mirror-backed, maple bar. Cards lay scattered on the floor where they fallen. Glasses sat half-full on the bar. People were still flooding dazedly up from cabins below, but the bar was empty. The barman had led his customers to their lifeboat stations.

A scent of male musk and green grass found her nose and she stopped dead. Matthew. Matthew was here. Now.

She swung around, but couldn't see him through the throng of pushing, shoving people.

She headed for the passenger stairs and someone grabbed her shoulder and swung her around.

"I need your help..." said a male voice.

She looked up into Matthew's vivid blue eyes.

He was here. Now.

He stopped in mid-sentence and his gaze widened in surprise. "Romy? Is it you?"

She nodded when she wanted to throw her arms around him. He looked good—as she remembered except for a few more wrinkles around the eyes. He was still tall, still handsome, still broad shouldered, but this time a band of gold decorated his hand.

She had to be aloof. Not let him know how long and hard she'd searched. How it hurt to see him like this. "Listen, I need to go. There's something I need to do."

His hand on her shoulder didn't let go. "I need your help. My daughter... My wife and I can't find her. We've looked everywhere."

Romy saw the confirmation then. The shape of his face. The blue gaze. Sarah with an H inherited them from her father.

"Sarah," Romy said and nodded. "Go to your lifeboat station. I'll find her for you."

She pulled away as surprise registered on his face. He caught the wrist of her injured hand. "You look good, Romy. I—I'm sorry about what happened all those years ago. My wife and I were going through a bad patch."

She yanked her wrist back and put people between them, then started down the passenger stairs.

He'd been married when they met? A bad patch was no excuse.

She'd left her people for him. She'd searched for him for five long years. She'd *left the water!*

The flood of passengers ended and she was alone. Still fighting back her anger, she hurried down the flight, but as she reached the next deck the lights went out. From above came the screams of the passengers. Thunks on the hull suggested lifeboats were lowering but inside the darkened ship, the darkness was like the deepest depths of the sea. She scrambled a flashlight from one of the emergency packs kept ready by the stairs and the light became a tiny point of life and hope. The passenger stairs were broad and filled the center of the ship. She leapt down them and down another flight to restaurant level—all black. And down again to the unheated vehicle decks and the cold, oily scent of diesel and gasoline. She stopped long enough to take her bearings, listening for the faint sounds of terror. Under the sea sound carried much farther and better.

The cries had subsided to sobbing below. Probably passenger stateroom deck, the first deck below the vehicles. Buried deep in the ship. How much farther could she go and not find herself in water? She got her answer as she continued down the stairs from the car deck and heard the gurgle and felt the chill of brine below.

The passenger cabin deck was flooding, which meant that the crew deck was already flooded. At the bottom of the passenger stairs she stepped out into freezing, ankle deep water as the sobbing stopped. She slid the light across the bulkheads and a cabin door swam into view replete with a glossy blue number fifty-two at eye level.

Chief Steward Pierce had said Sarah was in Cabin forty-seven with her mother and Matthew.

Down the hall water flowed around her calves as it overwhelmed the Borealis Queen. Darkness flowed like the water and the water rose. A few doors down number forty-seven appeared. She tried the door.

Locked. She knocked. "Sarah! Sarah, it's me, Romy. Open the door. We have to leave."

No sound came from within and she opened her senses again,

listening. Silence filled cabin forty-seven. Had something happened to Sarah? Had she drowned?

A soft whimper still echoed inside the hull of the ship like tides belling through coral. The child was somewhere, just not here. Chief Steward Pierce might have brought her back to her cabin, but she hadn't stayed. Something else had happened.

Romy closed her eyes and allowed the darkness to flood into her senses. In her youth it had been liquid dark, the inky cold of the ocean depths and still she could find her way to whomever was lost and find her way back, towing them with her if they were injured. Always she'd been a seeker and finder, until she'd turned her back on her skills and became a—a hider. A coward nursing her grief over Matthew's choices, away from her people amongst the cold steel of men.

And he had never wanted her as she wanted him! He was a liar. A thief of emotions.

Well she would not give herself to him, but she would find Sarah-with-an-H. For herself—to prove herself still the seeker. For the child.

She inhaled the ocean scent of brine and old wood and history carried in the shifting water. The Borealis Queen groaned and shifted, sinking deeper into the waves. The current around her ankles quickened and the cold brine swiftly rose to her knees.

But the water's echo carried with it the faintest sound of weeping from lower down.

By all the water in the ocean, what had the child done?

Romy waded the hallway until she found a crew door—one used by the housekeeping staff when they cleaned the rooms. She fought it open against the water's pressure and looked down into a deep well filled with black ocean. She could imagine it now. Sarah had left her cabin. She'd gone seeking Romy and had found the stairwell and had, for some reason, chosen to go down rather than up to the safety of the passenger decks. She'd seen Romy heading below and had thought that was where Romy would be.

The dark waves lapping around the steep crew stairs carried Sarah's scent, Sarah's call.

And there was no way Romy could get to her—at least not in human form. She shrugged out of her jacket and then wished she hadn't for the air had turned icy, but there was no way she could swim with the heavy garment on. She looked down at her trousers and boots. She would try with them. No need to tempt further transformation.

She stepped down on the first rung of the ladder and the metal sang at her step. She was up over her knees. Another step down and the water was up to her hips. Another step and she ducked under the oily surface and swam.

The flashlight was dim, catching on green plankton and algae, but her nictating eyelids helped filter the water and her eyes to gather light. The flashlight was a distraction as she reached the corridor that held the crew cabins. Dark water floor to ceiling. She couldn't imagine that the cabins would be much better, but somewhere ahead there was a pocket of life that suggested a pocket of air. She turned the flashlight out and stuck it in her shirt, then kicked her boot-heavy feet to drive forward. The cold threatened to leaden her human limbs. She wouldn't last long in this form. She had to get Sarah and get out of here. Her chest ached for air and she allowed the gill slits to form in her neck. At least breathing was easier, but the cold...

So cold.

The water belled in the hull around her, but the child's whimper was fading. She reached the first cabin with hands half frozen and felt the name plate on the wall. Four names. It was her cabin. Sarah *had* come seeking her. And now Romy was seeking her in return.

The door barely budged under her urging. Her hand throbbed as she fought the door open, bracing against the bulkhead and pulling until she'd made an eight-inch gap. She slipped inside into the darkness. Sarah's scent filled the water and Romy knew she'd been right. She stroked upward and found the barest of four inches of air along the ceiling. The open door was allowing the water to pour in, gradually swallowing that pocket of air.

"Sarah?" She brought her mouth to the surface and grappled on the flashlight with numb fingers.

Floating in the last bit of air above Romy's bunk Sarah turned terrified eyes toward her. Sarah's cheek was pressed against the ceiling.

"Ro—omy?" Her voice shook with cold and fear.

A sigh escaped Romy. She'd found the child. "I'm here, Sarah. Now we need to get you out of here."

But how could she do that? There was no way Sarah could hold her breath long enough to escape this cabin, let alone navigate the flooded halls beneath the vehicle deck.

She looked back at Sarah, only her nose and mouth barely above freezing water in the shrinking space.

The small, half-formed gills Romy had in this partial transformation might work for a short immersion, but this was clearly going to be more than that. The Borealis Queen had shifted further around them, Romy's bunk now listing forty-five degrees from normal. The ship could go down at any moment and breathing for two was going to require a great deal more than her partial gills could handle. There was only one chance.

She closed her eyes a moment, setting aside what this would mean. Then she loosed the flashlight in the gloomy water and fumbled her boots and trousers off with half-frozen fingers. Long ago one of her kind had gone to dry land to find her true love and had died because she could not return to the water. The girl had been a princess and much beloved by her people and so, as her legacy, her people had found a magic for a mermaid to return to them. Such a magic was hers.

If she wanted it.

The water against her naked limbs was a balm after the prickle of air. The flashlight slowly spun, turning the dark water amber green, and she ducked under the surface and inhaled. Cold water turned warm as it burned into her lungs. All the barriers against changing back to her old form were shocked away.

Her hipbones shifted downward, her legs grew soft and liquid as the flesh came together to become one. Knee joints disappeared and became a lovely continuous malleability that allowed her to flick the long translucent fins that her toes became. Her arms elongated and so did her fingers, pale webbing growing between them as her injured hand healed. Her nascent gills grew the long frill of membrane that helped her draw oxygen.

In the spinning light she glimpsed her beloved, green-gold tail. So many years she'd denied herself the water, because of Matthew, and for what? Her long fingers and their nails became claws. It was done.

It could happen only once and there was no going back. The land was beyond her now. She belonged to the sea.

She rose above the water and caught Sarah's hand. "Take a deep breath, as big as you can and kick with all your might. I'm going to pull us out of here. When you can't hold your breath anymore dig your nails into my hand. Do you understand."

"O—kay." Sarah's voice was half strangled by the water.

"Ready?"

A nod and the burble of a huge inhale.

"Close your eyes."

Romy caught her and dragged her down into the darkness. With Sarah in one hand, she left behind the flashlight, instead depending upon her transformed sight. The water glowed around her, all the tiny algae emitting the tiniest of phosphorescence as if they knew to light her way. Bulkheads loomed black and the current against her told her the ship was filling. Pressure on her skin said they were deep and getting deeper. They needed to get out of this metal tin.

If it dragged them down, she might survive, but the pressure would certainly kill Sarah.

At the bottom of the ladder to the passenger deck small claws in her palm said Sarah was desperate. Romy hauled her in close and exhaled the water from her lungs. Then she brought their faces close. She pressed her mouth against Sarah's and blew bubbles against her lips. Sarah opened her mouth and gulped air down. Romy fed her one breath, two. Her gills strained open. She felt blood vessels exploding as she fought to release the oxygen from her bloodstream into her water-filled lungs. Pain filled her chest, but then Sarah nodded. Romy released her and carried on. But she couldn't quite catch her breath. Her gills weren't used to fulfilling this dual need and her body wasn't capable of doing small transformations back and forth between forms.

Her tail sent them racing up the ladder. The door floated open to the passenger level. She ducked into the hall and propelled them down it to the passenger stairwell and turned upwards. At least this would get them to the car level. That had been above water when she went down.

She came out into the cavernous car level, but it was above the water no longer. Her head broke the surface. Sarah sputtered beside her.

"We made it! Romy, you saved me!"

Her voice echoed in the darkness. Water belled inside the cavernous hull. Above, the upper deck tilted forty-five degrees. Vehicles had smashed together at the prow of the ship, further weighting it in the water. It would not be long. The metal groaned against the imbalance of load. The rear of the ship must be out of the water. She had to get them out of here, but she couldn't take the passenger stairs that loomed above them.

"We have to go under water again. Hold your breath again, Sarah."

"Really? Again?"

"Again."

A sigh in the darkness, but then the sound of a huge gulp of air. Sarah squeezed Romy's hand and she ducked under, pulled them under and raced toward the crew ladder closer to the prow of the ship.

Cargo from the vehicles dotted the water, a tarp, a carboard box, a floating tire and too much plastic. She fought her way through, tugging Sarah after her until she reached the steep crew ladder.

She turned upward. If she could reach the main deck she could get Sarah out into the ocean and to one of the life boats. Then she would escape, back to her people.

The door to the first deck loomed before her, but that deck had no hatches to the exterior. She kept going up, following the ladder. Sarah's small nails bit into her hand.

The ship shifted around her, the prow turning downward. By all the fish in the sea, she needed to keep going, but if she didn't stop, Sarah would drown.

She stopped and repeated the breathing to replenish Sarah. As she finished, the ship lurched and began to move around them.

Not waiting to ask Sarah if she was ready, she fought the next door open and was in the main saloon on the main deck, the water full of floating cushions and passenger debris. She shoved them aside with her shoulders and headed for the nearest hatch. Please let it be open. That was their only hope.

The bulkhead loomed ahead and she felt the current as the ship began to slide deeper in the water. The hatch was open!

Her tail gave a mighty push and they were at the hatch. Water ripped past it, the ship was heading down. She grabbed Sarah and held her to her chest until the child held on. Then she lowered her head and swam.

There was every chance that the ship would catch them and they'd be crushed by a metal railing or something falling. Water ripped them down, in the suction of the ship's descent. Romy fought against it. Fought to get distance from the ship. Something grazed her side and she felt a blaze of pain as something stripped away a patch of her scales.

And then she was free of the sucking current. She hung in the water and turned as the Borealis Queen made a graceful final dive past them like a ghost beneath the darkened waves. They had made it.

Another breath for Sarah and then Romy started up through the darkness. Up through ship's debris and driftwood. Up through the pulse of the ocean. Up and up until in a final burst, she broke free and surged, head and torso, into the storm-filled night. Rain slashed her face. Wind howled in her ears. Waves fell over her head. Small lights bobbed on the waves as she hauled Sarah up. Sarah, eyes closed and limp in her hands.

"Sarah!" she shook the girl, but nothing happened and she could not lift herself out of the water and give artificial respiration, for her lungs were no longer capable. Simply raising her head into the air brought half her gills out of water.

"Help!" she called. "Help! I have a child here in the water!"

But there was only the roar of the waves.

She had to get Sarah to a boat. She had to save her. She'd given up too much for the child to die. With one arm she held Sarah's head above water. With the other and her tail, she swam.

A white life boat appeared in the gloom, bobbing like flotsam amid the spindrift of the waves. Farther off, shoreward, the bobbing lights of fishboats and pleasure craft cut through the water from the direction of Smokey Point. The Captain and First Officer had gotten the SOS out.

She came up beside a life boat and slapped a hand up over the gunnel.

"Help!" she cried and a face appeared above the rail. She lifted Sarah's limp body to waiting hands and then sank beneath the waves.

Then she turned tail and swam deep in dark water. Home. It would be home forever, now.

A year later and Romy had ranged far under the sea. She had returned home to her family and left again, for an aching restlessness was still upon her. Her mother said it was lovesickness. Her father said she was a fool. Her sisters said she was the bravest mermaid they ever knew.

She knew better. A brave mermaid could let go of Matthew. Instead regret and anger still occupied her mind.

Her mother was right. The ache for Matthew filled her bones.

That was why on a quiet summer morning she surfaced in the Inside Passage to watch a cruise ship ply past on its way to Alaska. The ship was white and tall as the clouds. Its decks were crowded with people enjoying the morning sun and the light on the green mountains that were forever beyond her now. The light waves glimmered. The ship's huge engine growled and its screws tore up the water behind it, just as the Borealis Queen's screws had. Along the shore sat the low, gray-weathered buildings of Smoky Point fishing village that had rescued the Queen's passengers that terrifying night.

These were the waters where she had last seen Matthew. These were the waters where she had last inhaled his scent. She swam through the glassy water toward the unseen shoal that had brought the Borealis Queen down.

All was quiet. The tide was partially in, the dangerous shoal treacherously hidden beneath a smooth expanse of water. The waves carried the taste of salt-rotten metal, so the Queen still rested in her watery tomb.

Romy had not been back since that awful night. What had brought her back now, she didn't know, but she still wondered whether Sarah had survived. How a visit here would give her an answer, she didn't know, but she had followed her heart and come. After all, it had been a year since she walked as a human. A year since she had last seen Matthew. It felt like an occasion.

If Sarah had died at least Romy knew that there had been nothing more that she could have done.

A bell's tolling and voices across the water brought her to the village. She coasted closer to the shore. There were more people there than the village seemed able to house, but a large yacht sat at the village pier.

Approaching closer, she saw that a group of people had gathered on the shore and a single voice rose above the others in what might be prayer. The crowd went silent as the voice went on, but the breeze kept the words from Romy's water-suited ears. A few minutes later the crowd broke apart and retreated up the shore to a large hall in the village. For a meal probably. They left behind a stone cairn and a small figure that ran down to the water and looked out into the waves. The chestnut curls said who it was.

Sarah-with-an-H had lived.

Relief flooding her, Romy ducked under the surface, but not

265

before she'd seen a man and woman join Sarah and look out into the waves. The woman she didn't know. The man was Matthew. The woman and Matthew gave Sarah a bouquet of flowers that she threw onto the waves. Then hand in hand, the three figures retreated to the village after the other humans.

The tide ran in around Romy as she hung in the water. Her heart ached at what she'd seen. It wasn't right. It wasn't fair. It should have been her with Matthew. But instead he'd had Sarah with another woman.

All day she hung there in the hopes of seeing him again. From the village hall came music and the sound of laughter and in the evening the crowd retreated to the village houses and to the cabin cruiser—Matthew, Sarah and the woman among them.

As darkness settled over the town, Romy swam closer to shore. The bottom of the cove was covered in smooth round pebbles. The cairn stood beside the entrance to the pier and smelled of new cement and metal. The water lapped around its base and she allowed the wavelets to float her to it. She sat up in the shadows and read the metal placard.

In Memoriam for the downing of the Borealis Queen, the bravery of her crew and the citizens of Smoky Point in the rescue.

She ran her fingers over the smooth metal and smiled. At least the disaster was remembered Though perhaps Chad had lied about her part in it.

Pushing off from shore, she coasted past the cabin cruiser hoping for a glimpse of Matthew.

"There's a second one, Romy," a small voice said.

Romy jerked around and spotted the small head poking halfway through the rails, night-darkened chestnut curls falling around Sarah's face. She grinned down at Romy.

"There's a second piece of metal. It remembers you and another officer who died on the ship. I told them you hadn't died, but Mommy said you had. Daddy said so , too, though he cried when he said it. I told them you changed into a mermaid and that was how you saved me and now you live under the water all the time. They didn't believe me about that, either!" she said in perfect childish disgust.

Smiling, she reached out a small hand and Romy couldn't help herself. Tears in her eyes, she reached up and lightly caressed Sarah's fingers.

The ache in her chest diminished. Sarah was safe and so was Matthew. Then she ducked her head, and with a flip of her tail for Sarah's benefit, she slipped away. She left behind only a ripple, like wind over water.

ABOUT THE AUTHOR

Karen L. Abrahamson is a well-traveled writer who has explored cultures and countries around the world but British Columbia, Canada is her favorite place to come back to. She is the author of literary, mystery, romantic and fantasy fiction including the highly regarded Cartographer fantasy series. She lives on the west coast of Canada with two Bengal cats that aren't quite as well-traveled as she is.

When she isn't writing she can be found with a camera and backpack in fabulous locations around the world.

Find out more about Karen at:
karenlabrahamson.com

g goodreads.com/karenabrahamson

BB bookbub.com/authors/karen-l-abrahamson

AFTER THE BALL

PAM MCCUTCHEON

"**C**inderella is a witch," Griselda declared in ringing tones. She ought to know, she was the ungrateful wench's stepmother.

Unfortunately, her announcement dropped with all the elegance of a dull thud in the silence of the glittering throne room. Perhaps if there had been more people present, her accusation would have had more effect, but the king had insisted on privacy for this interview. Only he, the queen, Cinderella, the prince, and a few of the king's advisors were present to hear Griselda's defense. And none of them seemed inclined to be sympathetic.

Griselda would have liked to think this semi-private audience was in concern for her own reputation, but she suspected the king and queen simply didn't want anyone else to hear the truth about Cinderella.

Luckily, Griselda had it on good authority that one of the advisors was a magic-sniffer—the tall, lanky one named Bern. She would keep his abilities in mind in case events went against her.

The king, looking regal with the golden crown on his equally golden hair, stroked his beard and frowned down at Griselda from his throne on the raised dais. "Cinderella, our son's future bride, is not on trial. You are."

Griselda seethed in silence. She and her poor, mistreated daughters were forced to stand humbled before the few members of the court while her stepdaughter was allowed to sit in the royal presence. It was so unfair. Cinderella had captured the prince's heart with her evil, deceitful spells and Griselda's daughters were left with nothing but ashes. Worse, they had to stay mute behind their mother and watch as she was unjustly humiliated.

Griselda raised her chin. "I have done nothing wrong. What am I accused of?"

The elegant dark-haired queen, who still retained the beauty she had been famed for in her youth, frowned. "You are accused of being a bad parent to an orphaned child left in your care, of treating a gentlewoman like a servant, and of being cruel to a gentle soul."

Griselda almost snorted in disbelief. Cinderella, a gentle soul? The conniving chit was more wily and crafty than anyone she knew.

And being a bad parent was no crime, or half the parents in the kingdom would be in the dungeons.

"She has bewitched all of you," Griselda said scornfully. None more so than the prince, who stared, besotted, at Cinderella's glowing beauty. And where, pray tell, did they think she had acquired her good looks? She certainly hadn't looked like that before the ball.

Besides, since when was it wrong to treat poor relations like servants? It happened in all the best families.

The king raised a condescending eyebrow. "You persist in these accusations?"

Griselda curtsied, trying to appear humble. "I must, Your Majesty...if you would hear the truth?"

The king and queen held a whispered consultation, then the king nodded. "Very well. Let us hear your tale from the beginning."

"Don't listen to her, Father," the prince cried. "She is the wicked one, and she is trying to turn you against my intended bride."

"Cinderella will have a chance to explain herself," the king said. "After we hear her stepmother's story." He glared around at the people present. "And I will brook no interference until it is told."

Griselda cast a triumphant glance at Cinderella, but the silly girl didn't even have the intelligence to appear afraid. She would soon regret underestimating her stepmother.

Casting her eyes down in an attitude of despair, Griselda said, "My dearly departed husband, bless his soul, was sadly deceived in his first wife, Cinderella's mother. He saw only her beauty and did not realize that the heart of a cunning witch lurked within her bosom."

Satisfaction filled Griselda as she glanced up and saw distress on Cinderella's face. The witch was right to feel so, for soon Griselda would unmask her true nature.

"You have proof of this?" the king asked.

"Yes, Sire. The village priests found Cinderella's mother guilty of practicing witchcraft and burned her at the stake." There—let Cinderella explain that away.

The queen turned to look at Cinderella. "Is that true?"

Cinderella's bowed head told it all, but at least the girl had the grace to nod and confirm the truth.

"I see," the king said slowly. "Well, being put to the torch is no guarantee of evil intent. We fear we have many overzealous priests in our kingdom, especially in the west, who have tortured and killed innocent women whose only crime was being at the wrong place at the wrong time. It is possible Cinderella's mother was one such."

Blind fool. But Griselda dared not utter her accusation aloud. Instead, she merely bowed her head, and said, "I am certain the record speaks for itself, Your Highness." She didn't know exactly what Cinderella's mother had done, but like mother, like daughter. It must have been heinous.

He waved that away as if it were inconsequential. "Well, we don't have the records available, nor the priests to question. Go on with your story."

"I met her father not long after. He was shocked and dismayed at learning of his first wife's true nature. Fearing his daughter would follow in her mother's footsteps, he moved as far east as he could and sought a sensible woman who would take Cinderella in hand and ensure she never indulged in such foolishness."

"You?"

Griselda bowed her head in modesty. "Yes, Sire, he hoped I would raise his child in piety and decency, as I have my own two daughters." And it hadn't hurt that Griselda had still been a fine figure of a woman. "But the child was inconsolable at her mother's death."

And, indeed, Cinderella looked greatly saddened now at the memory. Griselda almost gagged when the gullible prince put his arm around Cinderella and clasped her to his chest. If he knew what a viper she could be, he would not hold her so near.

The king nodded. "So I understand. And that is why you gave her nothing but rags to wear and made her sleep in the ashes?"

"I did no such thing," Griselda said in indignation. "It was Cinderella's choice."

The queen looked skeptical. "It was *her* choice to look like a beggar?"

"Yes," Griselda declared. "Their western customs require mourners to rend their clothing in grief and cover themselves in ashes. The child took it to extremes and persisted in mourning her mother for many years beyond the customary time. She even chose to sleep on the hearth to ensure she was always covered in cinders, then demanded we call her by the new name she had chosen—Cinderella. Indeed, she used her evil magic to make us forget the name she was born with."

When the queen continued to look skeptical, Griselda said, "I tried to coax her away from the hearth, to no avail. Cinderella stubbornly refused to give up her bereavement, no matter how poorly it reflected on the rest of her family. In fact, she resented me so much for taking her mother's place that I think she *wanted* to make me look bad to the other villagers. And it became much worse when her father died." She shook her head sadly. "He was stolen from us far too young by a fever, his last wish that I continue to watch over his daughter."

"So you honored your dead husband's wishes by working Cinderella's fingers to the bone to slave for you and your daughters?"

The poor, deceived queen appeared to be as enamored of Cinderella as her son. "It wasn't like that at all," Griselda protested. "Idle hands mean idle mischief, and no one can get into more mischief than my stepdaughter. Just look at my own daughters." Griselda made a sweeping gesture that encompassed Edda and Solvig, standing behind her. "Before Cinderella arrived in our household, my daughters were the fairest in the land, bidding fair to rival you, my queen, in their beauty."

The queen didn't seem flattered by the comparison, so Griselda continued, wondering what would convince her of the truth. "Now, as you can plainly see, my ungrateful stepdaughter has enchanted her stepsisters so that none will find them fair."

Indeed, they had been called downright ugly—Edda with her skinny beanpole frame, spotted complexion, and teeth like a horse, and Solvig whose girth had become such that she had problems fitting through most doorways.

"Are you saying my son's betrothed did this to them?" the king asked in disbelief.

What else could explain why her sweet angels had turned into such homely spinsters? "Yes, she did it out of spite, because they still had a parent, and she had none living. Plus she envied her sisters' beauty and wanted to spoil any chance of happiness for them. To keep her from plotting further harm, I had to keep her as busy as possible."

The members of the court didn't look convinced. "It was for her own good," Griselda explained. "I feared that if she had idle time, she would continue to practice her evil tricks. And if our neighbors had realized I harbored a witch child in my household, they would have ensured she met the same fate as her mother." Griselda sighed, righteous in the knowledge she had done her best. "My plan worked, and I kept her safe and the kingdom ignorant of her true nature."

"Oh, really?" the queen drawled. "If you are so concerned about maintaining your promise to your dead husband and keeping Cinderella safe, then why are you revealing this 'true nature' now?"

Raising her chin, Griselda declared, "Because there is a greater need at stake—the fate of the kingdom. As much as it pains me, I must tell the truth for your sake."

"If she was such a danger," the king said, "why did you not reveal this before?"

"Because she had done no real harm...until the ball was announced."

She stole a glance at Cinderella, but her face was still buried in the prince's shoulder—no doubt to keep the guilt in her expression from being seen by the king and queen.

Looking doubtful now, the king asked, "What happened then?"

Griselda hurried to follow up on her advantage. "Suddenly, Cinderella was seized with the conviction that she must attend the ball, ensnare the prince, and marry him."

"And what is so wrong with that?" the queen asked. "After all, your daughters had the same objective, did they not?"

"They did. What young girl would not? The prince is charming, kind, and fair of face and form. Of course they wanted to catch his eye." It couldn't hurt to pour on the praise for the royal pair's only child.

"Then Cinderella did just as they did," the queen said in triumph.

"I fear not, Your Majesty." Griselda shook her head sadly. "It was then that Cinderella finally gave up her mourning and turned calculating. Though Edda and Solvig were content to be themselves in hopes that the prince would see their natural sweetness show through the appearance Cinderella had doomed them with, my stepdaughter was determined to shine brighter than any maiden at the ball. And the only way she could do that was through...magic." Griselda whispered that last word, fearing the taint would stick to her if she said it too loud.

"How so?" the king asked.

"She rose from the ashes, washed herself for the first time in many years, and demanded that I provide her with a sumptuous gown." Griselda still felt indignation at the chit's boldness. "I refused, of course."

"Why?" the queen asked. "You dressed your daughters in the best money could buy, and said you had tried to coax Cinderella from the ashes. Why would you refuse to give her a gown when she finally did as you asked?"

"Because she made it quite clear that she was out to trap the prince and bend him to her will. I feared what would happen to the kingdom if she succeeded...and to Your Majesties, since you would be the only impediments standing between her and the throne."

The queen gasped. "You are accusing our future daughter-in-law of treason?"

Wary now, Griselda spread her hands. "You be the judge." Especially since Cinderella continued to hide her face.

"So we shall," the king said with a frown. "Explain this use of magic."

Griselda hid a triumphant smile. She'd be happy to. "After years of stubbornly living amidst the ashes on the brick hearth, you can imagine how awful and rough her skin and hair were." Seeing the queen frown thoughtfully at the obvious truth gave Griselda hope that she might listen to what she had to say. "None of the mundane remedies I tried would bring them to any semblance of beauty, so she did the unspeakable." Griselda paused and let foreboding enter her voice. "She used her black arts to call upon her mother's help."

"But her mother was dead by then," the king said, looking puzzled.

"Yes, that is why the act was so despicable. She brought her mother's shade back to help her. Oh, she said it was her fairy godmother—trying to make the apparition seem harmless and inoffensive—but I know better. From the description the servants gave me, this so-called 'fairy godmother' was, in fact, her mother, who taught Cinderella the dark arts."

"That's a very serious accusation," the king said. Even the magic-sniffer looked alarmed.

"Yes, Your Highness, I know. But I feel it my duty to warn you of Cinderella's true nature."

The prince shot her a murderous look as Cinderella moaned piteously and snuggled into his arms. *Well, when I'm through, you won't be so loving anymore.*

"She prevailed upon her mother's shade to use her ill-begotten power to make her beautiful, so radiant that she would eclipse any woman at the ball. When I saw what she had done, I was frightened."

Griselda hung her head. "I knew then and there I should have gone to someone and explained what happened, but I had grown fond of the girl and didn't want to see her hurt. So, I tried to keep her home instead."

"How?" the king asked.

"I set her impossible tasks, telling her if she accomplished them, she could attend the ball."

The queen scowled. "If she is as powerful a witch as you say, why would she agree to such a thing? She could just thumb her nose at you and your demands and do as she pleased."

"Because I threatened to reveal her secret if she didn't do as I requested. I felt bad about holding it over her head, but it was the only way to keep her from using her magical wiles on the prince." Griselda gave a rueful smile. "But I wasn't entirely cruel. I even let her believe there was some hope I would let her attend the ball. Unfortunately, she took full advantage of that."

The king stroked his beard thoughtfully and motioned for her to continue.

"I threw a bushel of lentils into the ashes and told her if she picked them all out, she could go with us."

"And did she?" the queen asked.

Griselda sighed. "I fear so. She brought them to me faster than humanly possible."

"So you gave her permission to attend the ball," the queen said in satisfaction.

"No, I—"

The queen leaned forward, as if pouncing upon her words. "You went back on your promise?"

Ignoring the queen's question, Griselda explained, "I wanted to know how she had done the chore so quickly. So, I threw two bushels of lentils in the cinders, saying she had to sort and clean them before she could go. Then I hid and watched to see what she would do."

"I imagine she picked them out of the ashes very fast," the queen said dryly.

"So I thought. But to my surprise, she called a flock of birds. They swooped in through the window and pecked all the lentils from the hearth then put them back in the baskets for her." Just in case someone didn't catch the significance of her story, she spelled it out for them. "Only witches have the ability to call animals and use them as familiars."

The queen sniffed. "It sounds to me as if the birds felt sorry for her. I know I would."

Griselda shook her head sadly. Cinderella must have put a spell on the queen for her to continue so adamantly in the girl's defense despite all the evidence against her. But it would be folly to contradict the queen. Instead, Griselda said nothing and glanced at the king and the magic-sniffer, who were deep in consultation. Good—it appeared they had not yet fallen under the girl's spell.

The king gestured at her to continue. "So, *then* you let her go to the ball...?"

"No, Your Highness. Seeing her use her powers in so audacious a manner, I feared she would balk at nothing to bespell the prince. And the queen," she added boldly. When the king raised an eyebrow but didn't say anything, Griselda continued in a more urgent tone. "I forbade her to go, and tried to keep her so busy helping Edda and Solvig with their preparations for the ball that she wouldn't have time to get ready herself." She sighed heavily. "I thought it had worked— when the coach carried us off to the ball, Cinderella was still at home in her unkempt rags. The only way she could have made it to the ball on time is with the aid of unholy magic."

"Aha," the queen exclaimed. "But if you didn't see what happened after you left, you have no way of knowing if she used magic or not."

"Oh, but I do. The cook told me all after the ball, quaking with fear for what she had seen."

She paused dramatically, but the king filled the silence with an annoyed, "Get on with it."

Disconcerted by his apparent lack of sympathy, Griselda said, "Cook described how Cinderella was white with fury, and called upon her mother to help her in her hour of need. This 'fairy godmother' appeared and with a single wave of her hand, made Cinderella and her complexion beautiful. Then, with another wave of her hand, she gifted my stepdaughter with a gown of spun gold and sparkling glass slippers."

There—let the queen explain *that* away.

The queen tried, tossing her head. "I imagine your cook had been imbibing too freely of the cooking sherry."

"Cook is a tea-totaler, Your Majesty."

"Then she was crazy with fever, or imagining things. Or, more likely, she's a liar."

Not wanting to call the queen herself a liar, Griselda said, "I've never had any problems with her before. But...how else would

Cinderella have acquired these items? And it gets worse. Seeing that Cinderella had no way to get to the ball, her mother changed a pumpkin into a coach, white mice into horses, and lizards into footmen."

"Utter nonsense," the queen declared.

"I might have thought so, too," Griselda explained. "But your own servants will tell you she arrived in a grand coach and four. The girls and I had taken the only coach our family possesses. How would she have been able to acquire such a lavish equipage with no money and very little time...save for magic?"

"There must be some explanation."

"Perhaps," Griselda conceded, not willing to offend the queen too much. "And I might be convinced of that...except for the other evidence of magical usage."

The queen looked wary now. "Such as?"

"Those glass slippers, Your Highness. Think about it. How could anyone possibly dance as Cinderella did without breaking them? Glass is a very fragile substance, and the dance figures were strenuous. Had you or I worn those slippers, they would have shattered instantly. Yet Cinderella wears them still, with nary a scratch on them. How could that be...unless they were enchanted?"

Everyone turned to look at Cinderella's feet which she tried unsuccessfully to hide beneath her gown. The truth was obvious.

Following up immediately on her advantage, Griselda added, "Luckily, the magical spell had a limitation. Didn't you wonder why she fled so precipitously when the clock struck midnight?"

"I assumed something had happened to upset her," the queen said. "Or that she was urgently required at home."

"Neither was the case. The magic was due to run out. To avoid being caught in her rags with nothing but a pumpkin and vermin to see her home, she had to flee." Griselda arched an eyebrow. "But wasn't it convenient that she managed to leave a souvenir behind with which the prince could find her?"

"Convenient?" the king repeated with a barking laugh. "It was damned inconvenient if you ask me   riding all over the land, being inundated by desperate spinsters, and inspecting every dirty, smelly foot in the kingdom. If she was so intent on being found, why didn't she make it easier?"

Griselda managed a graceful shrug. "I can only speculate. But Cinderella was well aware of the maxim that says a man prizes the reward he has to toil for far more than the one that falls into his lap." She gestured at the prince who still clasped Cinderella to his breast. "Apparently, it worked."

"Aha," the queen exclaimed. "If you knew the shoe belonged to Cinderella, why did you insist your daughters try it on?"

Griselda hung her head. "I'm ashamed to say I was afraid to admit I knew it was hers for fear she would be found out, that we would be reviled for harboring a witch in our midst. It would have looked suspicious if my daughters were the only two in the kingdom who weren't eager to try the glass slipper on."

"And you?" the queen demanded. "Why did *you* try it on? Don't you think you're a bit long in the tooth to be my daughter-in-law?"

She wasn't *that* old. "Of course," Griselda said soothingly. "But I never expected to wed the prince. I simply wanted to see if the slipper would fit. You see, Cinderella and I wear the same size. If it didn't fit, I knew it had to be enchanted so that it would fit only one person. And so it was."

Before the queen could interrupt with another objection, Griselda said, "I knew how unlikely it was that, out of all the women in the kingdom, the glass slipper would fit only one person. Sooner or later, someone else would have realized it, too, so I confined Cinderella to her room, trying to keep her from claiming it and making her witchery obvious to one and all."

Griselda sighed. "Unfortunately, she used her black arts to escape, made herself beautiful once more, and caught the prince wholly within her thrall when she put the shoe on her foot." She gestured at the two lovebirds, inviting everyone to see the truth for themselves.

"Have you anything more to add?" the king asked.

"Just one more thing, Your Majesty. Once she had thoroughly

conned the prince, Cinderella knew that all she had to fear were the people who knew her for what she truly was—me and my innocent little girls. That is why she made up this story and accused me of mistreating her." And just in case her logic hadn't convinced them, Griselda added, "If you don't believe me, have your magic-sniffer confirm my story. *And* hers—don't let her use magic to bespell you as well."

The king nodded in decision. He gestured the magic-sniffer, Bern, to his side, saying, "We shall ensure no magic is used in this room without our leave." He turned to Cinderella. "Please come forward, child."

The prince looked stricken. "Father, you can't—"

"Quiet," the king ordered. "There are some grave charges here and Cinderella must be allowed to speak in her own defense."

The prince bowed and sat back down, and Cinderella stood to face the king and queen. If Griselda didn't know better, she might have been fooled by the girl's demeanor. The picture of injured innocence, Cinderella managed to look stunningly lovely even as copious tears coursed down her face. If that wasn't magic, what was?

"What have you to say?" the king asked. "Is what she says true?"

Cinderella wrung her hands in such an obvious bid for sympathy that Griselda was surprised the entire assemblage didn't immediately condemn her.

"Some of it," Cinderella said in a small voice.

Surprised by the girl's admission, Griselda narrowed her eyes, wondering when the lies would come.

Cinderella gave the prince a nervous glance. "My mother's gentle spirit did use magic to reverse the effects of my mourning, but it was good magic, not evil. And she did it because she loved me, because she wanted me to look nice for the ball and the prince. You see, she knew how much it meant to me to win his heart...because I love him so."

What sheer, unadulterated pap. Why weren't they all gagging on this syrupy treacle?

"And your stepsisters?" the king asked. "Did you...alter their appearance?"

"No, Your Highness," Cinderella said with eyes cast meekly down. "They did that on their own. Solvig cannot pass by a sweet without putting it in her mouth and I understand Edda resembles her father."

"Ridiculous," Griselda declared. "How could my precious cherubs have grown into such hags without magical intervention? It is obviously a lie."

The king gestured at the magic-sniffer. "Your verdict?"

Bern descended from the dais and approached Edda and Solvig. They shrank back at his approach, but he did nothing more alarming than peer at them and sniff a bit. It was true, then. He really could smell magic.

Bern then went to Cinderella and took a whiff of her and the prince as well. But nothing showed on his expressionless face as he walked back to the king and stood by his side to whisper in his ear.

Griselda held triumph close in her breast. Now everyone would hear the truth, and she would be vindicated.

The king rose and perforce, the queen and prince rose as well. Drawing himself up to his full height, the king said, "We have made Our decision."

Griselda's heart leapt in her breast. Finally.

"Bern has tested all three girls and has found no residue of magic anywhere on Edda or Solvig. Their appearance is unfortunate, but is not due to magic." He glared sternly at Griselda. "I suggest you do as Cinderella said and look to your first husband's features and your daughters' habits for the culprits."

"Nonsense. Cinderella must have bewitched—"

"Nor has the prince been enchanted," the king continued inexorably, not letting her finish. "Furthermore, Bern has determined that Cinderella is, in fact, a witch."

Murmurs filled the room and Griselda turned smug. Finally, she would have justice.

"However," the king said, his voice rising above those of the court, "her magic is benign, not dark. There is no evidence that she has violated the law of three or that she has wished harm upon others."

"The law of three?" Griselda repeated in confusion. "What's that?"

Bern explained. "It is the law all witches abide by. They take a vow to harm none, for they know anything they do for good or ill shall be returned to them threefold."

"What? So you're saying she *is* a witch?" Griselda wanted to make this very clear.

The king answered. "Yes, but from your own testimony, it is obvious she used magic only to contact her mother's spirit, not for any personal gain. Her mother is the one who performed the rest of the magic, and benign magic at that."

Very confused now, Griselda could do nothing but sputter, "B-but, she's a witch!"

The king nodded. "Indeed she is, and a very good one. Tell me, what made you imagine we would object to having this talent in the royal family?"

"But all witches should be burned at the stake," Griselda protested. "Everyone knows that."

The king shook his head sadly. "Only the ignorant believe so. And we have been working hard to stamp out this sort of misconception in our kingdom."

The queen glared at her. "This wicked woman's accusations against the future princess pose a danger to Cinderella, my family, and the kingdom. We cannot let her continue to spread her lies throughout the land."

The king pondered for a moment, then nodded. "The queen has the right of it. Therefore, we find you and your daughters guilty of treason."

"Treason?" Griselda repeated in disbelief. "But—"

She broke off as she realized the king paid her no heed. Instead, he was listening to Cinderella who was now whispering urgently in his ear.

Nodding, he said, "Your stepdaughter has pleaded for clemency. As our wedding gift to her, we shall not order your execution.

However, to ensure you are not allowed to spread your venomous views, you are banished from the kingdom immediately."

No, no, this couldn't be. Was she in the middle of a nightmare? "But Sire, I—"

"Enough," the king thundered. "We have spoken. At Cinderella's request, we shall send you to join your sister in the land to the west."

The king waggled his fingers at them, and Griselda abruptly found herself and her daughters yanked out of the throne room and plopped into another place...a place with a strange-looking yellow pavement surrounded by low bushes and very short people.

The king is a witch as well? Why had she never suspected?

Suddenly, she heard Cinderella's disembodied voice, sounding concerned. "Be careful, stepmother. Watch out for flying houses."

As Edda and Solvig ran screaming down the road, Griselda folded her arms and scoffed, "Flying houses, indeed. As well I might believe in flying monkeys."

"Mama, run," Edda cried as a shadow blocked out the sun.

It was the last thing Griselda heard before the house landed on her head.

ABOUT THE AUTHOR

Pam McCutcheon is the award-winning author of romance novels ranging from fantasy, futuristic, paranormal and time travel to contemporary romantic comedy. She also has two nonfiction how-to books for writers in print, has written fantasy short stories, and writes the Demon Underground New Adult urban fantasy series under the name Parker Blue.

After many years of working for the military as enlisted, officer and civil service successively, she left her industrial engineering position to pursue her first love—a career in publishing. She can be found in beautiful Colorado Springs with her three dogs: Mo, Daisy, and Trixie.

Find out more about Pam at:
pammc.com

 twitter.com/pammcauthor

facebook.com/pam.mccutcheon.author

pinterest.com/pammccutcheon

bookbub.com/authors/pam-mccutcheon

THE CHARMING WAY

KRISTINE GRAYSON

B OOK FAIR.
The very words of the sign filled Mellie with loathing. Book
Fair indeed. More like Book Unfair.

Every time someone wrote something down, they got it wrong.
She'd learned that in her exceptionally long life.

Not that she was old—not by any stretch. In fact, by the standards
of her people, she was in early middle age. She'd been in early
middle age, it seemed, for most of her adult life. Of course that wasn't
true. She'd only been in early middle age for her life in the public eye
—two very different things.

And now she was paying for it.

She stood with her hands on her hips (which hadn't expanded
[much] since she was a beautiful young girl, who caught the eye of
every man) and looked at the pavilion, with the banner strung across
its multitude of doors.

The Largest Book Fair in the World! the banner proclaimed in bright
red letters. The largest book fair with the largest number of publishers, writers, readers and moguls—movie and gaming and every other
type the entertainment industry had come up with.

It probably should be called *Mogul Fair* (Mogul Unfair?). But they
weren't pitching Moguls (although someone probably should; it was
her experience that anyone with a shred of power [present company
included] should be pitched across a room [or down a staircase] every
now and then); they were pitching books.

This season's books, next season's books, books for every race,
creed, and constituency, large books, small books and the all-important evergreen books which were not, as she once believed, books
about evergreens, but books that never went out of style, like *Little
Women* or anything by Jane Austen or, dammit, that villain Hans
Christian Andersen.

Not that he started it all. He didn't. It was those Grimm brothers,
two better named individuals she had never met.

It didn't matter that Mellie had set them straight. By then, their
"tales" were already on the market, poisoning the well, so to speak.
(Or the apple. Those boys did love their poisons. It would have been

293

so much better for all concerned if they had turned their attention to crime fiction. They could have invented the entire category. But noooo. They had to focus on what they called "fairies" as misnamed as their little "tales.") She made herself breathe. Even alone with her own thoughts, she couldn't help going on a bit of a rant about those creepy little men.

She made herself turn away from the pavilion and walk to the back of her minivan. With the push of a button, the hatchback unlocked (now *that* was magic) and she pulled the thing open.

Fifty signs and placards leaned haphazardly against each other. Last time, she'd only needed twenty. She hoped she would use all fifty this time.

She glanced at her watch. One hour until the Book Unfair opened.

Half an hour until her group showed up.

Mellie turned her attention to the pavilion again. Impossible to tell where she'd get the most media exposure. Certainly not at those doors, with the handicapped ramp blocking access along one side.

Once someone else arrived to help her hand out the placards, she could leave for a few minutes and reconnoiter.

She wanted the maximum amount of airtime for the minimum amount of exposure. She'd learned long ago that if you gave the media too much time in the beginning, they'd distort everything you said.

Better to parcel out information bit by bit.

The Book Unfair was only her first salvo.

But, she knew, it would be the most important.

He parked his silver Mercedes at the far end of the massive parking lot. He did it not so that he wouldn't be recognized— he wouldn't anyway—but because he'd learned long ago that if he parked his Mercedes anywhere near the front, the car would either end up with door dings, key scratches, or would go missing.

He reached into the glove box and removed his prized purple bookseller's badge. He had worked two years to acquire that thing. Not that he minded. It still amazed him that no one at the palace had thought of opening a bookstore on the grounds.

He could still hear his father's initial objection: *We are not shop-keepers!* he'd said in that tone that meant shopkeepers were lower than scullery maids. In fact, shopkeepers had become his father's favorite epithet in the past few decades, scullery maid being both politically and familially incorrect.

It took some convincing—the resident scholars had to prove to his father's satisfaction that true shopkeepers made a living at what they did, and in no way would a bookstore on the palace grounds provide anyone's living—but the bookstore finally happened.

With it came a myriad of book catalogues and discounts and advanced reading copies and a little bit of bookish swag.

He'd been in heaven. Particularly when he realized he could attend every single book fair in the Greater World and get free books.

Not that he couldn't pay for his own books—he could, as well as books for each person in the entire kingdom (which he did last year, to much complaint: it seemed everyone thought they would be tested on the contents of said gift book. Not everyone loved reading as much as he did, more's the pity).

Books had been his retreat since boyhood. He loved hiding in imaginary worlds. Back then, books were harder to come by, often hidden in monasteries (and going to those had caused some consternation for his parents until they realized he was reading, not practicing for his future profession). Once the printing press caught on, he bought his own books—he now devoted the entire winter palace to his collection—but it still wasn't enough.

If he could, he would read every single book ever written—or at least scan them, trying to get a sense of them. Even with the unusually long life granted to people of the Third Kingdom especially when compared with people in the Greater World (the world that had provided his Mercedes and this quite exciting book fair), he would never achieve it. There were simply too many existing books in too many languages, with too many more being written all the time.

He felt overwhelmed when he thought of all the books he hadn't read, all the books he wanted to read, and all the books he would want to read. Not to mention all the books that he hadn't heard of.

Those dismayed him the most.

Hence, the book fair.

He was told to come early. There was a breakfast for booksellers —coffee and donuts, the website said, free of charge. He loved this idea of free as an enticement. He wondered if he could use it for anything back home.

The morning was clear with the promise of great heat. A smog bank had started to form over the city, and he couldn't see the ocean, although the brochures assured him it was somewhere nearby. The parking lot looked like a city all by itself. It went on for blocks, delineated only by signs that labeled the rows with double letters.

The only other car in this part of the lot wasn't a car at all but one of those minivans built so that families could take their possessions and their entertainment systems with them.

The attractive black-haired woman unloading a passel of signs from the van looked familiar to him, but he couldn't remember where he had seen her before.

He wasn't about to go ask her either. His divorce had left him feeling very insecure, especially around women. Whenever he saw a pretty woman, the words of his ex-wife rose in his head.

She had screamed them at him in that very last fight, the horrible unforgettable fight when she took the glass slipper—the thing that defined all that was good and pure in their relationship—and heaved it against the wall above his head.

Not so charming now, are you, asshole? Nope, not charming at all.

He had to concede she had a point—although he never would have conceded it to her. Still, those formerly dulcet tones echoed in his brain whenever he looked in the mirror and saw not the square-jawed hero who saved her from a life of poverty, but a balding, paunchy middle-aged man who would never achieve his full potential—not without killing his father, and that was a different story entirely.

Charming squared his shoulders and pinned his precious name badge to his shirt. The name badge did not use his real name. It used his nom de plume—which sounded a lot more romantic than The Name He Used Because His Real Name Was Stupid.

He called himself Dave. Dave Encanto, for those who required last names. His family didn't even have a last name—that's how long they'd been around—and even though he knew Prince was now considered a last name, he couldn't bring himself to use it.

He couldn't bring himself to use any name, really. He still thought of himself as Charming even though he knew his ex was right—he wasn't "charming" any more. Not that he didn't try. It was just that charming used to come easily to him, when he had a head full of black black hair, and an unwrinkled face, and the squarest of square jaws.

Prince Charming was a young man's name, in truth, and then only the name of an arrogant young man. To use that name now would seem like wish fulfillment or a really bad joke. He couldn't go with P.C. because the initials had been usurped, and people would catch the double irony of a prince trying to be p.c. with his own name change.

And as for Prince—that name was overused. In addition to the musician, princes abounded. People named their horses Prince, for heaven's sake, and their dogs, and their surrogate children. In other words, only the nutty named a human being Prince these days, and much as Charming resented his father, he couldn't put either of his parents in the nutty category.

So he told people to call him Dave, which was emphatically not a family name. Too many family names had been co-opted as well—Edward, George, Louis, Philippe, even Harry not just by another prince, but by some potter's kid as well.

Dave, not David, a man who could go anywhere incognito any time he liked. Gone were the days when people would do a double-take, and some would say, *Aren't you...?* or *You know you look just like that prince—whatsisname?—Charming.*

Now they nodded and looked past him, hoping to see someone more important. Which was why he preferred the Greater World to the Third Kingdom. In the Greater World, they knew he wasn't *the* Prince Charming. To them, *the* Prince Charming was a man in a fairy tale, a creature of unattainable perfection, or—more accurately (he believed) a cartoon character, an animated hero.

He was none of those things. True, he had a longer than usual life, but that caused longer than usual problems—like waiting for his father, who also had a longer than usual life, to kick the proverbial bucket (which in the Third Kingdom, wasn't as proverbial as you might think).

But as for magical powers, Charming had none. Besides that all-encompassing charm, which Ella had told him in no uncertain terms was gone now. Ella, who got his estates, half of his money, and custody of their two daughters because—true to form—his father wouldn't let him contest the divorce over *girls.*

He sighed and started across the monstrous parking lot. Several other cars were pouring into the first entrance, way up front, near the doors. The parking there, he knew from the e-mails he had gotten, was reserved for booksellers and the disabled—or the differently abled, as he had been bidden to say. The e-mails claimed he would need the close-in parking for the hundreds of pounds of books he would lug back to his car at regular intervals. But he had lugged chain mail and two injured companions over a hundred miles. He figured he could handle a few books.

The attractive woman had pulled out the last sign. He saw the initials—PETA—and felt a surge of disappointment. He'd seen what those animal rights lovers had done to his mother's favorite fur coat the one and only time he had taken her to the Metropolitan Opera in Manhattan. His mother had been horribly traumatized, although not so badly that she didn't implore him to bring the entire cast of the Met to the Third Kingdom at the end of every opera season.

He walked around the woman, and headed toward the pavilion,

ready for coffee, donuts, and some insight into this season's best-sellers.

Mellie watched the well dressed man walk the length of the parking lot. He wore what was known as business casual—a long-sleeved shirt and dark pants (no suit coat, no tie) but he still looked elegant. Some of that was the clothing itself; there was nothing casual about it. It was tailored to fit—and fit it did, over a well-muscled back, broad shoulders, and a nice tight—

She shook her head and looked away. If she really thought about it, she had to acknowledge that men were the source of her troubles. From her know-it-all first husband who had left her a young widow with two extremely young daughters to her beloved second husband who stupidly introduced her as a fait accompli to his own daughter starting a resentment that continued to this day, men had been the root cause of her dilemmas from the moment she hit the public eye.

Of course, she had handled things badly. She always thought that any publicity was good publicity. Little did she realize that once someone had defined you to the media, then it didn't matter how many charities you gave to or how many advanced degrees you had, you would always be the evil stepmother, the wicked witch, or worse, the aging malignant crone.

At least she had avoided that last category—for now, anyway. She felt it hovering around her, like the flying monkeys from the stupid Hollywood version of the *Wizard of Oz*. The Wicked Witch of the West. Now *that* was a misunderstood woman.

"Mellie?"

She turned. The man behind her was exceptionally attractive. He also left a trail of wet footprints heading west. He was a selkie whose real name she did not (of course) know. He carried his pelt over his right arm and this time he wore human clothing.

He had actually stopped their first protest earlier this year by pulling off his pelt and having nothing suitable on underneath it.

(Although she could see why the human storytellers had felt threatened by these creatures from the sea; not only were they preternaturally good-looking, they were also very well endowed.)

"As people show up, will you hand out signs?" she asked. "I need to figure out where we'll stage our protest."

She shoved the last pile of signs at him, not giving him a chance to say anything, and then she hurried along the parking lot.

Midway there, she realized she was trying to catch that ever-so-elegant man and she slowed her steps.

She had sworn off men decades ago.

She wasn't about to let one distract her now.

The coffee was bitter and only the inedible coconut-covered donuts were left. He should have arrived earlier. Still he poured himself a cup, grabbed one of the few remaining paper plates, and found a maple bar crammed against the back of the donut box. Then he settled into a chair at the back of the room.

The panel was already talking about social media and whether or not it meant the death of the book, a topic that always broke his heart. He understood the importance of stories—he'd been raised on stories. Bards had come to his father's court before Charming could even read. But the best stories were the ones he accessed privately—and a screen never really felt private to him.

Still, he listened politely, getting more and more discouraged, until he finished his maple bar and fled the room.

The doors to the main exhibition hall were locked, with guards standing out front. The guards didn't look that formidable—two fat security guards in uniform, and several bookish types with their arms crossed, trying to look tough.

He sighed and decided to explore. He knew from his convention packet that there were side rooms, meeting rooms, conference rooms, and the all-important media room where the famous people, from the writers to the politicians/actors/musicians who loaned their names to books gave interviews about whatever seemed important at the time.

The hallways were unbelievably wide so that they could accommodate crowds and wheelchairs, and yet he was the only person in them, except for the occasional publishing house salesman scrambling to put the finishing touches on a booth. From a distance, he caught the scent of cafeteria food, and remembered that they would all be able to buy lunch here if they were so inclined.

He was inclined, especially after that maple bar. There were no restaurants close, and he didn't want to lose his parking space.

The media wasn't a room; it was an entire wing, with smaller rooms designated as green rooms, and larger rooms with actual mini studios, all set up to record certain kinds of programming. Surprisingly, these rooms were unlocked, but they were filled with young attractive people who all looked important and busy.

He peered in one, only to feel someone against his back.

He turned. The attractive woman from the parking lot stood there. She was tall and thin and exceedingly familiar. Her eyes were filled with intelligence, accented by her very good bone structure. This was a woman who had been a pretty young girl and had become striking in middle age. She would be lovely even into old age, so long as she didn't let that mouth of hers remain twisted like that.

"Charming, right?" she said. "The question is which one?"

He leaned against the door jam, feeling startled. Not just that she had recognized him, but that she knew there was more than one Prince Charming.

Which meant she wasn't a native of the Greater World. She came from one of the Kingdoms. But again, the question was which one.

"My name is Dave," he said as dismissively as he could.

"Yeah, I see that." She grabbed his prized purple badge, looked at it, and then dropped it against his shirt. "Dave Encanto. You're not fooling anyone, 'Dave.' Why are you here? To shut me down?"

He frowned at her. Clearly they'd met but he couldn't remember when and he certainly didn't understand her comment. He didn't have the power to shut down anyone. Not in the Greater World, anyway.

"Listen," he said, "I know everyone has a right to their opinion, but I do think tossing paint on little old ladies going into the opera takes things a bit too far. When I said I would shut you all down, it was only because I was angry, and it was, after all, my mother's fur coat that you ruined—"

"You don't know who I am, do you?" the woman said.

"No-oo," he said. "Just that you're with that animal rights group."

"Clearly we need a new acronym," she said more to herself than to him. Then she sighed. "P. E. T. A. which stands for People for the Ethical Treatment of *Archetypes*, not animals. We had the acronym long before those animal people stole it from us. They were just better at getting press coverage. Like everyone else on the planet, including you, 'Dave.' You know everyone wants to find their Prince Charming. Everyone—women, gay guys. Even real men, they want what Prince Charming has. You don't need a publicist. You just need to bask in your princely charmingness."

He studied her, too stunned to say much. He was always stunned in the face of bitterness, although these days he was beginning to understand it. Bitterness and the feeling that no one else knew exactly what you were going through.

He could have given her his litany—the paunch that wouldn't go away no matter how much he exercised, the increasing irrelevance, the fact that he hadn't seen his girls in nearly a year—but he didn't. Instead, he frowned.

"You're not one of the fairy godmothers," he said. "They were always unbelievably happy for no apparent reason. Disney got that right at least. Bippity Boppity Boo and all that."

She tilted her head at him, obviously intrigued.

"You can't be one of the old crones either, because they do look like the witches in MacBeth—Shakespeare had clearly been to one of the Kingdoms, maybe more than once."

She raised her eyebrows.

"And you're beautiful, more beautiful now than you probably ever were as a girl." He wasn't coming on to her; it just wasn't in his nature. He was stating a fact. "So you're probably one of the stepmothers. I would guess Snow White's. Which means we met at a party, gosh, a century or two ago, when someone decided we should clear up the Charming mess and the stepmothers gossip and see if we could take care of those Brothers Grimm."

"*I* thought," she said. "It wasn't someone. It was me. I hosted that party."

He nodded, remembering now. It was one of the first large scale events ever held in the Greater World. There had been too many arguments about which kingdom would host so someone—this woman maybe?—decided to rent a castle in Germany of all places, that white one with the towers along the Rhine that Disney later used in one of its films—for the three-day catered affair.

Nothing had gotten settled, and in fact, he could point to the entire event as the beginning of the end of his marriage. Ella met the wives of the other Charmings, and they started talking about their marriages, and things got said. The other Charmings apparently treated their wives like princesses. Not that he hadn't. But he also expected her to think for herself, and do something other than spend the King's gold.

He'd said that more than once, and he'd made the mistake of saying it in front of his father, who then harped on it forever. Apparently—at least according to Charming's ex-wife, the other Charmings never said anything bad about their wives.

Charming thought that was just one-upsmanship. People—charming or not—said things they regretted. Maybe the other wives just hadn't been as sensitive to slights as Ella had been. Either way, Ella had been dissatisfied with the relationship ever since.

Charming looked at the attractive woman, who continued to stare at him. She really was beautiful. He remembered noticing that in Germany all those years ago. He had noticed and thought she had gotten a bad rep, considering everything. All she and the other step-mothers wanted was a little respect.

"You never answered me," he said. "Are you Snow White's stepmother?"

"Are you Sleeping Beauty's Prince Charming?" she asked, apparently not willing to show him hers until he showed her his. But in asking the question, he got his answer. She was Snow White's stepmother.

"I married Ella," he said. "The fairy tales still call her CinderElla, which really isn't fair. She never was covered in dirt, not even when I first met her."

"Thin and shapely and beautiful and oh, so, young." That bitterness again. "Why is it that men like you always go for women like her?"

"I was a boy," he said. "And she was a girl, not a woman. We weren't really old enough to commit to anything."

The woman let out a small "huh" of surprise. "So all three Charmings have divorced now."

That news made him grunt with surprise. He hadn't known that. He thought the other Charmings lived in perpetual wedded bliss. Happily ever after and all that.

The woman didn't seem to notice his surprise. She was saying, "Isn't that just the way of things? I suppose you blame the women's movement as well?"

The other Princes Charming had blamed the Greater World's women's movement? Seriously?

He knew where the fault in his marriage was, and it wasn't with some amorphous movement in another world.

"Ella and I weren't compatible from the beginning," he said. "She's very into the social whirl, the dresses, the dancing, and me, well..."

He grabbed his badge. He was going to shake it ruefully. Instead, his fingers closed protectively around it.

"I'm bookish," he said. "Quiet. A bit of—what do they call it here in the Greater World?—a nerd."

"A nerd," the woman repeated, as if she couldn't quite believe what she was hearing.

"And," he said, mostly to cover the blush he could feel warming his cheeks, "I'm certain my father didn't help any. He wanted sons, and he blamed Ella when we didn't have any. There was no explaining genetics to him. X and Y chromosomes are beyond him. He'd been urging me to throw her off after our first daughter was born. But then, he also wanted me to use the old-fashioned King Henry the Eighth method."

"Divorce," the woman said.

"No," Charming said, trying to be circumspect. He was conscious of the fact that the number of people around them was beginning to grow. "Henry's other method of disposing of his wives."

"Oh, my," she said. "He really is the tyrant, isn't he?"

Charming nodded, a bit uncomfortably. He tried not to look at his father's deeds—or misdeeds. Not that they were illegal. Whatever the King did was legal; that was the law of the land. But he didn't have to like it.

"I prefer it here," he said. "In the Greater World."

With books, books and more books being created all the time. Not to mention movies and television and games. He was even beginning to like Twitter novels, even though that panel this morning had shaken him more than he wanted to admit. He didn't want the book to die. He wanted it to live, in its lovely hand-held form, for the rest of his (exceptionally long) life.

"Of course you prefer it here," she said. "The Greater World loves you. You're an ideal. Everyone wants to be you or have you or marry you. You're not considered a bitter, witchy woman past her sell-by-date who's jealous of younger women and can't come to terms with her lost potential."

Well, they had the bitterness spot on, he thought, but didn't say. Still, he really didn't care about charming her. She had made up her mind about him on very little evidence—mostly on what other people thought—so he knew better than to try to change her mind.

Although, he couldn't prevent himself from saying, "Aren't you jealous, though? I mean, really?"

Her eyes widened. Had no one spoken to her like this before?

"Look," he said, holding out his hands. "You're the one who made the comment about me marrying a girl who was 'thin, shapely, and oh so young.' That's sounds a little bitter and jealous to me."

"Of course it would to you," she snapped. "I suppose you think I tried to kill Snow White, like the fairy tales say."

"No, I don't," he said. If she had tried, she would have been imprisoned when Snow White married the other Charming. Imprisoned or beheaded.

"People like you believe in the fairy tales. Why shouldn't you? You live one." Her tone got even more strident.

He sighed. He didn't think divorce was part of the fairy tale, but he couldn't get a word in. She hadn't stopped talking.

"People like you don't understand people like me. You have everything in life, and you don't understand people who have to fight for every scrap—"

"You're right," he said flatly.

She stopped, as if she was surprised at his words. Apparently, she didn't expect him to admit anything.

But he wasn't going to say what he really thought. He hated it when conversations veered in this direction. He was in a damned if he did and damned if he didn't situation. If he said he understood, he'd have to prove it, with life experience that she might or might not believe. And if he said he didn't understand, then she'd try to convince him. So he gave her his standard answer.

"I don't understand people who like to fight," he said. "I never have. So have a good book fair, and I'll see you around."

He slipped past her into the hallway, feeling unsettled and somewhat disappointed. He had liked her at first, anyway, and it wasn't often that he found a woman attractive any more. Most women his age had given up or had snared the right man and weren't interested in meeting anyone new.

Technically, he should marry a younger woman and give his father the heir that his father was clamoring for, but he'd already married a young woman, and that hadn't gotten him anywhere. And besides, he had children. Two lovely, intelligent daughters whom he didn't see enough.

And who was to say that a girl couldn't inherit? If his father died before Charming did, he'd make a decree that his daughters could take over.

It was the least he could do.

The doors to the main exhibition hall were opening as he walked past, and his heart took a small leap. He was still unsettled—he really hadn't expected to find someone from the kingdoms here—but he was getting past that. And considering how big this place was, he probably wouldn't see her again.

Which bothered him a little bit more than he was willing to admit.

Okay, so she had been unfair. She launched into her rant without thinking about who she was talking to.

Not that she could convince a Charming that Archetypes needed protecting. His archetype—handsome, heroic, *perfect*—was desirable.

Hers wasn't.

Still, she leaned against the door to the main media screening room, hoping her heart would stop pounding. She hadn't meant to yell at him. She'd learned over the years that no one responded well to the whole "you don't understand" thing, even if they didn't understand.

But she had years—no, decades—of unfairness trapped inside her, and it wanted to flood out. And she wasn't about to go into therapy. That would just be buying into another version of the stereotype.

It took her a moment to gather herself. She always said things she regretted later. No amount of living or practical experience could change that about her.

And she did regret yelling at him.

Maybe if she saw him later in the weekend, she would apologize.

Maybe.

But first, she had a group of protesters to organize.

This hallway was big enough, and it wasn't roped off. It was perfect. It would give her all the media attention she needed. She might even be able to stage an interruption on one of the panels being held in the studios.

She ran her hands over her hair (still naturally black, except for a Cruella de Vil white streak that she had to color so that she wouldn't look like her properly infamous cousin), and headed back down the hallway.

Time to gather the troops.

She had a book unfair to interrupt—

And she was going to do it with style.

~

He was beginning to understand the thinking behind parking close. He had already made four heavily laden trips back to the car, and it wasn't even noon yet. The day promised to be one of the hottest of the year so far, and if he didn't get some Gatorade, he might just perish—long life or no long life.

He carefully avoided the van, even though he saw no one around it. During one of his trips, he'd seen a motley gathering of people—some looking a little less human than others. He was pretty convinced he saw Rumplestiltskin there. The canny old dwarf had convinced most people he could spin straw into gold, but really his major skill was turning nothing into something—which wasn't that far from Charming's skill.

Not that Charming had ever used it.

But he wasn't going to think about PETA. Or anyone from the kingdoms. He had enough reading material in the car to last him the entire trip plus some, and he still hadn't gone through the first aisle in the first exhibition hall.

If he felt overwhelmed by the number of books before, he felt worse now. Booth after booth after booth, representing publisher after publisher after publisher, filled with book after book after book, all of them for this season's list or next season's. No one had back stock, except in the catalogue, although some of the evergreen books did have backers deeper in the pavilion—at least that was what his program said.

His program also gave him listings of panels. He could get into all of them with his lovely purple badge.

He was torn between listening to writers or picking up their wares. He wished he could do both. And in some cases, he could, since some of the panels were being filmed for—well, maybe not for posterity, but for people who hadn't attended at all.

Even with two more days of this, he doubted he would see much of it. Not just the panels, but the books, the related materials, the third and fourth exhibition halls. He was actually despairing of getting through the entire thing, even though another book dealer, seeing his sadness, commiserated.

Don't worry, chum, the other dealer said. *I've been coming for twenty years, and I've never once left the main exhibition area.*

As if that made him feel better.

For the first time in his life, he wished he had magic so that he had could explore every single one of the nooks and crannies. But even he knew that wasn't how magic worked. He'd have to pay some horrible price for that wish, and he wasn't willing to do it.

He'd already paid price enough when he married Ella.

He was just coming back into the hall when he saw her—that woman—Snow White's stepmother. What was her name? He didn't know for sure, which wasn't that unusual. In the kingdoms, names had power, especially to the magical.

And if his memory was right (and he wasn't sure it was), she had some magical powers.

How could anyone with magic be bitter? He wouldn't have been. Of course, he didn't understand how anyone with magic could be a failure either, but a bunch of them were.

More than a bunch really. Most of them.

Still, he found her strangely compelling and just a little sad. He actually understood her rant—a little, anyway. He'd seen the way that his father and others had treated Ella's stepmother, who hadn't been a bad woman. She had just been desperate. Her husband had died, leaving her with a stepdaughter she hadn't known about, a house that wasn't paid for, and two daughters of her own.

Sure she struggled, and yes, she had been verbally abusive to Ella —by Greater World parlance. In the Third Kingdom, she had been kind. She hadn't turned Ella out of the house. She'd fed her, clothed her (if poorly), and had given her a roof over her head, when she'd been within her legal right to abandon her.

As a wedding present to Ella, his father had imprisoned her stepmother, and Ella thought that just punishment. She'd been gleeful about it, which had disturbed Charming then even though he was besotted with her.

Now he was appalled—and a bit suspicious. He had a hunch the fact that the stepsisters got blinded at the reception by a pack of out-of-control birds had more to do with magic of the paid-for variety than the bad luck everyone had attributed it to.

He shuddered. Then he shoved the overstuffed bags in his car and headed back to the pavilion.

Halfway there, he saw one of the woman's PETA companions, who was—unless Charming missed the guess—a flying monkey. Only he had stuffed his wings into a 1960s Sergeant Pepper's coat and put on a hat, a fake ZZ-Top beard and sunglasses. He looked human enough, until you peered and realized that bluish fur covered not only the skin around his eyes and his forehead, but also his hands and forearms.

He carried two signs, and Charming gasped when he saw them: *Book Unfair! Destroy the Lies!*

As he got closer, he could smell the scent of fresh Magic Marker. The flying monkey loped ahead of him.

"Excuse me," Charming said. "Are you with PETA?"

He said it the way the animal rights group did—pee-tah—and the monkey's mouth tightened into a little frown.

"I'm with P.E.T.A.," he snapped. "People for the Ethical Treatment—"

"Of Archetypes, I know," Charming said. "What's this about unfair books?"

The monkey stopped. "You read these things?"

"Books?" Charming asked. "Of course. Why else would I be here?"

"You're being brainwashed," the monkey said. "You don't understand the evil being perpetrated by these horrible fairy tales."

"Fairy tales," Charming repeated. He knew that "fairy tales" were how the Greater World absorbed the history of the kingdoms. Some of the tales were wrong, and some were not quite as wrong. They were about as accurate as the dime novels from the old Wild West, just a lot more popular.

"That's right," the monkey said. "They're lies. Damn lies. And they've got to be stopped."

"The fairy tales have to be stopped," Charming repeated because he didn't entirely understand this. "Fairy tales have been around for hundreds of years."

"That's hundreds of years too long," the monkey said. "We've got to put an end to this madness."

"By protesting a book fair?" Charming couldn't keep the incredulousness out of his voice.

"We have to start somewhere," the monkey said, and loped even faster, so that he got ahead of Charming.

Charming watched him go. He was confused. They thought they could—what? Stop the spread of fairy tales? Make fantastic literature go away?

To what end?

He needed to go back to the exhibition hall, but he found himself following the monkey instead.

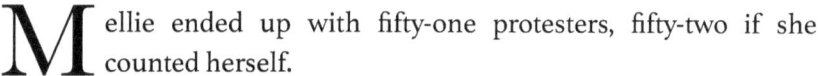

Mellie ended up with fifty-one protesters, fifty-two if she counted herself.

The problem was that they were the bottom of the barrel. The selkie no one had heard of, a few flying monkeys, Rumplestiltskin (who liked to be part of any kind of political action), and Bluebeard, of all people. None of the other stepmothers, none of the witches, none of the crones. The magical fish had sent their regrets, claiming they would take part if she held the next protest on the Santa Monica Pier—as if she believed that, which she didn't.

It seemed like every time she tried to rally the troops, the troops scattered to the wind.

Still, she decided to go through this, although she decided to shorten the protest to only a few hours for one day, instead of several hours over the life of the conference. Maybe she could get an interview—or better yet, some face time with some of the publishers and movie moguls. They would understand.

Forty-five of her protestors were already marching through the hall, shouting *Death to Fairy Tales!* The rest were handing out flyers explaining PETA's position on fairy tales and why they were evil, along with the URL of the website she had started back when she first conceived of the protest idea.

So far, all the TV people had done when the marching started was shut the doors to the studios, so the sound of the protests didn't drown out the panels. Once the flying monkey got back with the two extra signs she'd asked him to draw for her, she'd change the tone of the protest a little. She'd have the entire group yelling *Book Unfair!* which was bound to get someone's attention.

The hallway seemed smaller with fifty bodies in it, even if all fifty were of varying (and often smaller) sizes. She kept peering around the corner, waiting for that damn monkey, and she heaved a sigh of relief when she finally saw him.

Although the relief turned to dread when she saw who was following the monkey. Charming. Looking...angry?

For some reason she didn't think any of the Charmings got angry.

The monkey stopped when he saw her and handed her one of the signs. He started to go into an explanation of his lack of artistry—he really couldn't do proper calligraphy with Magic Markers—but she didn't care.

Instead, she stepped past him and right in front of Charming.

"You want to ban books?" he said, his voice strained. "Are you kidding me?"

"Not ban them, exactly," she said, hoping she sounded calm. "Just reduce the lies a bit."

"You think fairy tales are lies?" he said.

"Well, you clearly don't because—"

"Oh," he snapped, "don't start that 'people like you' crap again. People like me know that happily ever after is a crock. I'm divorced, remember?"

She bit her lower lip. She really hadn't put that together.

"You know what your problem is?" he said, his voice getting louder. "You don't know how lucky you are."

His arrogance took her breath away. "Lucky?"

"Lucky," he said. "You're beautiful, you're smart, you're successful enough to travel the Greater World, for heaven's sake, and all you care about is what people think of you."

"I do not," she said.

"You do too." He swept an arm toward the protestors. "Are you really an Archetype? Nowadays? Maybe a century ago, when women didn't have as many opportunities. And maybe when you couldn't choose your own identity. But who in this world knows who you are unless you point it out to them? And when you do, they think you're crazy."

"You don't know—"

"I do know!" He was yelling now. "Of course I know. Do you know what some officious little American government prick did when I told him my real name after I passed my driving test? Do you?"

She swallowed. "No."

"He laughed." Charming lowered his voice. "He laughed and said my parents ought to be shot."

She smiled. She couldn't help herself. She could picture that. She, at least, didn't have to go around introducing herself as the Evil Step-mother because that wasn't her real name. Never had been.

"Go ahead," he said, with some heat. "Laugh. But it's not fun. I actually prefer Dave. No one laughs when I say my name is Dave."

"Hey!" A door opened near Mellie. A man peered out. "Can you people pipe down? We're taping in here."

The nearest flying monkey—whose name she always forgot—raised his sign and waved it in the man's face. "This book fair is unfair!" the monkey said. "It's—"

"Yeah, yeah, yeah," the man said. "Someone is always publishing something someone else objects to. Whoopee ding dong do."

Then he slammed the door closed.

Mellie stared at it for a moment. Her heart sank. All this planning, to be dismissed with a single whoopee ding dong do.

The protestors had stopped marching and shouting.

"What do you want us to do, Mellie?" the selkie asked.

She didn't know. She had no idea any more.

So she shrugged. "Take a lunch break."

They set their signs down and bolted out of the hallway. She wondered if she'd ever see them again.

She didn't want to look at Charming. He would be laughing. He would gloat. Or he would be gone already.

But she couldn't help herself.

She looked.

He had an expression of compassion on his face. "It really bothers you what they think, doesn't it?" he said softly.

Her lower lip trembled, and she bit it. Hard. Evil stepmothers weren't supposed to cry. Nor were they supposed to care about the opinion of a Charming.

But here she was, on the verge of tears, in front of a Charming who actually appealed to her.

"Back when I was thin and shapely and beautiful and oh, so young, I didn't care," she said. "But then more thin and shapely and beautiful and oh, so young things showed up and I stopped being important, and I would say something a little sarcastic, and I suddenly got called old and bitter and jealous, and it just went downhill, no matter what I did. Words hurt, Charming. Words hurt."

He nodded. "So you thought you could control the words."

"Isn't that what you do with that golden voice of yours and that marvelously soothing manner? Don't you control the words?"

He gave her a rueful smile. "If I did, don't you think I would have ended up with custody of my daughters?"

Mellie looked at him, really looked at him, for the first time. He was very handsome. Elegant, not quite as trim as he could be, and just a hint of a bald spot that he might not even know about. A few lines around the eyes.

Not as young as he used to be either.

Seasoned.

Like her.

Only no one called him old and bitter and jealous.

But he had called himself a nerd.

"What are you doing here in the Greater World?" she asked.

"Me?" his voice squeaked just a little. "Getting books. I told you. I read a lot."

She picked up his badge. It was purple, not for royalty, like she'd initially thought, but for booksellers. "You got an illegal badge?"

"No," he said. "I sell books back home."

"You're a merchant?" She couldn't quite keep the incredulousness from her tone.

He straightened his shoulders as if by making himself taller he would become more powerful. "It's an honorable profession."

He was being defensive. That surprised her. "I just thought being prince was profession enough."

"Maybe in the Greater World," he said. "Here princes have to give speeches and do good works and have meetings with other princes. Back home, all I do is wait for my father to die."

He flushed a dark red.

"I didn't mean that the way it sounded," he said.

"I know what you mean," she said. "You like it better here."

He nodded.

"Why?"

He waved his badge at her. "People don't have any expectations of Dave the Bookseller. Except one."

315

"What's that?" she asked, actually curious.

"They expect him to know a lot about books."

And as he said that, he suddenly knew how to solve her problem. He held out his hand.

"Come with me," he said.

She frowned at him, then she looked down at his hand as if she expected him to be holding a dagger. "Why?"

"Because you're going about this wrong," he said.

"Going about what wrong?" she asked.

"Getting them to think better of you," he said.

"They need to know that we're not evil. We're just people, doing the best we could with a bad hand—"

"I know," he said. "I know what the perception is, and I know how wrong it is. But you can't change it by telling people they're wrong. That whole 'people like you' thing—"

"I'm sorry I said that," she said. "It's rude."

"So are these placards," he said. "They insult book people."

"They do?" she asked.

"But I know another way to convince them," he said.

"A Charming way?" she asked.

"Exactly," he said, and grabbed her hand. "Come on."

He dragged her to the exhibition hall. She had only walked past it; she hadn't looked inside. But she did now.

It was bigger than any castle audience hall she had ever seen, and it was crammed full of booths and books and people. More people than she could ever imagine.

One of the security guards looked for her badge, but somehow Charming got her past him. Something about an assistant. She didn't listen closely. She was too awed by the size of this hall.

She had no idea how many books there were.

"What do you think of vampires?" Charming asked as they hurried down an aisle.

It was such a non sequitur that she actually stopped. "Vampires?" she said.

"Or werewolves," he said. "Or zombies."

She shrugged. "Zombies don't exist," she said.

"Okay, then. Vampires. Werewolves. Creatures of the night. You think they're misunderstood?"

"I think they're scary," she said. "The handful I've met anyway. Predators. Real predators who think of us as prey."

"Yet they're half human, right?"

"Werewolves are," she said. "Technically vampires used to be human, and they have some vestiges—"

"So that's a yes," Charming said. "They care about their reputation too. About the time we started dealing with those Grimm people, they had to deal with someone named Stoker. He let the Great World know about them—"

"So?" she said.

"And the Greater World heard how evil they are," Charming said.

"And you think that's bad?" she asked. She didn't think so. Vampires scared her more than werewolves who were, at least, predictable.

"What I think is irrelevant," Charming said. "But what the Greater World thinks, now that matters."

He swept his arm toward a wall of books.

"Behold," he said.

She looked at what he was pointing at. Book after book after book about vampires. Not about how evil they were or how dangerous. But how sexy they were. There was even a movie magazine dedicated to the rise of the sexy vampire, and movie posters with the vampires looking longingly at young women—not like they were going to eat the women, but like they were in love with them.

"You're kidding, right?" she said.

"No," Charming said. "Vampires are all the rage now. Teenagers dress up like them. Prince Charming is passé. Now they all want to fall in love with Edward."

"Edward?" she asked.

"Long story," he said. "Suffice to say that the vampires used to be as angry about their own image as you are."

"So what did they do?" she asked.

"They started writing."

She blinked at him. Writing? Seriously?

He must have seen her shock, because he said, "You can't defeat the power of the book. But you can make it work for you."

"You think I should write about being an evil stepmother?"

"Why not? It worked for the Wicked Witch of the West." He grabbed a book off the shelf with a green witch on the cover. "She's got her own sympathetic Broadway play now and it's going to be a movie or so I hear, and she has her own soundtrack, not that horrible thing from the *Wizard of Oz*, and—"

"Me?" she said. "Write?"

"If you can't," he said, "I'm sure there are a lot of writers here who'll write the book for you."

"They'd do that?" she asked.

"For the right amount of money," he said.

"You're playing some kind of joke on me, right?'

"No," he said. "Ask anyone."

So she did. She started walking down the hall, asking people about vampires. She got a lot of opinions. Older people thought they were evil, but the younger ones talked about how sexy they were, and some even tried to shove vampire novels in her hands.

After a while, Charming showed up beside her with cloth bags covered in logos. As people shoved books at her, he took them and put them in the bags.

"Study materials," he said to her very softly.

"They give this stuff away?" she asked.

"Only to people they consider influential," he said. "Like me."

"So they know you're a Charming?" she asked.

He waved the badge at her. "I'm a bookseller. We're more important than any prince."

She tilted her head at him. "I really don't understand this place."

"I know," he said. "Why don't you let me show it to you?"

He slung the book bags over his shoulder and tucked her hand in the crook of his arm. Together they walked through the exhibition hall. She saw vampires, vampires, and more vampires, followed by werewolves and even a few zombies as romantic leads, no matter how fictitious they were.

And she saw people talking about books and arguing about them. Occasionally Charming would join them. He didn't seem like a prince. More like a really nice man.

A man who didn't believe in happily ever after.

But then again, neither did she.

Although she did like learning a thing or two.

And he had a lot to teach her about the Greater World. And books. And transforming wicked stepmothers into romantic heroines.

Sexy heroines.

Women who deserved their own princes charming, even if those princes were a little older, a little balder, and a whole lot nerdier than expected.

ABOUT THE AUTHOR

Called "The Reigning Queen of Paranormal Romance" by *Best Reviews,* bestselling author Kristine Grayson has made a name for herself publishing light, slightly off-skew romance novels about Greek Gods, fairy tale characters, and the modern world.

Her novel *Utterly Charming,* won the *Romantic Times* Reviewer's Choice Award. Her novel *Wickedly Charming,* which appeared in May of 2011, is based on "The Charming Way."

WMG Publishing will be releasing a series of omnibuses from her popular Fates Universe novels starting in March 2019, with a new novel, *Hidden Charm,* releasing in June 2019.

As Kristine Grayson, she also edits the romance volumes of *Fiction River: An Original Anthology Magazine,* including a special edition, *Summer Sizzles,* coming summer 2019.

Find out more about Kristine at:
kristinegrayson.com

BB bookbub.com/authors/kristine-grayson

OTHER COLLECTIONS

I f you enjoyed the stories in *Innocence and Deceit*, check out *Beauty and Wickedness*, the first volume in the *Ever After Fairy Tales* anthology series. Read a modern day retelling of Tam Lin, complete with motorcycle-riding faeries. A struggling lawyer's new client asks for her help to protect Sleeping Beauty. A white star nebula goes on a quest to find love. Enter the world of fairy tales, where dragons fly, trolls are real, and revenge can be achieved—for a price.

Learn more about *Ever After Fairy Tales* at:
blackbirdpublishing.com/series/ever-after-fairy-tales

I f you love stories about faeries as well as fairy tales, check out the anthology series *A Procession of Faeries*! This series includes *The Faerie Summer*, *Midwinter Fae*, and *Doorway into Faerie*.

Learn more about *A Procession of Faeries* at:
blackbirdpublishing.com/series/a-procession-of-faeries

www.ingramcontent.com/pod-product-compliance
Lightning Source LLC
Chambersburg PA
CBHW071055250626
47159CB00002B/474

* 9 7 8 1 9 3 9 9 4 9 0 9 7 *